JOHN MCNALLY

INFINITY DRAKE

THE FORBIDDEN CITY

Harper Collins

HarperCollins *Children's*

First published in Great Britain by HarperCollins *Children's Books* in 2015
HarperCollins *Children's Books* is a division of HarperCollins*Publishers* Ltd,
1 London Bridge Street, London, SE1 9GF

The HarperCollins website address is: www.harpercollins.co.uk

1

ISBN 978-00-0-752165-4

Typeset in Berylium by Palimpsest Book Production Limited,
Falkirk, Stirlingshire

Printed and bound in England by Clays Ltd, St Ives plc

FSC™ is a non-profit international organisation established to promote the responsible management of the world's forests. Products carrying the FSC label are independently certified to assure consumers that they come from forests that are managed to meet the social, economic and ecological needs of present and future generations, and other controlled sources.

Find out more about HarperCollins and the environment at
www.harpercollins.co.uk/green

To my mother and father, with love
and thanks for all the books.

FILE NO: GNTRC 9447549 [redacted] -OP/DRAKE~∞

TOP SECRET - MOST CLASSIFIED - RESTRICTION ULT9

FILE ABSTRACT: NARRATIVE ACCOUNT OF OPERATION FORBIDDEN CITY 操作故宫

(.1) BASED ON DEBRIEF INTERVIEWS CONDUCTED BY [redacted], TECHNICAL SURVEILLANCE DATA FROM 来源 中国技术情报报告# [redacted] SUPPLEMENTED BY [redacted] UPDATED [redacted] (.2) TO REFLECT TESTIMONY AND INTERROGATION OF [redacted]. FULL OPERATIONAL DETAILS. DECISION-MAKING PATHWAYS. FULL PSYCHOLOGICAL/EMOTIONAL CONTEXT.

ACCESS: PRIME MINISTER/CABINET SECRETARY/SECRETARY OF STATE DEFENCE/SECRETARY OF STATE FOREIGN/CHAIRMAN JOINT CHIEFS OF STAFF/CHAIRMAN GNTRC.

LIFETIME ACCESS: A. ALLENBY/ ∞DRAKE.

STUDY ACCESS: LEADERSHIP AND TACTICAL COMMAND LEVEL 009.

FILE MOST SECURE - NOT TO LEAVE REGISTRY

And the Lord said unto Moses, Say unto Aaron, Stretch out thy rod, and smite the dust of the land, that it may become lice throughout all the land of Egypt. And they did so; for Aaron stretched out his hand with his rod, and smote the dust of the earth, and it became lice in man, and in beast; all the dust of the land became lice throughout all the land of Egypt.

Exodus 8:16-19

Carbon will take over.

Mildred Dresselhaus

PART
ONE

ONE

September 28 23:58 (GMT+1). Hook Hall, Surrey, UK.

Midnight in the heart of England. The witching hour. In the woods an owl screeched, then ripped through a mouse, beak blood-wet in the moonlight.

The great old house of Hook Hall stood empty. It had not been used as a home since the day it had been requisitioned by Her Majesty's Government to become the top secret headquarters of the Global Non-governmental Threat Response Committee[1]. It lay now at the heart of a complex of modern laboratories and military installations

[1] Aka the G&T, formed by an alliance of international powers in 2002 to deal with extraordinary threats to global civilisation.

that spread around it in the darkness like the still, silent courtiers of a grand old lady.

The silence did not last. A low hum penetrated the dark and along the great drive the largest of the buildings began to glow.

Inside the cathedral-like space, the massive Central Field Analysis Chamber (CFAC), power surged and a great stone circle of particle accelerators, each the size of a shipping container, came to life.

"My Henge," as Dr Al Allenby, the dishevelled genius behind the machine, called it. "Everyone should have a Henge."

From the windows of a laboratory overlooking the henge a very small boy sent up a mad private prayer.

Finn (full name Infinity Drake) was about to turn thirteen. He had sand-coloured hair that grew in several directions at once (like his father's) and deep blue eyes (like his mother's). He had been orphaned two years before. He was into gaming, mad science and most lethal pastimes, like any other boy. But unlike any other boy, thanks to getting caught up in Operation Scarlatti[2] the previous spring, Finn was now only 9.8mm tall.

With a deafening electrostatic crack and hum, white lightning began to spin like candyfloss around the core, the hoop of accelerators whipping up a cyclone of pure energy. With one last push they would form a perfect subatomic magnetic field.

Perched above the Henge, crammed into his cockpit command

[2] See FILE NO: GNTRC 9437549-OP/BLAKE~∞ TOP SECRET: an attempt by transnational terror czar D.A.P Kaparis to blackmail the G&T into handing over the secrets of the Boldklub process by releasing a doomsday bioweapon, the Scarlatti Wasp, and threatening Armageddon. The attempt was thwarted by a military kill team shrunk to hunt down the wasp, and by the heroic actions of Infinity Drake.

pod, Dr Allenby (known to all as Al), recited the snatch of poetry he used to remember the crucial sequencing equations he kept secret from the world –

"But at my back I always hear
Time's wingèd chariot hurrying near
And yonder all before us lie
Deserts of vast eternity..."

(... adding in his head: *where B is acceleration and E opens and closes brackets and where all other vowels are disregarded*).

Several calculations ran at once inside his brain and in an instant he typed a series of numbers into his control terminal... *WHOOOOOOOMMMM!*

The spun lighting became a continuous arc, then, with a flash, the Hot Area was created – a throbbing orb of white light within which the distance between the nucleus of any atom and its electrons would be reduced, thus shrinking all matter to a fraction of its original size. Called the Boldklub[3] process, it was a remarkable feat of physics that only Al really understood.

"OH YEAH, BABY!" he cried, incongruous given the surroundings and the presence of so many distinguished scientists, soldiers and political functionaries.

His boss, Commander James Clayton-King, Chairman of the Global Non-governmental Threat Committee, sighed and briefly lowered his eyelids.

[3] Named after the Danish football club Akademisk Boldklub, who Nils Bohr, the father of subatomic physics, used to play for.

It had taken months longer than Al had anticipated to reach this point and there had been many mistakes along the way, but finally he thought they'd got it right. In a few moments he would be able to prove that he could shrink a living mammal, then reverse the process and successfully return it to its normal size. Alive. Countless tests had been run with countless objects – up to and including living plants.

All that remained was a live mammal test.

A white mouse had been selected, sedated and encased in monitoring devices.

It had been named 'Fluffy'.

It was for his nephew Finn, and his three Operation Scarlatti team mates, that Al had worked so hard day and night in the hope of being able to return them to their normal size.

A technician up in the Control Gallery, on a command from Al, started the conveyor that fed items into the Hot Area. Fluffy moved along the belt and slipped into the perfect light.

Finn watched, transfixed, as the Hot Area rippled and the white mouse was reduced to 'nano' scale, just a 150th of its original size, just like Finn. Next, the process would be reversed, bringing Fluffy back to normal 'macro' scale. If it worked, the four nano-humans, including Finn, would be resized next.

They watched the show together, hopes looping the loop.

"Come on, Fluffy," whispered Captain Kelly of the SAS from where he stood beside Finn – six foot six of muscle and scar-tissue, currently reduced to 13mm, and so convinced the experiment would work he'd booked a flight to Scotland where he planned to spend the next few weeks sailing around the Western Isles accompanied by a crate of whisky.

"Kick it, Fluff!" agreed 11mm-high Delta Salazar from behind her Aviator shades – the best and coolest pilot in the US Air Force. She'd grown as close to her nano-colleagues as she had to anybody in her life, but she couldn't wait to fly back home to see her younger sister, Carla.

Even 10mm-high Engineer Stubbs, ancient and given to doom and gloom, had boiled an egg in case things went well (party food would just upset his stomach).

"Reverse the polarity!" cried Al.

Finn's heart beat like a drum. He could not wait to be big again, to open a door, to hug his stupid dog, Yo-yo, to kick a ball around with his best friend Hudson. To—

Suddenly everything went purple as his view of the action was eclipsed by a gigantic, well-preserved lady of sixty-four in matching top and slacks.

"Now, does anybody want more Welshcakes?"

"GRANDMA! GET OUT OF THE WAY!" Finn screamed.

Nobody in the universe had a more uncanny ability to interrupt than Finn's grandma – and Al's mother – Violet Allenby. She was drawn like a magnet to hoover in front of any given TV and always asked too loudly who was on the phone.

"Oh, am I in the way?" she said, towering over them like a colossus.

"YEEEEES!" Finn wailed until she moved along to offer yet more cake to the technical staff, her way of taking her mind off everything that could possibly go wrong.

The Henge reappeared just as Al cut the power to the Hot Area, everyone watching as the spinning cyclone evaporated into a million specks of light.

As the sparkles faded Fluffy's test rig was revealed at centre of the Henge... at full size.

There were whoops from technicians. A smattering of applause.

"Yes!" shouted Finn.

Delta got him in a headlock-come-hug.

Kelly began to dance a jig, then got Stubbs in a headlock too.

Out in the CFAC Al popped the perspex lid on his command pod and hurried down the ladder.

Beeeeeeeeeeeeeeeeeeeeeeeeeep... went an alarm.

Al ran into the middle of the Henge.

Beeeeeeeeeeeeeeeeeeeeeeeeeep...

Fluffy was very still.

Beeeeeeeeeeeeeeeeeeeeeeeeeep...

Al examined her.

Beeeeeeeeeeeeeeeeeeeeeeeeeep...

Seeing the angle of his uncle's shoulders, Finn knew at once.

Beeeeeeeeeeeeeeeeeeeeeeeeeeeeeeeeeeeeeeeeeeeeeeeeeeeeeeeeeep...

Fluffy was dead.

TWO

September 29 07:04 (Local GMT+8). Song Island, Taiwan (disputed).

Dawn broke over the South China Sea.

Song Island stood roughly 150 miles southwest of Taiwan and 150 miles southeast of Hong Kong, part of a forgotten archipelago – uninhabited, untouched, undisturbed, except for the occasional visit from a mad nationalist or a passing naval patrol. Three countries lay claim to Song and it had been the subject of a United Nations disputed territory process since 1948, though Song's file lay at the very bottom of the pile, uncared for by a diplomatic community with better things to do. After all, it was just a Karst Limestone sugarloaf – a big conical rock stuck like a sore thumb out of the deepest azure ocean, baked by the sun and whipped by typhoons, with barely a

scrap of life upon its rocky surface. True, there were some nesting seabirds, patches of vegetation, but mostly it was just a sheer 200-metre column of barren, bare rock…

… within though?

Kaparis settled down. There was nothing quite like moving into a new HQ: they always had that irresistible 'new top secret operations facility' smell. And this place, even Kaparis had to admit, was special. The creation of his eccentric personal architect, Thömson-Lavoisiér, it boasted 2km of tunnels, bunkers and laboratories built into the seabed, a submersible weapons platform, a sub-aquatic escape vehicle and – the pièce de résistance – a personal recumbent operations chamber for Kaparis and the iron lung he'd spent his life in since he was totally paralysed by a medical 'accident' in 2001.

The chamber was set into the sugarloaf itself and featured not only 'the usual' domed screen array and cranial panopticon (allowing a 360 degree field of vision and eye-track control of all screens) but also: a window. Unremarkable, until you realised the whole chamber could move up and down like an elevator within the stick of rock. Kaparis could enjoy a commanding view of the South China Sea and the surrounding islands one minute, then descend to a point six metres below sea level to watch the local sharks the next.

All in all he was delighted. His eyes spun round the opticon as he sought out his butler.

"Heywood?"

"Yes, Master?" Heywood stepped forward – bald, immaculate.

"What do you think to something local for dinner?"

"Of course, Master."

Heywood pressed a button. For mood music, Kaparis flicked his eyes across the screen array and called up a performance of The Mikado *by Gilbert and Sullivan.*

The sharks circled.

A portal opened on the seabed and an official of the Taiwanese Coastguard – who had attempted to report his superiors for accepting bribes to keep clear of the island – was expelled. He began to swim desperately for the surface.

The sharks exposed their teeth, then expressed their delight… in the only way they knew how. And the chorus sang –

"Behold the Lord High Executioner

A personage of noble rank and title

A dignified and potent officer

Whose functions are particularly vital!

Defer! Defer!

To the noble lord, to the noble lord

To the Lord High Executioner!"

Blood bloomed through the waters and what remained of the coastguard official drifted down to the ocean floor.

Kaparis ordered his chamber to rise then checked the progress of his agent in Shanghai via a live video feed. It was all so nearly over, the Vector Program so nearly complete. He could imagine the weight lifting from his shoulders. The long months of struggle, the long months of effort and excellence in his secret factories beneath the deserts of Niger had resulted in the production of fifty-two of the most devilishly sophisticated robots ever conceived.

Finally he was on the road to recovery, putting distance between himself and the memory of Infinity Drake and all the damage he'd managed to inflict during the Scarlatti episode.

Finally, he was to master mankind and take over the world...

All that remained was to enjoy the yields of his genius. As the chamber broke the surface of the water, sunlight flooded in and momentarily Kaparis felt free again, as free as the Booby Birds and Great Crested Terns now wheeling around the rocks. And in that moment he forgot himself and a thought bubbled up through his mind: I... am... happy...

Beeeeeeeeeeeeeeeeeeeeeeeeeeeeeeeeep...

An alarm sounded.

The bubble burst.

September 29 07:22 (Local GMT+8). Kung Fu Noodles, Concession#22, Food Hall D, Sector 9, Forbidden City Industrial Progress Zone, Shanghai, China.

The food hall was vast. At dozens of outlets staff in ridiculous paper hats served hundreds of customers, night workers just off shift. The air was hot and street-food aromatic.

Baptiste spotted the plain-clothes cop as soon as he walked in – neat, serious, casually checking out the handful of westerners in the food hall. Including Baptiste. The cop glanced down at a palmtop screen, then immediately walked across the seating area towards him.

As he approached, Baptiste touched his phone and initiated emergency contact. His free hand felt instinctively for the fountain pen in the front pocket of his bag.

The cop flashed his ID and said something in Mandarin Chinese.

Instantly, Song Island relayed a translation back to an audio device embedded behind Baptiste's ear. *"He's asking your name."*

"Jaan Baptiste."

Baptiste. It had started as a nickname. Many religious scenes remained on the walls of the Kaparis seminary, a school for Tyros housed in an abandoned monastery high in the Carpathian Mountains, including an icon of John the Baptist. With greasy hair that dripped as far as his shoulders and a soft-as-silk teenage beard 'Baptiste' was a dead ringer for the dead saint. Aged between twelve and seventeen, the Tyros were the foot soldiers of Kaparis, secretly selected from care institutions across the world and brought to the Carpathians for training and NRP[4] indoctrination.

"Passport?" the cop asked, in English now.

"At hotel." Baptiste answered in a Bulgarian accent, mentally checking off the six ways he could kill the cop with his bare hands.

"Hotel name?"

"Tiger Star."

[4] Neuro-Retinal Programming aka NRP – an accelerated learning and personality control process whereby a probe, inserted directly through the eye, connects to the optic nerve and delivers information (specialist knowledge, emotional association, ideology, etc.) straight to the brain's cerebral cortex.

* * *

"This just received by Shanghai Police Command..." Kaparis heard Li Jun report.

From her bank of screens at the edge of his operations chamber, Li Jun posted the image of Baptiste that the cop had just sent to his headquarters. She was an unassuming young Tyro who had became Kaparis's chief technologist.

Kaparis seethed.

"Happy..." His brief moment of sentiment had been punished. By fate. The following moments would determine the outcome of the entire project.

What to do?

There was a fifty-fifty chance Baptiste would be exposed as his agent. Half the world's security services were on the lookout for the Tyros and their telltale retinal scarring. Baptiste's cover could be blown. But if they aborted the Vector operation now and started again they would waste months, years even, of careful planning and preparation.

How close were they? Never been closer. Fifty-one of the fifty-two bots were already in place. The last bot, the one full of executable[5] data, was about to be released. The brain of the entire operation. The ace.

What to do?

You make your own luck, 'they' say, but fate, according to Kaparis, was different. Fate you have to assault, coerce. Kaparis prided himself on being its master. One of the very few. Like a god on Mount Olympus.

[5] In computing an executable file contains actionable program code rather than just data. It's the bit that says Do This, Do That, and Stop Complaining.

He felt a delicious shiver.

"Play the ace."

"Have you visited this restaurant before?" the cop asked.

"I do not remember," said Baptiste.

The cop pulled up a grainy CCTV image on his palmtop screen of Baptiste at the Kung Fu Noodle counter.

"This is you last week. Six times in the last month. Come with me," the cop said, leading him out of the food hall and into the back seat of an unmarked police car. Baptiste reached instinctively into his bag. He was not yet under arrest. The cop got in the front and picked up the radio, waiting for his orders.

But Baptiste received his first.

"Release it. Complete Vector at all costs."

Baptiste relaxed. The point of action had arrived. He took a luxury Mont Blanc pen out of his bag and flipped off the top, as if he were about to make a note.

The Prime Executable Bot woke.

XE.CUTE.BOT52:BORN

An order came in from Kaparis Command on Song Island.

KAPCOMM>>XE.CUTE TERMINATE LIFE FORM LOCATION COORDINATES: 4578377/46294769

XE.CUTE.BOT52:KILL

The cop finished his radio message and turned his head to speak to Baptiste, but before the first word made it out of his mouth –

Ttzxch.

The smallest sound as it entered his brain.

The tiniest entry wound at the temple.

His face went into spasm, then froze.

THREE

September 29 10:14 (GMT+1). Hook Hall, Surrey, UK.

The morning after the night before was 150 times more disappointing than any previous morning at nano-scale.

Finn, Delta, Kelly and Stubbs sat in silence at a tiny table that had been specially made for them and stared at nothing in particular for a good long while.

The Sons of Scarlatti (one technically a daughter) as they liked to call themselves, lived in an 'apartment block' fashioned from cellular seed trays that sat inside a biohazard bubble, which protected them from insects and other threats, inside Laboratory One. It was known as the nano-compound. First they were going

to be there a week. Then they were told twelve days. Then three weeks "tops".

So far, five months had passed.

On the upside, the longer they'd waited for the one thing they wanted most, the more they got of everything else. They could come and go as they pleased from the biosphere (as long as they followed elaborate safety procedures) and anything they wanted could be shrunk in the new accelerator array, so they enjoyed the finest foods, consumer goods and high-end leisure activities. Finn had his own private zoo full of his favourite insects, a laboratory and a skate park, and there was even a ski slope inside a macro freezer in Lab Two. Best of all a perspex-covered road and model rail network had been laid that allowed them safe access to the entire complex. Finn had been gifted a red Mini to drive around, which he adored (even though its speed had been restricted at Grandma's insistence).

But right now none of that helped.

Various people had already called to reassure them: Grandma, Commander King and, over a video link, the Prime Minister. Even Hudson had been sent for. Not many kids could ruin the 'jeans and hoodie' look, but with his long hair, massive glasses and uncomfortable expression, Hudson was one of a kind. He was in on the Boldklub secret because he'd been dragged into the climax of operation Scarlatti and proved himself an unlikely hero.

"What a bummer... That's so rubbish. Bet you were looking forward to being tall again?" said Hudson when he arrived.

"Mmmm," said Kelly, looking round for a gun to shoot him with.

"It must really eat away at the back of your minds..." Hudson mused.

At which point Delta politely asked that they be left alone "to suck things up a while".

"At least he didn't offer to write one of his poems[6]," said Finn when the nano-team were alone again.

Stubbs grunted. "We are at the very margins of human comprehension. We might be stuck here for years and years..."

"What do you know, old fool!" Delta said to Stubbs.

"Quite a lot, actually," said Stubbs defensively.

Doubt stirred like a great black eel in the pit of Finn's gut.

Be yourself. Trust yourself. Just keep going. These had been his mother's Big Three rules. But how could you *be yourself* when you were stuck in the wrong-sized body? What was the use of *trusting yourself* when you were totally dependent on other people? And how could you *just keep going* when you were so obviously stuck? When he'd complained about this to Christabel, their local vicar and a good friend since his mother's funeral, she'd said, "Use it. Just like your mum left you three lessons, see what lessons you can learn from what you're going through."

All he'd learned so far was that *the more you wanted something, the further away it got.*

"I expect you've had better birthdays, Finn," said Stubbs, looking more than ever like a dejected tortoise.

[6] Hudson had won a Hertfordshire Schools anti-bullying poetry prize for 'Willow: Bowed, Yet Ye Stand'.

Kelly gave a hollow laugh and slapped the old man on the back for being such a grouch. Stubbs could fix anything, but didn't have much clue when it came to 'being a human being'.

"Thanks – it's not until tomorrow," said Finn.

"Hey – a birthday is still a birthday. What do you want to do?" asked Delta, trying to brighten things up. She didn't normally do 'close' but her younger sister Carla was the same age as Finn so he'd become a de facto younger brother.

Finn shrugged. What was there to celebrate at 9mm? He didn't even get to skip school. Instead he was attending via Skype, Hudson dutifully carrying him around on a laptop (the official explanation for Finn's absence being he had a highly-contagious skin disease). Grandma insisted on the arrangement. "So he can live a normal life, like any other boy," she had said, to which Finn responded, "IN WHAT POSSIBLE WAY COULD MY LIFE BE CONSIDERED NORMAL! I'M NINE MILLIMETRES TALL!"

"At least you lot get to go to work..." Finn complained.

There was a military research project that Finn wasn't really supposed to know about called the 'nCraft'. One great problem of being a centimetre tall was the time it took to cover even a modest distance and a new vehicle was being developed to take full advantage of the massively improved power-to-mass ratios at nano-scale. Al disapproved of *any* military application of his technology but Finn knew, that out of sheer boredom, Stubbs and the others had been working on it.

They felt for him.

"Don't sulk, you'll get over this! You can get over anything," said Kelly. "You know how many cars I'd stolen by the time I was thirteen? I spent half my teens in youth custody – and look at me now!" he boasted, opening his massive, battle-scarred arms as if he was a model citizen.

"This is what I tell Carla," said Delta. "Between thirteen and seventeen you do a lot of suffering, then life gets much, much better."

"Oh great," said Finn, sarcastically.

"People always say things like that to teenagers," said Stubbs, "but as I recall you never really get over the trauma of your teens. The bullying... the heartache... the loneliness..."

"The being nine millimetres tall..." added Finn.

"Hey! If I got over a childhood in a Philadelphia children's home, you can get over this. You just need a little help and support – am I right?" said Delta, glaring at Kelly and Stubbs.

"She's right," said Kelly, then added generously, "and if you need things livening up, just say the word! One of us can always tie you to the train tracks, or shoot at you..."

"I could drop you out of a plane?" offered Delta.

"Or ostracise him. Mental cruelty," added Stubbs.

"You'd really do that for me? Thanks, guys," said Finn, smiling at last.

A pulse came from Finn's nPhone[7].

[7] Reducing matter collapses the electro-magnetic spectrum in such a way that nano radio transmissions cannot be picked up on macro radio receivers and vice versa. An nPhone is a tiny macro phone carried in a backpack with a keypad that allows texting on the regular phone network. It also allows constant tracking.

He opened the pack and checked the screen.

U there? Skype?

"What's wrong? You look like death."

The girl who on a daily basis filled his Skype screen with dark hair, bright eyes and wisecracks, peered into the lens at him, suspicious.

"Wrong? Nothing's wrong," said Finn, wondering how Carla's emotional radar could possibly work at this distance.

The background usually showed her bedroom in the States, but right now he was looking at a hotel room in Kunming, China, where Carla was on tour with the Pennsylvania Youth Orchestra. Her luggage and a cello case lay on the bed behind her.

What she saw from China was a mock barrack room that had been built especially within the nano-compound. Carla thought Delta was stuck at an airbase in England working on a secret project and that Finn was just a kid who lived on the base with his uncle. They had hit it off as soon as Delta had introduced them, not so much soul mates as complementary opposites. Carla knew everything Finn didn't know – and much he didn't want to know – about art and life, and Finn knew everything she didn't know about the natural world.

What Carla also didn't know was that everyone she saw on camera was about a centimetre tall.

"Something is definitely wrong."

"I lost a pet," said Finn for cover.

"A pet? They let you have pets on an airbase?" she said, sceptical.

"Only a mouse."

"A *mouse*? What was its name?"

"Fluffy. It doesn't matter."

"Of course it matters. I had a hamster die on me; it nearly broke my heart. Does Delta know?"

"Sure. She told me 'life is much better than you think'."

"How patronising! They think we're just kids! They have no idea what 'life' is like for us," bemoaned Carla, who enjoyed being disgusted with her sister and with grown-ups in general.

"What happened? Was it old age?" she asked, gently.

"No, my uncle killed it," said Finn. "It was late, they'd been drinking, a fight broke out..."

She laughed despite herself.

"Oh HA HA – you're avoiding your emotions."

There was a call off-screen. "Carla, we have to go!"

"OK!" she shouted back, and turned to Finn.

"That's it. We're going to the airport. You should have seen this place we passed – there's this actual *dwarf world* here! A theme park full of little people to gawp at. Can you imagine anything so cruel?"

"Honestly, I can't," Finn said without a hint of irony.

Finn wished he was going with her, wished he was going anywhere, with anybody.

Carla grabbed her things and went to shut down the screen, then paused and confessed, "You know, I often wonder if you two are locked-up in some theme park – isn't that the weirdest thing?"

"Ha! Why?" Finn stalled.

"I don't know, the crazy stories and everything. Plus I've never even seen outside this barrack room..."

"Well it is a *secret* base," said Finn.

"Exactly. Always the big mystery with you two!"

"Carla!" called the voice off-screen again, and she waved goodbye.

Phew, thought Finn.

As Finn walked out of the fake barrack room back into the nano-compound, Delta, Kelly and Stubbs suddenly stopped talking. He hated when grown-ups did that.

"What?" said Finn. "What were you talking about?"

"Nothing," said Delta.

"Liar," said Finn.

"We said the main thing is we've got to stick together as a team. Everything takes time," said Kelly.

"I know," said Finn. At least he could be sure of that.

"Your uncle will eventually find the answer," said Stubbs, almost reluctantly.

"You better believe it!" came a familiar booming voice, as a shadow, like a huge cloud, fell across them.

The four tiny figures looked up at the giant, praying for good news.

"I just don't know what the answer is yet," Al finished, to a chorus of sighs. "Now, who's up for Sunday lunch?"

* * *

For want of anything better to do, Finn agreed to spend Sunday at Grandma's with Al and they razzed along the country lanes between Hook Hall and the village of Langmere in Al's incomparable De Tomaso Mangusta sports car[8], happily outrunning the Mercedes of the security detail and scattering autumn leaves.

Finn sat in a nano-den (or 'nDen' as Al liked to call them) that was clipped to Al's top pocket.

A way had to be found for the nano-crew to be housed, heard and taken out of the lab complex from time to time and nDens were the answer. This particular nDen was a typically eccentric choice of Al's: a vintage Sony Walkman cassette player. About the size of a book, it had been adapted to hold nano-humans: there was a sofa, tinted glass for them to see out of, a line to Al through the earphones, and a built-in loudspeaker for when they needed to make themselves more widely heard.

"Tell me what went wrong with Fluffy. Maybe I can help," said Finn.

"About three grams," said Al.

"Three grams?" said Finn.

"That's right," said Al. "We reduced Fluffy, then we rescaled Fluffy – in perfect form, every atom, every molecule in the right place – and yet... somehow Fluffy ends up stone cold dead and three grams lighter. It's as if the electrical relationships and reactions that run a body – *the stuff of life* – somehow disappeared. We just have to isolate

[8] "The greatest thing to come out of 1969, after the moon landings by NASA and *Abbey Road* by the Beatles" – Al.

why, what, where and when, and then we'll be able to do something about it. But at the moment we haven't got a clue – just three missing grams."

The conversation continued as they walked through the woods with Grandma later that afternoon – another headache for the Security Service. Al was thought to be a prime target for kidnap, but Grandma refused any extra security. For her there was no appeasing villainy – and no mystery in Al's missing three grams, either.

"The three grams are obviously the Soul," said Grandma. "The divine."

"Mother! As the wife of one scientist, the mother of two more and as a medical professional, do you *really* think that—"

"Don't you dare be rude about simple faith!" squawked Grandma. "People have the right to experience mystery!"

"Let's not have this argument again!" Finn pleaded, as it was one that had ruined at least three mealtimes a week for most of his life.

Yap! agreed Yo-yo, running ahead and making Finn wish he'd opted to ride with him instead. He often did this, sitting in the fur just under Yo-yo's ear, guiding him with simple commands. Yo-yo was the best, most uncoordinated mongrel ever born. He couldn't fathom the mystery of Finn's physical disappearance – just as he couldn't fathom what clouds were – but he could still smell Finn and hear him, which was all he needed.

Grandma and Al lowered their guards, warily.

"If it isn't supernatural, what's your best guess on the missing three grams?" Finn asked Al from the nDen.

"My best guess is there's a relationship between dark matter, the speed of light and the timing of electrochemical reactions within a body," said Al.

"Dark matter?" said Grandma.

"Yes, dark matter, also known as dark energy. It's mystery stuff that makes up nearly all of the Universe, but no one knows what it is or how it works. No one except *us. We* have discovered that when you shrink ordinary matter – atoms and stuff – there must be a proportionate shrinking of dark matter, otherwise you'd be incredibly heavy; as heavy as you were when you were big."

"But where is it?"

"Who knows? It's unobservable, we can't even begin to experiment – and without experiment we are nothing but apes groping around in our own excrement."

"Charming!" said Grandma.

"Think of dark matter as a shadow – in this case, a shadow that makes up ninety-five per cent of our weight. When you get smaller, the shadow gets smaller. But that's just a guess."

"Didn't my dad work on dark matter?" asked Finn.

Grandma stiffened and called to Yo-yo, who had reached the house and was scratching at the back door.

Grandma didn't like to talk about Finn's dad, Ethan Drake, who

had disappeared in a lab accident before Finn was born, fire consuming him so completely that only the sphalerite[9] stone he wore around his neck was recovered. The same stone – that Finn's mother had worn until she died of cancer two years ago – now hung around Al's giant neck, next to the nDen.

"Nobody knows exactly what your dad was doing just before he passed away," said Al. "We have some of his notes from around then, but your mum had just had you and most of his assistants were sitting exams."

"I didn't know he'd left notes. Can I read them?" said Finn.

Al frowned. He'd spent the best part of thirteen years crawling all over them. He could probably recite them.

"Tea! We must get in and put the kettle on before it gets dark," Grandma interrupted, trying to move things on.

But Al was in the moment, and it was clearly an uncomfortable one.

"They're complicated, Finn. A mess, in fact. Lots of stuff that looks like answers but isn't. It's not what you want," he said, cryptic and awkward.

"And cake! We have plenty of cake," Grandma said, taking out her keys to let them in.

"What's that supposed to mean? Will you show me or not?" said Finn.

"Maybe. One day."

[9] Sphalerite possesses a quality called triboluminesence, which means it glows when scratched.

"Sherry!" concluded Grandma, hurrying them into the house.

By the time they got back to Lab One it was late.

Al opened the Sony Walkman and said goodnight to Finn at the edge of the nano-compound.

"We'll try the experiment again tomorrow, and every day, till we get it right," he said, winking and walking away.

Finn took comfort as he watched him go. His uncle might wear glasses held together with tape, but he was reassuringly massive, in brain as well as bulk.

Everything was dark and Finn supposed the others had already gone to bed.

Then he heard a voice.

"Feeling any better, Noob?" Delta asked, using her nickname for Finn.

Suddenly – *POP!* – all the lights came on at once, dazzling him.

"What the…?!"

As Finn's eyes adjusted to the light, he could make out three figures, some balloons, and… a Thing.

"Surprise!"

FOUR

September 29 22:58 (GMT+1). Hook Hall, Surrey, UK.

Delta slapped Finn on the back.

"Happy nearly-birthday!" grinned Kelly.

"Thought we'd cheer you up," said Stubbs, deadpan.

They stood back and let Finn take in the Thing.

The others had been testing it for the last month. He'd glimpsed parts of it before, designs on-screen, but he'd never seen the whole thing.

"The nCraft?" said Finn.

"I see you've been paying attention," said Kelly.

"Say hello to the X1 Experimental Nano-thruster," murmured Stubbs, reverentially.

Delta bit her lip excitedly, like they had pulled off the best birthday surprise ever.

"Guy's a genius," said Kelly, roughing Stubbs's remaining hair.

"It's fast as a whip and can turn on a pin!" said Delta.

"It's –" Finn tried to put it into words – "a little ugly."

Three faces fell at once. He thought Kelly would cry or hit him. "This isn't a beauty contest!" he yelled.

It was, thought Finn, like one of those weird deep-sea fish that had evolved in the perpetual gloom of an ocean trench. Roughly the size of a limousine at their scale, it had a gawping front grill like a great mouth and two headlamp eyes. It had multiple stubby wings and rudders that looked like fins, and a tail section with a scorched and nasty-looking exhaust, and its underside was regularly pockmarked with clusters of small thruster units.

"I'm not being mean," said Finn, apologetically. "I'm just saying it looks like an ugly bug and when you go into production—"

"It's the prototype!" shouted Kelly. "You think we'd let you *near* one of the new X2 models?"

"So shallow," sighed Delta.

"Hey, I'm still twelve –" Finn checked his watch – "just. I'm meant to be shallow!"

"Well then I don't suppose for one moment," said Stubbs, "you'll be wanting a go."

And with that he flicked a switch on the outside of the craft. Computers and gyroscopes woke within, turbines turned over and the Bug came alive. Lights blazed all over its body and it floated off the ground, suspended on a cushion of air, flexing its tail and wings to keep absolutely steady.

"Wow," said Finn, gobsmacked.

"We've 'borrowed' it for one night only. Not a word to anyone, especially not to Al," warned Kelly.

"Note the extraordinary stability," Stubbs began, gearing up to explain the technicalities. "A central jet runs a compressor that feeds cold gas rockets all over the body controlled by an intelligent thrust-vectoring syst—"

"OK, OK, I want a go!" said Finn.

With a high-pitched hum from the jet engine beneath them and the hiss of collective thrusters, they rose steadily towards the roof of the Central Field Analysis Chamber. On top of the Bug was an open cab with four seats, a roll cage, a windscreen and some crude controls. It was like sitting in a fat flying sports car, thought Finn, yet with a ride so gentle they might have been in a bubble. There was also a mount for an M249 Minimi light machine gun, to defend themselves against insects and any other threat they might face in the outside world.

They had to be careful, the craft was supposedly strictly out of bounds in Lab Three, but the Duty Techs were in Lab Two and Stubbs and Kelly had nobbled some of their monitoring equipment, smuggling the Bug out through the model rail network, first to the nano-compound in Lab One, then into the vast, empty spaces of the CFAC.

Finn was just admiring the view as they rose above the stone circle of particle accelerators when Delta said, "OK, brace," and punched her arms forward against the dual joysticks.

Finn's head snapped back and the roof rushed by, his insides galloping hopelessly to catch up with his skeleton, as Delta turned hard to avoid hitting the far wall of the hangar. They shot back across the CFAC at roof level, then dived and... *SLAM!* Halfway to the ground Delta made the Bug turn 90 degrees without bothering to slow down, the nCraft morphing to deliver thrust at all the right angles at once. Finn was left gasping.

Delta then plunged towards the rows of benches crammed with computers surrounding the accelerator array. Down they went, skimming along the desks, slaloming the accelerators and monitors, whipping up paperwork, then down again to rollercoaster beneath benches and between chair legs, then up again into empty space.

Finn's mind was spinning. They were not flying: they were motion itself. Pure euphoria battled memories of his terror-flight, trapped on the back of the Scarlatti wasp the previous spring, till – *SLAM!* – Delta opened up the reverse thrusters and stopped the Bug dead. Finn was thrown forward so hard he thought he was going to bring up his lungs, never mind his dinner.

In sudden stillness, he took a gulp of air and looked at the clock on the lab wall. It was midnight, his birthday: his turn. He grinned.

Finn climbed across and took the controls, and for one minute and forty-nine seconds he had the best birthday ever.

Delta ordered him not to think too much. "Just point and shoot."

He took hold of the twin sticks, looked at the far wall of the CFAC and pushed them forward.

The Bug shot forward, so he eased back, getting a feel for the power as he coasted the entire length of the building, rising all the time. He felt a surging joy and remembered sitting on his mother's knee steering her old Citroën 2CV around a beach car park in the rain.

He accelerated and made a turn, arcing back around, just below the roof, then more turns.

Then he began to throw the Bug around like rodeo horse. *It was easy.* The speed and distance you could cover was awesome and the handling was amazing – it felt as though you had thrust from a thousand places at once.

It felt alive. This was almost better than being big.

He flew up towards the Control Gallery that overlooked the CFAC, then dived and curled to fly around the circle of accelerators like Ben Hur around the circus maximus, laughing and loving it, until…

POP! POP! POP!

For the second time that night he was dazzled by sudden bright lights.

Delta leapt across and snatched the controls from him, pulling the Bug to a halt and leaving them hanging in mid-air, staring down at a group of incoming officials, hurrying across the CFAC towards the gantry steps of the Control Gallery.

"What's happening?" asked Finn.

"Oh no..." said Stubbs. "King."

Finn looked over. The great hanger doors of the CFAC were whirring open and Commander King was crossing the chamber, trailing aides and flanked by General Mount of the British High Command on one side and the head of British Intelligence on the other. Then, even more remarkably – *VROOOOM! SCREEEEECH!* – in roared a 1969 De Tomaso Mangusta, and out hopped Al.

"Good evening, Dr Allenby," uttered King, trying to ignore the showy entrance.

"Peter. Wendy. Tink," Al said to the trio. All three, used to his odd sense of humour, ignored it and carried on up the steps.

Finn's heart was in his mouth, he looked at the others and they were already grinning.

"It's the G&T. It's meeting."

They should have been afraid, they were absent without leave in the Bug. But suddenly the normal rules didn't seem to apply any more.

After the months of tedium and frustration *something was happening.*

Nine miles away, Grandma was finding it difficult to sleep. She had been on her way to bed with her cocoa when she'd heard Al's car pull up in front of the house, only to take off again immediately. Perhaps he'd forgotten something and gone back for it? Perhaps he'd decided to go back to his bed in London for the night? Perhaps anything, really. She'd got into bed and tried to put it out of her

mind, but the moment she closed her eyes a maternal sixth sense had kicked in. What if something was wrong?

She called Al. Straight to voicemail. She called Commander King. Straight to voicemail.

She smelt a rat.

FIVE

DAY ONE[10] 00:03 (GMT+1), September 30.
Hook Hall, Surrey, UK.

"HEY!" Kelly called out as they descended. "WHAT'S THE BIG DEAL?"

Al's head snapped up. Did he hear something? A high-pitched whining? A wasp? No... it was a nano-jet.

"HERE!" came the shout again and Al saw a lit-up fat bumblebee-sized Thing dropping towards him.

"Woah!" Al shouted. "We've got the nano-crew in the house! Nobody move!"

[10] G&T official history, Forbidden City operational timeline starts: DAY ONE Sep 30th 00:00 (GMT+1).

Everybody in the CFAC, from Commander King down, froze. This shouldn't be happening. The nano-crew was supposed to be tracked at all times.

Al held out his hand and the Bug landed on it. Four tiny figures disembarked and were quickly surrounded by angry giants.

"I can explain…" Kelly started.

"What the hell?!" Al said. "I was about to come and wake you all. And you, young man," he said to Finn, "aren't supposed to know this vehicle even exists!"

"It's his birthday present! We were just taking the kid for a ride!" said Kelly.

"I'm telling my mum!" Al said.

This sent a bolt of fear through Finn.

"That's a top-secret, prototype nano-vehicle of incalculable value and you have just put all your lives in danger," Commander King hissed from on high.

"Ah, nuts. He's thirteen years old. What were you doing at thirteen?" said Delta.

"I was at Eton," said Commander King.

"This country needs a revolution," said Kelly.

"We don't have the time," said Commander King, turning smartly to lead the way up the gantry. "Come."

They entered the Control Gallery as it was blinking to life, the place crammed with computers and control systems. Various members of the Global Non-governmental Threat Response Committee were already settling themselves around a giant horseshoe-shaped table.

As Al sat, he placed the Bug on the table in front of him then carefully transferred all four of the crew to the Sony Walkman nDen, which he hooked to his top pocket and tapped to switch on the loudspeaker.

Commander King called the meeting to order with the words: "Lock us down".

Doors locked and blinds whirred down across the long gallery windows. Numerous screens switched on, showing live feed images of the UK Prime Minister and the other world leaders who sat on the G&T. For the first time in *ages*, Finn tasted danger and, with only a hint of guilt, felt a growing excitement.

Commander King turned to the main screen. On it appeared the two most powerful men in China: the President of the People's Republic and his security chief, Bo Zhang.

"Zaoshang hao daren." Commander King addressed the President with courtly authority.

"Good morning from Beijing," replied the President in perfect English.

"Mr President," King began, "on behalf of the Global Non-govern—"

"Yeah, it's late here," Al interrupted. "Let's skip the diplomatics and catch up at Christmas instead. What have we got?"

"Thank you, Dr Allenby," sighed King, and ordered: "Slide."

A picture appeared on the central screen.

It was of a Chinese police officer inside his car.

Dead.

"Shanghai, China, twenty-four hours ago. A dead police officer with no obvious sign of injury. He'd been running a simple ID and security check on a young foreigner."

Blurred CCTV footage appeared on-screen.

"White Caucasian male, false Belgian passport, no fingerprints, nothing to trace. We think late teens. He popped up enough times on both the Airport and Forbidden City CCTV systems to provoke a routine stop-and-search enquiry."

"The Forbidden City? I've been there with Her Majesty the Queen and it is most certainly not in Shanghai," asserted the Prime Minister with idiotic certainty. "It's in Beijing – look it up."

"Correct, the Forbidden City was the Imperial Palace of Chinese emperors for centuries, but it's also the name of the 23rd Industrial Progress Zone of Shanghai, a massive purpose-built, high-tech hub to the South of the city."

Pictures flashed up on-screen of a factory complex, miles of production lines, thousands of masked workers in shiny white facilities; then of the whole huge industrial area from the air – laid out like a complex crop circle. A diagram was then overlaid, illustrating the layout and adding numbers.

"Genius!" said Al.

"It's a picture of Pi!" Finn called out, delighted.

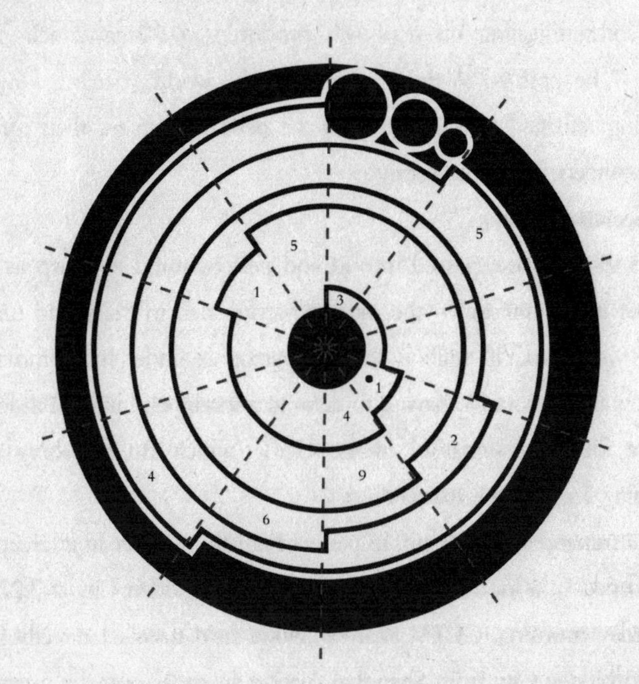

"Correct," King said. "The city is laid out as a circle divided into tenths. The ratcheting out of each arc, or sector, expresses the number Pi in multiples of one tenths of a rotation, thus – 3.141592654 recurring – the ratio of a circle's circumference to its diameter."

"You worked that out?" said Al, amazed at Finn's insight.

"We got shown it once in class," Finn admitted.

"It's the densest area of computer manufacturing in the world and the site of several advanced research plants," King continued. "A newspaper dubbed it the Forbidden City when it was being built and the name stuck. Nearly every piece of technology we're using and communicating on now was produced in China, much of it here –" he pointed to the screen – "in the world's hardware hub."

King returned to the picture of the dead policeman, then turned to the video feed from China.

"Secretary Zhang?"

Bo Zhang rose, poised, proud and perfect, mind as sharp as the creases in his uniform – the most powerful man in the world under forty, with some 10 million security personnel under his command. He was uncomfortable having to defer to a foreigner, but his President was a founding signatory of the G&T (which Bo had only that morning learned the existence of).

"Commander," he began, in perfect English, "Officer Ju intercepted the suspect in a food hall in sector 9 of the Forbidden City at 7:22am yesterday morning. CCTV analysis shows he'd travelled directly into the Forbidden City from Shanghai Airport six times over the previous five weeks. When questioned, the suspect contradicted this surveillance information and Officer Ju made a decision to bring him in. Last contact by radio was at 7:24am. An assault of some kind then took place. There were no marks on the body apart from a pinprick wound on the right temple. When the cranium was opened, massive nerve damage was observed in a clear path from the wound."

An animation flashed up, a revolving 3D CAT scan of a human head, with broad red lines marking the projectile's devastating progress through the brain.

It was like a child's scribble inside someone's head, thought Finn, and it reminded him of something...

"No weapon known to our analysts could have caused such damage. Given the global strategic importance of the Forbidden City complex, this committee was informed."

"Weird..." Al said, and got up to look more closely.

"What could have done this?" asked the UK Prime Minister.

"The most extraordinary bullet in history..." Al muttered as he studied the diagram. "How big was the projectile?"

"One point five millimetres square," Bo Zhang replied.

Then Finn remembered. "It's like what a grub would do to an apple! Or if a human botfly gets trapped in a human skull and eats and eats through the brain till the person goes mad and eventually dies."

"A *what*?" asked the Head of British Security in disgust.

"A human botfly," came the voice from the box on Al's top pocket. "I've always wanted one. How long was he under attack?"

"Less than two minutes. Who am I addressing?" asked Bo, confused.

"One of the nano subjects," explained King.

Al popped open the Sony Walkman before a camera to reveal the four tiny people ranged across the sofa. They waved. Bo, who had been frankly disbelieving of their existence to this point, gave the tiniest nod back.

"But an insect didn't do this," said King, returning to task. "This is the suspect arriving on a flight from Macau." He called up an image of a man in an airport security line. "And this is his hand luggage."

An X-Ray image of his bag appeared. King zoomed in on a

bright but tiny dot that seemed to be inside the top of a pen. Al went right up close and screwed up his eyes.

From the nDen it looked like nothing Finn had ever seen. A piece of magnified metal plankton. A black shell, some kind of square eye, a whip-like antenna, an ugly open hole (a mouth?) with a protruding rail and dangling beneath: spilled steel guts, tentacles, tools and connectors. A sharp squid of a thing.

"A robot?" Finn wondered aloud.

Al took off his glasses and gave them a clean.

"Whatever it is," said Al, "it's been shrunk."

There was an awful silence.

"Are you sure?" asked the Prime Minister, appalled.

"Well, I can't see exactly, but it looks like an incredibly sophisticated machine. The only way, in my opinion, to engineer something like that would be to build it at full size and subject it to the Boldklub shrinking process. Kaparis escaped Scarlatti with a chunk of my crucial Boldklub sequencing code[11]. We always suspected he had an accelerator, maybe he's figured out enough to take it this far. He won't have cracked the key fractal equations, and I doubt he's anywhere near shrinking living things, but crude, rude, oily machines he may have mastered."

Everyone but Bo Zhang knew who he was talking about.

"You have a suspect?" Bo asked.

King called up an image of a young, able bodied, jackal-handsome

[11] See Operation Scarlatti.

Kaparis trying to avoid a camera flash in Basel, Switzerland in 1994. Jet black eyes, jaw taut with suppressed anger.

"David Anthony Pytor Kaparis," said King. "Born 1965. A brilliant young scientist brought low by a nervous breakdown following the collapse of a crackpot theory of super-organisms. Went into banking and finance for a decade till he was paralysed as the result of some kind of accident circa 2000 and confined to an iron lung. He disappeared into the criminal underworld from where he rigged the markets and caused the financial crash of 2008, making himself the world's first trillionaire in the process. Bent on world domination. He was the man behind the Scarlatti emergency and is the global public enemy *par excellence.*"

"You think Kaparis would attack again so soon?" said the Prime Minister.

"Who else?" said Al as he studied the photograph. "Who else would have the audacity to imagine it, let alone the resources to pull it off?"

"Can we take another look at the killer?" asked Finn.

A copy of a false Belgian passport flashed up. A bearded face, hard and determined.

"Check his eyes," said Finn, sitting forward.

The shot zoomed in. Up close the iris was pure photo-shop blue.

"The iris in this shot has been erased and retouched," said Finn. "He's one of Them."

"The two Kaparis field agents we recovered during Operation Scarlatti showed severe damage to the cornea," Commander King

explained to Bo, "with scar tissue running through the optic nerve into the brain, consistent with the insertion of some kind of probe. We suspect some kind of brain conditioning. Here the scarring has been disguised."

"What's Kaparis doing in China? What's he after?" asked Kelly.

"Industrial espionage?" the Head of Intelligence suggested.

"But only the tech is built in Shanghai. The design work goes on in Silicon Valley – that's where a spy would be," said General Mount.

Commander King turned and addressed Bo Zhang again. "Not to be indelicate, but is it true there's a new supercomputer at Qin Research at the heart of the Forbidden City? The 'Shen Yu'? A quantum computer that's being tested as we speak?"

Bo Zhang said nothing, but there was thunder behind his eyes. Someone would suffer for this.

The Chinese President simply nodded. "A perfectly legitimate research project."

"A *what* computer?" asked Finn.

"A quantum computer," said Commander King, "designed to take advantage of the strange behaviour of matter at the quantum level – super-positioning, or the ability to be in two states at once. A single 'bit' of conventional computer memory either holds a 0 or a 1. A single 'qubit' in a quantum dot can be both 1 and 0 at the same time. In theory that makes it capable of processing contradictory information and thinking for itself – at 4000 times the speed of conventional computers."

"Thinking for *itself*? As if it were *alive?*" said Finn.

"Correct," said Commander King.

"Governments and companies waste buckets of money on them so that clever young researchers can ask them 'what's the meaning of life?' and so on. They have had no useful application thus far," said the Head of Intelligence with contempt.

"Only because at the moment so much conventional computing is needed to figure out what they're saying," said Al.

"We don't want Dr Kaparis anywhere near this technology," insisted King.

"*If* that's what he's after. We know nothing for certain," insisted General Mount.

"True," agreed Al. "It's speculation at this stage."

"So what's the next stage?" asked the Prime Minister.

Al pondered a moment.

"This kid has made six visits, so we have to assume he's released six nano-bots of the kind pictured here. Only one of them has to get inside your quantum computer and at the very least Kaparis will have stolen its design. And that's probably only the start of it. We have to stop him."

"But how?" asked Bo Zhang.

Then Al said the words Finn was virtually bursting for him to say.

"If there *are* half a dozen nano-bots flying about, they'll show up plain as day on our nano-radar rigs[12]. I say we go out there. We

[12] Nano-radar is limited in range but because nano-material is so dense even the tiniest objects shrunk by the Boldklub process are easily detectable in flight.

find them, then we destroy them."

"We can hunt them down in the new nCraft..." said Delta, almost breathless.

"YES!" said Finn.

Tap tap tap! came a knocking from the main door. *Tap tap tap!*

One by one, committee members turned to see what was happening. There, pressed up against the blacked-out 20mm-thick bulletproof glass was a face. The peering, distinctive, concerned face of a woman in an overcoat and slippers.

Grandma.

She was rapping on the glass with the handle of her umbrella and saying quite distinctly – "NO!"

SIX

DAY ONE 21:56 (LOCAL GMT+8). The Forbidden City, Shanghai. Nano-Botmass:*52

XE.CUTE.BOT52:GO

The colossal black concrete barn that housed the Shen Yu quantum computer lay at the very heart of the Forbidden City.

After tunnelling out of the dead policeman's brain, the XE. bot had flown through the Forbidden City and located the barn, entered its air-conditioning system, then spent many hours eating through layers of dust-filter membrane.

Once through the filters, the XE. bot flew along through six metres of aluminium ducting finally to emerge inside the Shen Yu Hall itself.

XE.CUTE.BOT52:STOP

Ranks of hyper-servers were arranged like city blocks over an area the size of a football pitch.

The XE. bot hovered, mapping the Hall and aligning itself.

At the very centre of the server blocks stood the Quantum Hub itself.

XE.CUTE.BOT52:GO

The XE. bot flew directly to the Quantum Hub. It landed on a pipe through which liquid nitrogen coolant was being pumped. It cut into the pipe and entered the liquid, sealing the breach with an expanding polymer plug, and allowing itself to be pumped along into the quantum core.

Inside it raised its body shell and flew into the crystal cluster at the great quantum computer's heart, exposing its own crystal core to the perfect light – photonic nano-beam laser light – and captured it. Stole it.

The light of life.

And the XE. became a new thing.

Infected with intelligence.

It navigated its way back out through the coolant pipes, leaving the Quantum Hub unharmed and intact.

Then it thought:

I CAN FLY.

And the bot flew. It flew up to the ceiling, back the way it came, squeezing out through the air filters into the night and across the rooftops of the Forbidden City, a secret fire dancing within. A fire that would spread.

SEE XE.CUTE FLY.

The bot flew all the way back to Food Hall D in Sector 9, all the way back to the Kung Fu Noodles concession.

I STOP.

It waited near the ceiling until the cash tray of Till Number 3 was opened by the cashier, then it dropped into it before it was closed again.

I SEEK.

When the cash tray closed, the bot crawled through a seam in the housing at the back of the tray and inside the till. Into its electronics. It made its way to a position on the till's circuit board near the power supply unit.

I FIND.

There it found the fifty-one other bots of the Vector Program, arranged and interlinked into a production suite, waiting for it. The final piece of their jigsaw.

The XE.CUTE bot connected itself to the head of the assembly.

Then it established a communications link with Kaparis Command on Song Island via the secure Confetti[13] network.

[13] An unbreakable radio-signal-fracturing program that allows Kaparis's operatives to communicate securely across the globe.

Then it instructed the Vector assembly suite to start self-replicating.

XE.CUTECONNEXBOT(ALL)> RUN

SEE VECTOR RUN...

Kaparis watched data dart to and fro across his screens.

He glowed.

A quantum mind was at work within the crystal belly of the XE.CUTE bot. It could think in a way that would allow it to operate without constant instruction. It could adapt. Survive.

It could pass on its stolen light.

Success... Kaparis let himself savour it a moment. All his victories were private. Selfish.

Exactly how he liked it.

The fifty-two prime bots would replicate themselves, then replicate themselves again, then replicate themselves again – on and on ad infinitum. And every time a bot was made, a tiny crystal would be created too, just a few atoms thick, and that crystal would glow with the same photonic light that the Prime XE.CUTE bot had just stolen.

It would allow that bot to think, would allow it to make a simple choice[14].

[14] Boolean logic, the system of logic that allows binary computers to process information, does not accept paradox (e.g. two different right answers to the same problem) thus computers can never choose between answers of equal value (I mustn't eat the chocolate it will make me fat vs I must eat the chocolate I will feel good): therefore computers can never be independently intelligent. Only humans can pull this trick off (mostly they eat the chocolate). And quantum computers (mostly they don't).

It might make a wrong choice and be destroyed, any number of bots might, but eventually one would make the right choice and the community of bots as a whole would learn and progress.

All that was needed was an inexhaustible supply of bots.

SEVEN

DAY ONE 17:54 (GMT+1). Hook Hall, Surrey, UK.

For eighteen hours after the G&T meeting broke up, Hook Hall was in full swing.

Secretary Bo Zhang and Commander King quickly struck up a bureaucratic rapport. King would take overall control, with Bo Zhang in charge of implementation. A Hook Hall team was to fly out to Shanghai and set up nano-radar in the Forbidden City, with cover particularly thick around the Shen Yu experimental quantum plant. Suitable headquarters and accommodation would be found. Signatories to the G&T agreement the world over were informed that a preliminary investigation was taking place and that the threat level was judged AMBER.

A team of technicians in the CFAC prepared to fire-up Al's Henge for the second time in twenty-four hours in order to shrink more radar systems and nano-supplies.

Stubbs supervised final adjustments to two brand new X2 nCraft – aka 'Skimmers' (way prettier than the Ugly Bug, like torpedoes crossed with flying fish) – while Kelly and Delta stocked up on supplies and went through tactical and fallback procedures with military planners, both loving the 'mission focus' after so many months idle.

In southwest France, as a precaution, eleven members of the Equipe Bleu of the Commando Hubert[15] cancelled a long lunch and a game of pétanque as they were scrambled to join the special operations vessel A645 Alizé then 200 miles West of French Polynesia, now diverting north to Chinese waters.

And Finn...

Finn spent his thirteenth birthday struggling against a Gale Force 7 sulk.

Grandma held a unique position within Hook Hall set up by dint of being Al's mother, Finn's grandmother, and Totally Formidable (she'd spent half a lifetime caring for the criminally insane as Lead Nurse at Broadmoor, the UK's most high-security hospital) and there was absolutely no way she was going to let Finn go on the mission with the rest of the nano-crew. She hated her grandson to be unhappy, but it was preferable to him being dead.

And Finn certainly was unhappy. He had refused to 'go' to school with Hudson, refused to help any of the crew or Al with their

[15] Special martime commando force co-opted to the G&T following assault action in the Bay of Biscay during Operation Scarlatti.

preparations, even refused to accept a Skype call from Carla (as she had the audacity to be in China herself, if a good 1000 miles south of Shanghai).

He spent most of the day in his nano-room, torturing himself by checking out epic Chinese bugs online. He had a classic green praying mantis in his collection already, but China boasted extraordinary multi-coloured versions, striped like tigers and poised like kung fu masters ten times his size. Not that he was going to see one. Not that he was going to see anything…

He reappeared at teatime to make one last desperate appeal.

"I *am* going!" he demanded.

"No!" repeated Grandma.

"It's not fair!" said Finn.

"Nothing is fair," Al confirmed, "but this is just an exploratory investigation."

"So I'm involved in everything we do – but I'm dropped as soon as anything exciting happens?!" said Finn. "*Everybody* is going to be there!"

"I'll still be here!" said Grandma. "And Hudson's coming for a birthday sleepover!"

"No he isn't! I'm going to China! I have medals from three countries! Look around, do you see any Scarlatti wasps?" asked Finn.

"Firstly," said Al, wagging his finger, "you weren't meant to be involved in Scarlatti. That was an accident from which we're still trying to recover and, secondly, think of me, Grandma and Yo-yo. We nearly lost you once, we're not going through that again."

"Hear hear!" agreed Grandma. "God saves the world one soul at a time, and you're next."

"I'M THIRTEEN YEARS OLD AND NINE MILLIMETRES TALL – GIVE ME A BREAK!"

"And we're not going to make it worse for you by allowing you to get killed!" Al replied.

Finn threw an empty nano-water bottle up at him. It bounced off his chest.

"Come on," pleaded Al. "If this is a real attack, and it's probably not, but if it is? Kaparis is behind it."

"It's YOU he wants, Finn. That ridiculous man..." said Grandma, having to repack Al's bag to cope with the thought.

"When a man that crazy, that powerful, is focused on taking over the world – that's bad enough," said Al. "But when he's gunning for revenge against a thirteen-year-old boy? Let's not go there."

"I've already beaten him once and I'm not afraid of death!" said Finn.

"Infinity!" cried Grandma.

Al snapped his fingers and pointed straight down at him. "That's the Drake family problem right there – like father like son. No temporal fear. On the Allenby side, we live in constant terror. Your mother was the only one of us with any guts."

"So – what, I'm always going to be hostage to *your feelings*?! You're going to leave me behind *all my life*, I'm *never* going to be allowed to do anything, is that it?" Finn was so angry he thought he might burst.

"Yes," confirmed Grandma.

"No!" said Al, "because Kaparis will soon be caught and you will soon be macro again and we're all going to live happily ever after."

"Oh yeah? When *exactly* – and how about the truth for once. Because you've been promising that for a while and all we've got so far is a dead mouse!"

Finn stormed back towards the seed tray tower block.

Al sighed. "Finn, stop… Truth is, there is a possibility that we may never be able to bring you guys back to size," Al said.

A moment stretched in silence. Finn felt weak at the knees. It felt strange having someone speak your worst fear out loud.

"But it's one possibility out of many," said Al, leaning into the compound. "I want you to look at me…"

Finn looked up into Al's clear, crazed, curious eyes.

"Your father used to say 'we are bound only by the speed of light and our imagination' and no matter what it takes, I will find a solution and bring you back – so help me Richard Feynman."[16]

Grandma appeared over Al's shoulder, eyes filling for all three of them. "Before he could walk or talk your Uncle Al could work a television remote control. He'll find a way to fix things."

Al paused. "You are precious to us, see… And we're never going to put you at risk again."

Finn bowed his head, resigned. While they loved him he was their prisoner; that's just the way it was with families.

"And stop behaving as if it's the end of the world," insisted

[16] Fun physicist par excellence.

Grandma. "This is not an 'end of the world' situation – it's term time."

When it came time for goodbyes it was all a bit of a rush.

"Happy birthday, kiddo," said Kelly and scuffed Finn's hair, offering his great block of a fist to bump – an action that usually deteriorated into a punch to the side of Finn's head as Kelly pretended to forget how to do it. "Sorry you're not coming with us."

"No you're not," said Finn, taking the punch.

"True," Kelly lied. "But someone has to stay at mission control."

"Think yourself lucky," said Stubbs. "I don't travel well at all."

"We're supposed to be a team!" said Finn.

"And you're supposed to be thirteen years old," said Delta, hugging him. "What matters most is you staying in one piece."

Finn watched them climb aboard a model train bound for the CFAC exit.

"We'll be back before you know it!" said Delta.

"I'm not going to think about any of you!" Finn called as they pulled away. "I've got Yo-yo, I know he loves me!"

"Yo-yo doesn't love you," came Al's voice from on high, "he's just the dumbest connection of nerve endings, protein and hair ever thrown together by a random universe."

Al saluted and winked.

"Text me updates – and Skype as well – and bring me back a kung-fu mantis, not just a green one but something special! And don't you dare have any fun!" Finn yelled.

"Moi?" grinned Al, all innocent.

"Sir, the Commander is waiting," called a technician.

Al's last words were, "Look after Grandma!"

Then Finn watched his uncle disappear.

Up on a monitor he saw him getting hurried across the CFAC to a waiting chopper. Soon they'd all be on an overnight flight to Shanghai. Power was leaking from the building.

At least he and Hudson could spend the rest of his birthday repeatedly blasting their way through successive digital war zones while consuming snack food. It would give him time to process his emotions and the events of the day. *There are limits on everything when you're thirteen years old*, he thought… A thought immediately interrupted by—

WHUMP! The sides of the biosphere shook.

"Hey. Birthday greetings," said Hudson.

Without fail, and despite repeated warnings about vibration, Hudson would chuck down his school bag whenever he came into the lab, sending a minor shockwave through the nano-compound that could shake Finn clean out of bed.

Hudson collapsed into the beanbag next to the compound, fringe flopping over the top of his glasses as he emitted the latest playground gossip. "Guess what? Skeggy's older sister took him to get a tattoo of a phoenix but his mum found out and stopped it halfway so now it just looks like a chicken with worms coming out of its butt."

He stopped at the sound of the helicopters overhead.

"Hey, where's everybody going?"

"Secret mission. Can't say or I'd have to kill you," said Finn.

"I thought we were meant to be a team?" said Hudson, indignant.

"Tell me about it," said Finn.

"We are a team!" said Grandma, catching the end of the exchange as she bustled into the lab, dragging Hudson's sack of sleepover bedding after her. "We're the three musketeers! It's me, you and Hudson!"

Yap! added Yo-yo, bouncing in her wake.

"And Yo-yo. And guess what I've got tickets for?" Grandma looked very pleased with herself.

"What?" Finn hardly dared ask.

"Bulb Expo! Tomorrow!"

"Bulb Expo?" said Finn.

"Turns out Commander King is *very* senior in the Royal Horticultural Society and he's given me three tickets. We'll have a marvellous time!"

"Is it a light show?" asked Hudson

"No, silly," said Grandma, "it's garden bulbs! Like *The X Factor* for flowers."

Garden bulbs? Finn felt something snap inside.

"I am not going to a poxy flower show!" he yelled.

"Nonsense. I can't just go with Hudson. We can't be two musketeers, we must be three!"

"Yes you can – he can tell you about his butt worms."

"Goodness. Have you got worms, Hudson?" asked Grandma.

Hudson looked stricken.

"Not me!" cried Hudson. "Skeggy!"

"Who on earth is 'Skeggy'?"

Hudson regarded her in terror, knowing he was about to undergo ruthless cross-examination.

Finn was about to storm back to his quarters when suddenly he was struck by a brilliant idea.

"Hold on," said Finn. "Grandma, where exactly is this flower show?"

"Chelsea."

He was going to do it...

Because he had learned a lesson after all today – *you have to take your chances ...*

Kaparis received intelligence reports of helicopters heading north from Hook Hall towards Heathrow and the holding of a China Airlines flight.

Tedious, *he thought and felt a tingle of irritation.*

They must have spotted Baptiste was one of his and decided to act. They would be too late, of course.

Should he bring bot distribution forward? He had the time. He would soon have the numbers.

Or maybe he just needed to create a little distraction?

To muddy the waters and give Allenby a shock he would never forget?

"Prepare a Viper squad," he ordered Li Jun.

Two and a half hours later, Dr Allenby, Commander King and the thirty-three other members of the Hook Hall detachment were cruising at 35,000 feet in a Boeing 747 bound for Shanghai. The evening meal had been served and the cabin lights had been dimmed.

The flight would take eleven hours and they would move seven hours forward in time. Al was reading *The Art of War* by the ancient Chinese warrior, Sun Tzu, to get into the right mood. "The General who wins makes many calculations in his temple before the battle is fought," he informed anyone who'd listen.

Out of the window the endless night passed, deep with secrets.

DAY TWO 07:00 (LOCAL GMT+8). Cash Till#3, Kung Fu Noodles, The Forbidden City, Shanghai. Nano-Botmass:*25765

SEE VECTOR RUN...

Sparks flew as carbon was fed into spark gaps at one end of the production suite. It was consumed, worked and transformed as it was drawn along an assembly line.

***25766...**

An instruction from an XE.CUTE bot at the head of each suite determined which of the fifty-two types of bot would be replicated.

*25767...

There were now forty-three production suites fixed like leeches to the electronic innards of the cash till, each a miniature factory, each running at full capacity. Eleven more were partially constructed across cash tills #2 and #3.

*25768...

Bots crawled and flew through the three cash tills and constantly swapped data and power through long whip-like antennae, bots of every kind and colour, waiting to slot into place to form a new production suite on the crammed motherboards.

*25769...

Desperate to replicate.

The PRIME XE.CUTE sat at the head of suite #1. Like every other XE.CUTE in the botmass it passed on the photonic light of life as each new bot emerged. With a quantum kiss.

It was endless.

*25770...

*25771...

*25772...

*25773...

*25774...

EIGHT

DAY TWO 17:43 (Local GMT+8). Shanghai, China.

The late afternoon sun threw itself off the glass cliff face of a hundred skyscrapers and a twenty-first century metropolis spread out before them like a cloth of gold.

Shanghai. The Pearl of the Orient. The largest city on earth.

Gold, King noted, because sunlight was filtering through a haze of airborne pollutants, through a haze of energy and effort. A city of a thousand cranes, of a million cars, millions more bicycles and countless busy people – yeast in the global economic dough.

The Hook Hall team were transferring from Pudong International Airport into the city aboard twin Z-15 PLA helicopters. From parks and green spaces tethered dragons curved up towards them, extraordinary

stacks of multi-coloured box kites, part of an annual festival. Looking south the team saw the Forbidden City industrial complex laid out before them, a crazy dartboard of radial roads and white-walled factories.

Bo Zhang, who had welcomed them with a faultless snap of a salute, explained that at the centre of the Forbidden City, where security was tightest, were the government and military research institutes and cutting-edge companies such as Qin Research.

"We will establish ourselves at our headquarters and then go to the city," Bo Zhang explained, and the helicopters banked to fly into the heart of Shanghai.

"Wow..." said Al.

It was clear the Chinese were going to look after them.

The spanking new Siam Towers Hotel was a bejewelled stalagmite: ninety-nine stories of luxury (including a helipad). The top three floors of the hotel had been turned over to the G&T, including the five-star Roof of the World restaurant, which had been transformed into an operational centre that was already up and running. Feeds to world leaders connected on one screen array. On another live CCTV and intelligence feeds from across the city were at their disposal. A huge central table had been set up for the most important players.

There was more to come as they were shown their rooms.

Commander King hated hotel rooms, thought them vulgar, and relied on handmade silk pyjamas for a sense of quality and comfort whenever he was travelling, but even they seemed cheap in the suite he'd been assigned.

Al loved hotel rooms. The minibar, gadgets and gizmos, the complimentary snacks and toiletries. His suite on the ninety-eighth floor did not disappoint. It was fitted out for the super-rich, with three dazzling rooms that boasted an interconnecting tropical fish tank – who could live without one? – and a bed the size of a tax haven from which he could look down on the Shanghai Bund riverfront. The cityscape that bloomed beyond looked like something out of a comic book. It looked like the future.

He must tell Finn. He took a picture, adding:

View from the top – Shanghai. Wish you were here, kiddo.

Then he focused on a little food van parked on a street corner, below. There was a queue. What was it selling? Dim sum? Ice cream?

Whatever it was, Al thought, *I'm going to get me some.*

A minute later, seized by the moment, he was travelling down the rapid elevator.

DAY TWO 18:16 (Local GMT+8). Song Island, Taiwan (disputed).

Activity increased on Song Island, and not just among the birds battling for nesting space on its craggy outcrops.

"Move fast," snapped Kaparis.

"Vipers One, Two and Three in position," reported Li Jun from her bank of screens.

Each Tyro in the field had a direct camera and data feed relaying information back to Song Island.

"Target approaching – hot hot hot," reported another voice.

"Viper Four, you have visual?"

"Visual," confirmed Viper Four.

The screen array above Kaparis became a clash of city images as his team closed in.

"Vipers One, Two and Three?" asked Li Jun.

"Visual..." "Visual..." "Check – visual..." came the response.

Kaparis could see the operation coming together, could see his quarry, could see his squad drawn up and ready to strike.

His pulse rose. Microprocessors instructed his iron lung to increase respiration.

"Command?" prompted Li Jun.

"Commence Viper," ordered Kaparis.

He watched as the Tyros moved as one.

DAY TWO 10:16 (GMT+1). London, UK.

The number 11 bus made its way down the King's Road, Chelsea, heading towards the Bulb Expo, and up on the top deck Finn was happy, looking out of the window and remembering all the times he was brought up to London as a treat by his mum – to go to the zoo, see a show, or visit Al.

They had taken the bus on Grandma's insistence and Finn was perched in Grandma's nDen, an adapted brooch pinned to her coat. He would transfer to an even smaller nDen on Hudson's baseball jacket (disguised as a button badge that read 'Be alert – your country needs lerts') later.

As the bus stopped Hudson rose, nervous. He was not good at breaking rules. He lumped down the stairs of the bus, carrying Grandma's wicker basket. Three undercover Security Service Officers – 'Suits' – followed. The boys' secret plan was to escort Grandma into the show for the bare minimum of time before being "free to do their own thing" and visit the museums for a couple of hours, or as free as one could be with the Suits hovering. But little did Grandma or the Suits know that hidden in the mouthpiece of Hudson's asthma inhaler was the X1 nCraft – the Ugly Bug…

They'd bagged it the night before just after lights out. Finn had said, "Hudson. Don't go to sleep yet. I've got an idea for tomorrow."

"Is it about flowers?" said Hudson.

"No. Ever stolen a car?"

Later, after much debate and reassurance, Finn had directed Hudson to crawl below CCTV range in order to slip into Lab Three where they'd nabbed the Bug. They would both be in terrible trouble if they got caught but, as long as Hudson held his nerve and avoided a major asthma attack, they wouldn't get caught.

For once Finn was going to be selfish. For once he was going to be free – even if just for an hour. They would find a way for him to board the Bug unseen and, while Hudson made his way around the Science Museum, Finn would fly around London – looping the Albert Hall, racing around Hyde Park and even dive-bombing the Changing of The Guard...

VROOOOOOM!

The moment Hudson and Grandma stepped off the bus Finn heard the screams of over-revved moped engines. In the microsecond blur before the first Vespa hit the curb and knocked Hudson flying, Finn saw all three Suits reach for their guns.

"Grandma!" Finn yelled, but before she could react everything went red, white and blue – *SLAM* – she hit the pavement and all Finn could hear was screaming, all he could see were shoes and smoke and tyres...

Vespas circled, engines buzzed, gushing out coloured smoke like the Red Arrows – one red, one white, one blue. Each moped was driven by a Tyro, each with a passenger, infrared visors giving them clear vision through the fog.

Kaparis caught sight of Hudson unconscious in the gutter. He could hardly believe it. His pulse leapt, his mouth watered... Drake. Why else would the Allenby woman be dragging the idiot Hudson around London except as a companion? He felt something bloom through his consciousness: Fate. He could almost smell the boy.

"Take her down fast! Get her into the container!"

Tzzzzzooft. Tzzzzzooft.

Silenced bullets spat from sidearms. Down went two of the Suits.

The third stood over Grandma to protect them, yelling into his radio. People on the street were scattering or screaming.

The three Vespa passengers dismounted. One aimed at the last Suit and shot out his knee. The Suit collapsed in agony but returned fire, felling one of the attackers.

Two remained. As they flipped up their visors Finn saw them. Identical twin girls, Thai, but with albino-white skin, flat eyes and fixed grins. One had a scar across her face, the other had chrome spikes sticking through pierced ears and lower lip.

"WHAT on EARTH do you think you are doing?" Grandma thundered at them from the ground.

For a moment they seemed surprised. Then, still grinning, they kicked themselves into the air to assault her.

With a sling-shot of her handbag – *WHUMP* – Grandma caught Scar in the solar plexis and sprang up. A snap pirouette (learned in the Miss Ellis Ballet School circa 1958) avoided Spike's incoming fist and was followed up by a D'artagnon-like swipe of the umbrella – *DOINK* – across her throat.

There was a moment of relative calm as the twin attackers reeled at Grandma's feet.

"Woah," said Finn.

But then –

"Go Viper Four!"

Just behind the bus a street sweeper detached himself from his cart and ran towards Grandma, swinging his broom like a majorette, clipping Grandma's ankles and sending her back to the pavement (she never expected such a thing from a local council employee). Spike and Scar seized her and sprayed something in her face.

"NO!" Finn cried as all three began to manhandle her into the street sweeper's cart.

He kicked open the nDen and was immediately hit by a sweet chemical smell... then everything slowed down and went black.

NINE

Within minutes all routes out of West London were subject to extensive roadblocks as police scoured the capital looking for the three scooters.

Nobody noticed the street sweeper and his cart emerge from the smoke. His passage south was uninterrupted. When he reached the river he pushed the cart to the end of a jetty and transferred it to a waiting speedboat.

Moments later the boat was cutting through the grey-brown water of the Thames.

DAY TWO 18:38 (Local GMT+8), Roof of the World, Shanghai.

Al headed back up in the elevator surrounded by a team of Chinese State Security Officers who had appeared in alarm while he queued at the ice-cream van.

On the top floor King and Bo Zhang waited for him to arrive. King had been alerted to the misdemeanour – "Allenby has left the building! Without an escort!" – and had agreed to talk to him about his conduct. Eccentricity might be seen as a marker of genius (or just an annoying trait) in Britain, but in China it bore no such association.

Then an emergency call came in and King had to step back and pick up a phone.

The elevator doors slid open and Al stepped out.

"Doctor! I insist we follow security protocols!" said Bo Zhang in polished distress.

"Take a chill pill, or at least get yourself one of these," said Al, indicating the ice-cream cone. "If we're going to work together, you have to understand my only rule is – 'there are no rules'. Frees up the mind, y'know? Helps to think." Al gestured expansively.

"Your working methods are your own. I am responsible for your personal safety!" snapped Bo Zhang.

From his phone, Commander King cut across them both.

"Gentlemen –" he looked grave – "we have a problem."

DAY TWO 23:59 (Local GMT+8). Kung Fu Noodles, The Forbidden City, Shanghai. Nano-Botmass:*249994

***249995...**

***249996...**

***249997...**

***249998...**

***249999...**

***250000: NANO-BOTMASS = DISTRIBUTION MASS**

Production continued while the datum was transmitted to Song Island.

A response code was received.

Immediately the PRIME XE.CUTE gave the order.

SEE VECTOR DESPATCH.

Bot group by bot group, the tiny army, packed so tightly into the three Casio QT6600 cash registers that they were in danger of overheating, began to come to life.

Miniature turbines turned in earnest.

Over the next few hours the bots left their electronic hives. They proceeded to the maximum altitude allowed by the food hall ceiling then drifted down to land on the heads of the workers, crawling down through their hair to hide.

The unwitting workers then carried them back to factories across

the Forbidden City. There the bots crawled out of the hair, cut their way through protective hairnets, and flew off in search of fresh electronic circuitry. Having located one another through a simple signal and colour-coding system they formed fifty-two new bot production suites. And began again.

SEE VECTOR MULTIPLY

*250001...

*250012...

*250019...

*250034...

*250041...

*250056...

*250077...

PART
TWO

TEN

DAY THREE 11:28 (Local GMT+1). Altitude 30,000 feet, speed 560mph.

Finn was sweating and running – he was lost in a supermarket, he was little, he was calling out, but no one could hear him, and—

A scream woke him. An everlasting dull scream.

Panic shot him to life – darkness, suffocating heat, his weight piled on his shoulders, thick cloth walls pressing in on him – a sack? He gasped in panic and kicked himself around, as he did so the cloth gave way and he got a lungful of fresher air – not a sack. He was in the folds of something…

He breathed some more. Let his panic drain. Still he heard the scream. An engine. A jet engine.

His eyes adjusted to a dim light and detected LED pulses of red and green. He pulled himself up the wall of woollen cloth, Grandma cloth... He could smell home. He had been caught in the hem of her 'smart-but-not-evening' skirt.

He reached her knee. She was laid out and strapped into some kind of white crate. Tubes and wires came off her chest and connected to a small life support unit, its LEDs blinking.

Finn ran up her prone body and scrambled over the hissing, humming medical apparatus clustered over her head until he reached her ear.

"GRANDMA!"

Nothing. He yanked on some of the downy hair on her lobe, scaled her soft splendid face and tried to haul open her eyes. She was out cold. Drugged.

Kaparis. The kidnappers had been Tyros, no question. But what did Kaparis want with Grandma? Finn knew the answer; it was in his heart. We love her. Blackmail... The thought of her being hostage to such a man made him sick.

Finn could feel pressure growing in his ears. They popped. The jet was descending. He had to do something.

Down the side of the white crate he could just make out something – a ziplock polythene bag.

Finn headed for it, unclasping Grandma's RHS visitor badge on the way. He used the pin to puncture the bag, then put both hands in the hole and forced it to split.

Inside were the crazed contents of Grandma's handbag – notes, nuts, make-up, coins, elastic bands, stamps, dog treats, a small china bell, a Cambridge University snow globe, a cheap string of pearls, an emergency sewing kit, a single cufflink and also everything they needed for their nano-day out – six nRation packs[17], his nPhone backpack (battery dead) and, crucially, *Hudson's inhaler.*

Finn kicked open the cover on the inhaler's mouthpiece.

There was the concealed Bug, its pockmark thrusters showing through the cotton wool wadding.

Finn pulled away the wadding and climbed on to the Bug. He snapped on the ignition switches and, with a sudden suck, the turbines turned over and the Bug lit up – rising to suspend itself, headlights alive.

He eased it out of the mouthpiece and loaded up the nRations and the nPhone. Instinct told him to haul a pin from the sewing kit too, just in case.

He climbed back aboard and was pulling on the harness when he felt a sudden jolt as the aircraft they were in touched down. There was a fierce braking and rumbling of wheels, loud enough to wake—

"Aaaaaaaargh!"

"Grandma!"

The giant old woman woke in a panic, trying to lash out but constrained by the straps. The whole crate shook.

Finn turned the lights up and shoved the controls forward. The Bug forced its way through the split in the polythene bag, then,

[17] Nano food and water packs that had been shrunk in large quantities to keep the Sons of Scarlatti fed and hydrated wherever they were.

thrusters hissing as automatic systems fought to keep it stable, it rose over Grandma's struggling legs, each the size of a blue whale, and flew up towards her head.

All Grandma saw was a glowing fiend approaching fast.

"Aaaaaaaargh!"

"GRANDMA! It's ME!" Finn yelled.

Grandma's terrified, giant eyes fixed upon the Bug.

"Infinity?" she demanded, words muffled by the mask.

He flew nearer to her ear. "We've been kidnapped. By Kaparis. But I don't know where he's taking us."

Grandma let out a yodel of distress.

"We're all right. I'm all right. I don't even know if he knows I'm here."

The engine noise wound down and they felt the aircraft stop completely.

"We have to decide what to do," said Finn. "We need a plan."

"Don't do anything!" insisted Grandma.

Metallic clunks were heard as doors were opened. Voices. East Asian.

"Grandma, if they lift the lid on this thing I've got to go and get help."

Footsteps began to draw closer.

Finn put the Bug into whisper mode and probed Grandma's soft grey hair until he found a hairgrip just behind her ear. "Grandma, keep your eyes closed and play dead. I have to escape and find Al – he'll rescue you!" he said quietly.

Grandma groaned as if in a deep sleep – a moan of protest.

Finn grabbed the nPhone pack off the back seat of the Bug.

"I'm going to leave the nPhone on your hairgrip. It's out of battery, but all you need to do is put it by any live wire to charge. Just by being on, it will send a signal so Al will know exactly where you are."

CLACK! CLACK! The clips holding shut the crate were sprung open.

Finn twisted the Bug out of sight and Grandma snapped her eyes shut in terror.

The lid of the crate lifted and a highway of light opened up down one side of it. Two pale, identical teen heads appeared.

Spike and Scar.

Scar took out a powerful torch and Spike took out a smart phone, studying the screen intently. Nano-radar of some kind? The searchlight started at Grandma's feet and crept up her body, towards her head.

They're looking for me, thought Finn.

He watched the light creeping up Grandma towards him. He could hear his heart beat in his chest. He and the Bug were bound to light up any nano-radar. He was a sitting duck. He slapped open the chamber on the M249 machine gun in front of him. There was ammo in the block ready to run.

As the searchlight hit him a bright spot showed up on the screen of Spike's phone. She shrieked.

Finn gritted his teeth and punched the controls forward, and accelerated towards a spot between Spike and Scar's ghostly faces, taking them by surprise.

The Bug shot out into the cramped cargo hold, engine

SCREEEEEEEEEECHING to reverse-thrust before it hit the fuselage, the seat harness nearly tearing through Finn's shoulders.

"Yaaa!" screamed Scar and dived for a cargo net, grabbing one and brandishing it.

Finn shot back past them, over the large white chest he'd just escaped, slaloming through a landscape of personal luggage and crated cargo, darting around, looking for any kind of exit.

Spike span with her phone until she captured the dot on her screen again. "Zhyaa!"

"It's on the tracker. Confirmed nano," reported Li Jun.

"Get it!" hissed Kaparis.

Nano-radar had been fitted into every Tyro phone to track the nano-bot army. They hadn't been able to search the body properly in the haste to escape London, but now, after hours of waiting, Kaparis congratulated himself. The boy would soon be in his hands.

Scar flew through the cargo after the Bug, agile and vicious, a cat after a bird.

Finn pulled the controls up hard and fast to loop above her, but she cast the cargo net.

THWACK! It caught the edge of the Bug and sent it spinning.

Finn clung to the controls as gyroscopes fought to stabilise the spin.

Scar and Spike leapt as one to grab the spinning, glowing Bug, but as they did so a whole section of the fuselage suddenly shifted.

All three were dazzled.

Bright sunshine.

The cargo bay was opening. Finn, back in control of the Bug, jammed the sticks forward and shot towards the light.

With a hot wet wallop he hit the air of the tropics. Eyes adjusting in the rich sunlight, he flew out beneath the belly of the huge airliner they'd been trapped in, then corkscrewed around until he found himself rising above it.

As he climbed higher, an airport spread out beneath him, its runways ending where they met the sea, while beyond, steep mountains framed skyscrapers that ran in a crest around a natural harbour.

Finn's mind jumped to the old kung fu films Al used to insist they watched.

And at once he knew exactly where he was...

ELEVEN

Hong Kong.

The city clung to the hills about the harbour. Cargo ships and junk boats busied themselves on the waters. Old and new, land and sea.

Finn looked back down at the airport runway. Spike and Scar were on the tarmac, searching for him, pointing the radar into the sky. The white crate was already being unloaded on to a forklift.

Grandma…

He had to get help.

At the edge of the artificial island that was the airport, he saw a fast train approaching.

Twenty minutes later Finn was riding its roof as it ran back into the city, like a desperado in the old Wild West, the Bug jammed into an air vent. Finn's plan was to find a British official – there must be an embassy in Hong Kong – who could make contact with Uncle Al. Though what he would say, and how he would say it, he had no idea.

After another ten minutes of buffeting, the train stopped at a station called Kowloon. Finn recognised the name from a Call of Duty map, and got off.

He floated the Bug out of the station and flew to the top of a road sign where he tried to take in the scene. Dozens of images, sounds, sensations hit him. It was *busy.* The traffic was busy, the people were busy, the buildings were busy... even the air was busy, infused with aromas of Asian food, exhaust fumes and the sea. Then, penetrating the cacophony around him, Finn heard a tinny, high-pitched, stop-start buzzing.

DZZTZT-ZZZTZTZT-ZTZTZ-TZZZ-ZZZSZ-TSTS-TZZZTZTZ...

He looked up.

Incoming. His least favourite insect: stooped in profile, lazy in flight and responsible for the annual death of half a million people from malaria. A mosquito.

It swung down towards him, body swollen to the size of a Labrador, its wingspan the same as Finn's height, arrow-thin proboscis pointing at the open side of the Bug, ready to run straight through him... *DZZT! DZZZT!*

Finn snatched up the pin he'd taken from Grandma's bag and using it as a sword he parried the incoming stinger with a healthy smack, before thrusting forward to nick the mosquito's swollen

abdomen. *BOOOSPLOOSSHHH!* Its guts – full with blood harvested that morning – burst spectacularly.

Not since Finn had totalled the pinata at Max Campbell's ninth birthday party had he seen such a multi-coloured explosion. *Yuk*, he thought, drenched in blood and guts.

But there was no time to recover, straight away...

DZZTZT-ZZZTZTZT-ZTZTZ-TZZZ-ZZZSZ-TSTS-TZZZTZTZ...

A dozen or so more mosquitoes appeared, from all directions, alerted by the smell. Finn aimed and fired the Minimi machine gun – *DRRRRTT!* – and a pair ahead of him exploded in a haze of haemoglobin. The scent would throw the others briefly off his own, but he had to get clean or he'd never get rid of them. He fired the turbines and took off.

There was a fancy skyscraper hotel opposite: The Ritz Carlton. Bingo.

Finn headed for the automatic doors, and following a businessman, he slipped into the sudden, air-conditioned cool and entered a large atrium.

Sanctuary.

He headed for the reception desk a few feet above the businessman, mind a blur, one half thinking: *I'll follow the man to his room, find water, wash the blood off, then fly out and find the Embassy*, while the other half thought: *How? How? How? Ho—*

And that was when he saw it. At the reception desk, one leaflet among a hundred others: The Pennsylvania Youth Orchestra Proudly Presents...

DAY THREE 16:03 (Local GMT+8). Roof of the World, Shanghai.

For Commander King, for Bo Zhang, for the team of technicians and experts of every kind, these hours were the worst of times. The waiting and the not knowing were far worse than fighting and losing a battle, far more sapping of the human spirit.

Al, who had long since burnt through his reserves of patience, was having the worst of it. Every newsless moment was torture. He watched the surveillance footage they had of the attack on Grandma over and over – the clouds of coloured smoke obscuring most of the screen. Nearly twenty-four hours had passed.

The boy stays safe. The one thing he'd promised himself – the one thing he'd promised his mother. *The boy stays safe.*

Al would never forgive himself. What was he doing here, miles out of place, hours out of time? But what was the alternative? This was Kaparis, Kaparis all over, and if it was Kaparis then by now Finn and Grandma could be at any point on the globe undergoing who knew what...

Whatever this was, it must be something to do with the G&T being in Shanghai.

He also knew that this would not end until he could get to

Kaparis. That meant watching and waiting. That meant holding his nerve.

He swallowed his fear, scratched the sphalerite stone that hung at his chest with his thumbnail. Secretly it glowed.

Kelly was angry, restless. Delta electric with upset. Stubbs withdrawn. But there was nothing to be done but deal with the task in hand, while security agencies scoured the globe for any sign of Finn and Grandma.

A network of nano-radar sites had been set up in the heart of the Forbidden City and Kelly and Delta had flown countless sorties in the X2 Skimmers, making high-speed sweeps, zone by zone, spiralling towards the centre of the tech metropolis. But so far they hadn't located any sign of a nano-bot.

Bo Zhang's technicians had pored over weeks of CCTV footage and established that nine other unknown teenagers had visited the Forbidden City over the previous eight weeks, they had all visited Sector 9, and it had to be borne in mind that many more than six nano-bots could have been released. But again, there was no direct evidence they were Tyros and as yet no sign of any nano-bots.

Commander King was detached and rational. "Time. The more time that passes, the closer we get."

Bo Zhang nodded in agreement. "We will find them, it's all just a matter of—"

"Scale," Al interrupted. He jabbed a finger out across Shanghai and did the maths.

"Somewhere out there, on a sphere with a surface area of more than half a billion square kilometres, is a boy only 9mm tall. Right now he may as well be lost in the infinity of space."

TWELVE

DAY THREE 18:06 (Local GMT+8). Song Island, Taiwan (disputed).

"First of all, Mrs Allenby, my apologies for keeping you waiting..."

An apology. He was opening with an apology. How English.

He had planned an awesome first meeting. Violet Allenby was to be led in as he listened to Bach's D Minor Toccata and Fugue *and the chamber rose out of the coral sea and spiralled to its highest point in the sugarloaf. He would then say, "Good day, Mrs Allenby." Instead, as the chamber rose in darkness, he was forced, upon his honour, to apologise.*

He'd spent the intervening hours mobilising the Hong Kong Triads[18] *and*

[18] Organised criminal gangs, often violent, based in Hong Kong but operating through East Asia, akin to the Italian Mafia.

organising the search for Infinity Drake, air-dropping into Hong Kong as many nano-trackers as could be spared. A vast effort, a vast expense. And so far: nothing. The boy had clearly gone to ground.

"My duties have delayed me. Also, I understand my operatives were negligent and omitted to restock the life support unit. Fresh opiates should have been added. I understand you may have been awake for part of the journey. Distressing. I wanted you to wake as if in paradise."

"I was as comfortable as could be expected, under the circumstances," snipped Grandma, determined this ridiculous man should not have the pleasure of being right about anything.

"They will be punished."

"Not on my account. I was quite happy. As a girl, I memorised 'Hymns Ancient and Modern':

"Love divine, all love's excelling

Joy of Heaven to Earth come down..."

...warbled Grandma rather beautifully.

Good grief, *thought Kaparis.*

"I hope from now on you will be more comfortable. A room has been prepared. As long as your son and his employers see sense, you should not be detained here for long."

"How do you know I haven't already raised the alarm?" said Grandma.

"Nobody will hear you cry for help out here," Kaparis assured her.

"Nevertheless," said Grandma, "I must inform you, it is my duty as an Englishwoman to attempt to escape."

Kaparis sniggered, sounding like a slowly deflating balloon. "That, I look forward to."

Mindful, as always, that every last soul was worth saving, Grandma took in the wretch on the raised dais. The hissing lung. The distorted head encased in optics. The screen array and the mysterious thirst for global dominance. It all added up to unhappiness (it so often did). She must try and be positive. She trotted across to the windows, adjusted the blinds and switched on a lamp to create a warmer atmosphere.

Heywood, the butler, froze in terror. Ditto her two female Tyro escorts. As Grandma rearranged a sculptural masterpiece, Li Jun physically shook at her bank of screens.

"Stop that!" Kaparis gasped. "This chamber has been designed with great care and at great expense by the finest – Do not touch! That's a Matisse!"

"Well, it's all wrong in here. You know, Doctor Kaparis, whatever misfortune befell you, a disability does not have to be a disaster—"

"MADAM! I am exactly the same in character now as I was the day I was born, never altered by expediency, circumstance, injury or experience – not even when members of your family tried to destroy me. I have endured and I remain and I—"

"Our local riding centre does marvellous work with the Cerebral Palsy Pony Club. Come along and you might surprise yourself. The ponies don't have the palsy, of course, the riders do. The point is to embrace life. I mean, look at Tanni Grey-Thompson and all the Paralympians—"

"Heywood!"

"If madam would—"

"Ah, it's Heywood is it – fresh flowers on top here." She patted the iron lung. "An arrangement around a tropical theme, I think. Do you have a

florist? I don't see much in the way of native flora, do you?" she said, peering out at the moonlit rockface.

"Kindly refrain from addressing my staff!" snapped Kaparis.

"Would you like to be alone?" asked Grandma.

"... Yes."

Kaparis tried to say it in a way that it implied it was all his idea, yet succeeded only in sounding chastened.

"Shall we go then?" she said to the two terrified Tyros and began to sing again.

"He who would valiant be, 'gainst all disaster

Let him in constancy, follow the Master..."

Grandma was taken to her room beneath the waves. It was beautiful, done out very much in her style, with a big brass bed and a selection of cakes. There was even a supply of wool, knitting needles and patterns.

"He should be running a hotel, not trying to take over the world," she remarked to one of her 'girls'.

Why's he looking after me so well? *she wondered.*

But there were cameras too and, as the girls left, she heard the suck and click of a heavy lock.

She thought about having a short cry, then decided not to let the side down.

She very carefully removed her hairgrips, leaving the nPhone, barely the size of a pea, against the lead of a lamp.

Then she settled down to knit and think.

Knit one, purl one, knit one, purl one, knit one, purl one...

DAY THREE 20:49 (Local GMT+8). Hong Kong Cultural Centre, Hong Kong.

Time.

Finn had spent the afternoon biding his time and playing it safe. After he'd managed to clean himself up in the hotel he'd found a tourist information map and headed straight to the concert venue. His strategy: to hide in the auditorium until the start of the concert.

He had thought about trying to find a friendly embassy. He had even thought about hiding in the hills with some exotic praying mantis. But anywhere in the open meant the Tyros could find him using their nano-radar.

Better to wait for Carla. At least she knew his voice, even if she didn't know he was only 9mm tall...

Once Finn made it into the venue he had hidden behind a light fitting above the stage. When at last he heard the concert start (with the theme tune from *Superman*) he emerged from his hiding place to watch the show.

He spotted Carla at once among the pristine members of the orchestra – kooky and pretty with hair and clothes that looked like they'd dropped out of the sky and just sort of landed on her.

He felt a wave of relief. She looked how he always thought she would – fun.

She sat in the second row of strings, scraping the hell out of her cello, and gave *Superman* everything she'd got.

The evening wore on and he even lost himself in the music once or twice, briefly forgetting the situation he found himself in.

But the relief was short-lived.

When the show came to an end, the conductress collapsed into a deep bow and the audience erupted. Then slowly the auditorium began to clear.

Finn waited for his big moment.

The musicians were packing up. Carla was putting things in her backpack and a side pocket lay open. When she put it down to help someone with a trombone, Finn hit one quick burst of thrust and dropped right into it.

DAY THREE 22:02 (Local GMT+8). Song Island, Taiwan (disputed).

An alarm sounded.

"We've got something. Sector Four," reported Li Jun from her terminals.

Kaparis felt a tingle of excitement. The search matrix in Hong Kong had finally got a bite.

A voice babbled in Mandarin. Li Jun translated. "Hum Hong district. Just a flash. Possibly aboard a coach. They're trying to track it through the traffic."

"Contain it. Investigate," ordered Kaparis. He watched the live video feeds, seeing Spike and Scar sprinting down a crowded, neon-lit city street, barging pedestrians aside and dancing through traffic.

On the ECG monitor his pulse quickened.

THIRTEEN

DAY THREE 23:01 (Local GMT+8). Harbour Grand Hotel, Hong Kong.

"Oh, hey Carla!" Finn rehearsed and paced. "Whatever you do, DON'T FREAK OUT, but it's me. Finn. Infinity Drake. I…"

He dried up. This was going to be hard. How do you to explain to someone you are 9mm tall?

Finn had flown the Bug out of the backpack and was hiding behind a marble bowl of potpourri in Carla's hotel room as she pulled a brush through her hair. As soon as she settled down, he would fly to her bedside table then, very calmly, make the speech of his life. That was the plan, anyway.

Carla put down her hairbrush and climbed into bed. As Finn got back on the Bug, he saw her check her phone.

Is she going to make a call? he wondered, then she plugged in her earphones and switched off the light. *Oh great, she's listening to music. Now how am I supposed to...?*

Then another thought struck him – screen-lock!

Quick as a flash, he fired the Bug across the room, dismounting as he hissed to a halt beside the smartphone. He jumped up and skidded across its touch-sensitive surface *just* before the screen-lock kicked in and it lit up beneath him like a dance floor.

He felt butterflies battle in his stomach. Before him lay a girl 150 times his size. If he got this wrong, she could swat him in a moment. How could he talk to her through the earphones? Finn moonwalked across the screen, scrolling the apps until he found an answer – the Voice Recorder.

Squeals and sounds of commotion came from the corridor outside. A shout. He heard a woman say, "Excuse *me*, young man!"

It suddenly occurred to Finn that it might be trouble. That it might be Tyros. He had to be quick. In a two-step shimmy, he paused what Carla was listening to and lit up the Voice Recorder.

"Hey, Carla! It's me," Finn said into the phone mic.

Her huge head turned in confusion.

"What...?" she said.

"Sorry to interrupt. It's a military thing," he said, thinking on his feet. "You can jump someone's phone without them answering. Crazy, huh?"

Carla sat up looking supremely puzzled. He dived off the screen and prayed she didn't notice him before he was good and ready.

"You're kidding?! People have rights!"

"That's what I said."

"I was almost asleep. Is it Delt? Is she all right?"

"She's fine. It's… me."

"What's wrong?"

There was more commotion in the corridor.

"I've got to tell you something, Carla, and it's pretty freaky so I want you to promise to stay calm," said Finn.

"What?" she almost spat, suspicious.

"No sudden movements even – OK?"

She looked like she was ready to kill.

"OK… Tell me."

"It's like this. Me and Delta and some others… What you think has happened to us – that she's doing some research and I'm some kid off the base? – that's not exactly true."

Carla gasped and sat up. "I knew it! I knew you were lying to me!"

"Only because something has happened to us that is so unbelievable you wouldn't have believed it even if we had told you the truth. But right now you're going to have to cope, because I'm in big trouble and you're the only one who can help me."

"What are you talking about?"

"See, I'm right here. With you. Now. I can hear those noises out in the corridor, I can see Hong Kong out the window, everything."

Her face was a picture of concerned incomprehension.

"We had our atomic structure altered. We were *reduced*."

"What?!"

"Have you ever seen *Honey, I Shrunk the Kids*?"

"Oh, ha, ha! You think that's funny? You know what my sister does? You know how much we worry?"

"I AM NOT JOKING – we had our atomic structure altered. I know it's hard to believe, but the distance between the nucleus and the electrons in every atom of us was shrunk. I'm just over 9mm tall, Delta's just over ten and, if you look to your left, I'm standing on your phone... right now..."

Finn held his breath and climbed back up on to the screen. It came to life, revealing him in a pool of AMOLED[19] phone screen light.

Carla held her head absolutely steady. She glanced over. Just once. Nothing. No reaction whatsoever. And then...

"ARRRRRRRRRRRGH!"

Finn had heard the term 'hit the roof' many times in his life but he had never actually seen it happen.

He did now.

Carla shot up out of bed with a scream any siren would be proud of.

"NO!" Finn shouted, but instantly found himself spinning through the air as the phone was yanked upwards by the earphones.

By the time he hit the bedside table again – "Oooof!" – there was a hammering at the door.

19 Active Matrix Organic Light Emitting Diode.

Finn leapt on to the Bug, like a cowboy mounting a horse, and shot it straight back into the open backpack, just as the door burst open.

"GET ME A DOCTOR!" Carla yelled.

There was a lot more yelling before any sense could be made of the situation. Ms Kampinsky – the orchestra's conductor and tour manager – was yelling about some unknown teens breaking into people's rooms, while Carla was yelling about having been seized by what she would only describe as "a medical emergency".

After a tennis rally of firm enquiry versus hysteric insistence, Ms Kampinsky decided that Carla did indeed need to see a doctor. Carla dressed and picked up her bag, but refused to bring her phone when it was offered, claiming it was "possessed".

Then at around 11:24pm Carla, Ms Kampinsky, two Chinese Cultural Officials and Finn (still hiding in the backpack) left the hotel in the back of the ambulance, arriving at the Queen Elizabeth Medical Centre four minutes later.

Within another ten minutes Ms Kampinsky and the officials were filling out forms and making calls while Carla, much recovered and thinking herself quite sane again, waited on a bed in a private room to see a psychiatric registrar.

Finn left as long as he dared before emerging again. He hadn't actually seen Scar or Spike in the hotel, but from what Ms Kampinsky had been saying, he was convinced the 'unknown teens' were Tyros searching the hotel for him. He had to get through to Carla.

Finn flew the Bug up to a spot just above her right ear.

"What did I say about *not freaking out*?" he said.

Carla wanted to scream again, but realised that she was in a 'Safe Place' now. She just needed to stay calm until the doctor arrived.

"I'm not listening," Carla whispered. "You're not real."

"Carla, this is real," said Finn, "and what's more, there are people after me, people called Tyros, those teenagers Ms Kamp—"

"Not listening!" insisted Carla.

"You're *not crazy*. You've been confronted with something very, very unusual and you're trying to figure it out. You need time, but I'm sorry, there isn't any. My grandma has been taken hostage and a bunch of people are trying to kill me! You have to alert someone who can get a message to the British authorities – to Delta and my Uncle Al."

"You think the *psychiatrist* is going to believe me?" she said.

Finn brought the Bug round to hover just in front of her face and looked her straight in the eye.

"Carla. I need your help."

She was looking past him. Then back again. Testing her senses. Finally her eyes fixed on him.

"Is it really you?" she whispered.

A wave of relief was just about to wash over Finn when –

SHHHHHHHHHCT! – the curtains round the bed suddenly flew back.

On one side stood Scar.

On the other stood Spike.

Cruelty in double exposure.

"RUN!" Finn screamed.

Too late. Twin hands – kung fu swift – snatched out: Scar plucking Finn and the Bug out of the air and Spike slapping a hand over Carla's mouth.

Finn just managed to reach the fire button of the Minimi as the world closed around him – *DRTDRTDRTDRTDRT!*

The giant hand was stung open. Finn found himself falling in the Bug towards the tiled floor. He reached the controls just in time and pulled the Bug round to corkscrew back up towards the Tyros' heads, finger on the fire button all the way – *DRTDRTDRTDRTDRT!*

Pinprick bullets struck Scar's face, raked Spike's neck, causing squeals of protest. Carla sprang out of Spike's hands and in a split second was off the bed and across the room, bursting through the doors, checking behind her for Finn, who was following in the Bug, surfing her slipstream.

She was as quick on the ground as her big sister was in the air, feet barely skimming the hospital floor as she shot down the corridor followed by the staccato slap and squeak of Tyro sneakers as Scar gave chase, Spike a moment behind, screeching into a phone.

At the end of the corridor were two sets of double doors. One left. One right.

"Which way?!" screamed Carla.

"Left!" called Finn, trying to remember, and *BANG* – through they went.

Bad call. No exit, just another empty corridor. Mean girls closing in fast.

Finn reversed the Bug's thrusters, turned 180 degrees and fired – *DRTRTRTRTRTRTRTRTR!*

Spike and Scar protected their eyes from the bullets, but barely slowed.

A porter appeared ahead of Carla pushing a trolley with a patient aboard.

"HELP!" she screeched, but the porter spoke no English, so *BANG* – on they flew through the next set of doors. This lead into a wider corridor, open stairwell and...

"People!" called Finn, hoping they might be safe, but as soon as he did he realised they weren't the kind you would want to meet in an alleyway on a dark night.

A dozen-strong gang of gritty, hooded Triads.

Spike screamed in Mandarin at them and they moved as one straight at them.

"LEFT AGAIN!" yelled Finn, lighting the Bug up as bright as Tinkerbell so Carla could track him.

They entered a stairwell. Finn whizzed ahead, Carla followed. Round and round and down and down the stairs they went, falling like Alice, until they flew through the doors at the bottom to arrive in...

The basement. Deserted, but for themselves and the incoming Triad hoods. For a moment it seemed like the end. Footsteps boomed down the stairs behind them. Then Finn spotted what looked like an emergency door at the far end. "OVER THERE!" he yelled, leading the way, and in a dozen strides Carla hit the release bar and was out into the tropical night.

She rolled a heavy bin across the door to slow their pursuers, then gritted her teeth and ran and ran and ran at full pelt, arms pumping back and forth, back and forth – a sprinter following a firefly.

But however fast Carla ran, the Tyros and the Triads kept up the chase, catching up to twenty, fifteen, ten metres behind.

Up ahead loomed a large building. Carla passed a sign reading WEST KOWLOON XTR – PERSONNEL ONLY and ran into the service area of a brand new railway station. One or two bemused railwaymen looked up as she leapt the barriers, but were too distracted by the strange twins and gang of Triad hoodlums in her wake to try and stop her.

Carla ran on, reaching the main concourse. Up ahead, a train was pulling away from a platform. As she and the Bug sped towards it, an electric luggage cart pulled out across their path.

"WATCH OUT!" yelled Finn, but Carla was way ahead of him, leaping and vaulting the piled luggage like an Olympic gymnast, hitting the platform on the other side.

Spike and Scar and the Triad gang tried to follow but the cart slowed them and protests rang out from station staff around them, whistles blowing.

Carla ran on. The back of the train was retreating, accelerating away. With a final lung-bursting dash she ran alongside and reached for the last carriage door. Her hand caught the handle. For a split second it opened before – *SLAM* – the rushing air shut it again.

Flying parallel, Finn urged, “AGAIN!”

Again Carla grabbed at the handle, opening the door the merest crack. Again the air pressure resisted – but Finn and the Bug, giving it all the power they’d got, drove themselves into it with thrust enough to hold the door open *just* long enough and *just* wide enough for Carla to leap like a salmon through the gap – *SLAM* – and land in a heap on the carriage floor…

Finn flew up to the window and watched as the last Triads giving chase ran out of platform, features snarling as they disappeared from view.

Hardly believing their luck, Finn floated back down to Carla as she panted it all out.

“Wow. You’re good. Not for a girl or anything… Just good,” said Finn managing to ruin the compliment.

A moment further ruined as they heard the chilling words –

“Tickets, please!”

FOURTEEN

DAY FOUR 00:23 (Local GMT+8). Hong Kong-Shanghai Sleeper Express.

Diddly-dee diddly-daa, diddly-dee diddly-daa...

The 23:55 non-stop XLR overnight train to Shanghai headed relentlessly north at never less than 165mph. As swift as it was luxurious, it was also the newest sleeper rail service in China. It had twenty coaches with each coach containing eight cabins. Beautifully designed and fitted to the highest specification, demand was high – even at RMB1900 (around £200) a berth – and foreign passengers had to book in advance to pass all security and transit checks. For their trouble, they could expect to arrive in downtown Shanghai for lunch the next day, completely refreshed.

Diddly-dee diddly-daa, diddly-dee diddly-daa...

Carla and Finn held their breath.

A rotund, uniformed attendant finished checking the bathroom at the end of the last carriage for stowaways and made his way to his own guard's compartment. The cleaners must have left the door open again. He shook his head, then paused in the doorway to check his phone. He was expecting a message from his wife regarding his daughter's exam results.

Nothing yet.

From her position on the luggage rack 20cm above his head, Carla was so close she could see his protruding eyebrows and generous belly. She tried desperately to control her breathing.

The attendant stepped inside. It was a simple office, with a messy desk, a CCTV screen and a digital graphic that displayed the status of each of the cabins in the five carriages he covered. Before he could sit down, a buzzer sounded. Cabin 6 in Car 3 lit up on the display. The attendant sighed, then opened a cupboard and hung a key with a yellow metallic fob on to one of many empty hooks. Then he left, locking the door behind him as he made his way back down the train to Car 3.

Carla gasped. Finn, hidden deep in the thicket of her black hair shouted: "Go!"

She leapt down from the rack.

"What did he put in the cupboard?" asked Finn.

She opened it and looked inside. There was only one key. It read '2:2'.

"Car 2, Cabin 2... it must be empty!" said Finn. "Come on! Take the key. We can lock ourselves in before he gets back."

An instinct of Carla's protested. "We should pay."

"What? How!"

"It's dishonest!"

"You want to wait up there all night? Or get arrested? What are you waiting for? Go!" said Finn from her hair.

Taking a deep breath, Carla pocketed the key, unlatched the lock on the guard compartment door and they stepped out into the corridor. A divider door into Car 1 hissed open. The corridors were quiet and air conditioned, but they were also narrow. Passengers moved back and forth to the bathrooms and restaurant car, most of them excited tourists and family groups.

Just as they stepped into Car 2, the attendant appeared at the far end of the corridor, making his way back towards them, smiling at the passengers, answering questions.

"Oh my God..." said Carla.

"Make friends! Make friends with that family! Quick!"

"Hi!" said Carla to a pair of blond-haired children waiting to use the bathroom. "Do you guys speak English? Do you know if there's a shower in there?"

"Sure," said the older girl in a Swedish accent.

"We never had a shower on a train before!" explained a boy of eight or so, excited, holding up his phone, which had a Batman case. "I take pictures!"

His older sister rolled exasperated eyes at Carla, making teen-to-teen contact.

"We're here with our parents. Did you like Hong Kong?" the teenage girl asked. The attendant was only a couple of metres away. Carla willed herself not to look at him and literally wrung her hands as she spoke.

"Hong Kong was great, but we had to run like crazy we were so late, so..."

"Are you on holiday?"

"I was playing in a concert!"

The attendant was now literally squeezing past them. Through the curls of Carla's hair Finn looked directly into his eyes.

"The cello. I'm a soloist!"

"Cool," said the teenage girl. The little boy took Carla's picture with a flash of his camera.

"Are you famous?" asked the boy.

"Not really, I'm just—"

"Go!" said Finn, seeing the attendant disappear. "We've got to get in before he makes it back to his office!"

"Oh I think I hear my mom calling me!" Carla said, stepping towards the door of Cabin 2 and inserting the key with a little prayer. The key clicked home. She turned it and shot inside.

The attendant arrived back at his compartment.

All was well, no more cabin indicators were flashing, and the passengers were settling down for the night. Hold on... He paused for a second as he hung up his jacket. He could have sworn he locked the door before he left? He checked the room quickly... All the passports and papers were as he'd left them. Good. But still he could have sworn—

Beep.

His phone sounded. He checked the text. His daughter had passed!

He picked up a dragon head the size of a dice from the mess on his desk, a charm a cleaner had found that morning that must have fallen from a bracelet. He blew on it, blessed his luck, then texted back his congratulations.

Diddly-dee diddly-daa, diddly-dee diddly-daa...

DAY FOUR 00:39 (Local GMT+8). Roof of the World, Shanghai.

It came in a package delivered by a uniformed courier, one of sixty the driver delivered during the all-night shift from the depot in FEDEX/#41/SHANG. It was unusual in that it was unexpected, after midnight, and addressed to 'Dr A. Allenby, Long March Suite, Siam Towers'.

Bo Zhang was furious. Al was a top-secret personage whose whereabouts were meant to be a state secret.

For Al, for all of them, it was if a great balloon of tension that had been filling for the past thirty hours had been popped.

Suddenly things were moving very fast. Technicians gathered round the package, instruments sniffing for poisons or explosives. Al examined every minute detail, then opened it.

It contained a single item. A chess piece. A king. And it came with a note in elegant handwriting that read: *"Check. Unless you'd prefer an exchange of queens?"*

"Typically flamboyant," remarked King as Al screwed it up, suddenly deflated.

"What does it mean?" asked Bo, alarmed at Allenby's flagrant disregard for the rules of evidence.

"It means 'do nothing,'" said King. "Sit this one out."

"He knows we're on to him," said Al as he began pacing and thinking.

"And the 'exchange of queens'?" asked Bo. Before King could answer –

"Sir!"

Three minutes later, Al and an undignified rabble of policemen, uniformed security chiefs, scientists and two flying nano-warriors in X2 Skimmers raced each other down the Nanjing Road to look at the large display window of Yolo Electronics.

They reached it, panting.

On a screen in the top right ran a gif of a woman in her sixties sat in a rocking chair, knitting. A thoughtful look upon her face.

Grandma.

Al leant against the glass and drank her in – the woman who had brought him into the world, had softened its sharp edges, had defined and ennobled his experience of it. Who loved him.

"You fool..." he said out loud.

Not to himself. Not to her. *To Kaparis.*

Meanwhile, back at the Roof of The World operational centre, the youngest Chinese technician seconded to the G&T team, Shi Jian, approached Major Stubbs with a new piece of evidence and in a state of mild terror.

Shi Jian had never addressed a 10mm-high person before.

"You asked, sir, for any unusual activity? Does this qualify?" he said to the tiny, owlish figure who looked up, sceptical.

With shaking hands Shi Jian held out a plastic evidence bag containing the charred remains of a nit comb.

"I doubt it. I doubt most things and it's an attitude that's served me well," said Stubbs.

He indicated the bag should be placed on the table where he could examine it.

Shi Jian briefly explained. Apparently, a woman's hair had caught fire in a factory bathroom. First responders had managed to beat out the flames and an investigation had begun. She had finished her shift and suspected she had lice. She had been pulling a nit comb through her hair when it combusted.

Stubbs stuck on his glasses and peered at the burnt teeth of the comb. Some of the 'lice' had become entombed in the melting plastic.

Stubbs had seen head lice before.

These were definitely not head lice.

"Oh dear," Stubbs said, looking up at Shi Jian as if it was all his fault. "I suppose you better raise the alarm."

As Al led the charge back up to the Roof of the World in one of the express elevators, he explained his excitement to Bo and King. "He's overplayed his hand!"

At last he felt free. At last he felt vital. Let battle commence.

"He hasn't got Finn. If he had Finn he'd show him to us," said Al, convincing himself. "That woman would happily die a thousand times before she saw a member of her family – or anybody else's – come to harm. We nix whatever this is, we find Finn, we hunt Kaparis down, and *only then* do we look for her... Any other way round she'd never forgive us."

"Damn right," said Delta, hovering beside him in a Skimmer.

The elevator doors opened to a space suddenly alive with activity.

"What's going on, people?" Al demanded, and he was led to where Stubbs had begun to hold court at the large central banqueting table, Delta and Kelly flying up for a ringside seat.

In the hubbub, Bo Zhang was taken aside. "Sir, Hong Kong on the line..."

The news from Hong Kong brought Delta to a crashing halt.

"Your sister has gone missing."

"What do you mean 'missing'?" she finally grunted at Commander King, having to force the words past her own fear.

Al had never seen her like this. She was tiny on the table before them, but still somehow terrifying, eyes wide, teeth gritted, ready to run or kill. Probably kill.

"She disappeared from a hospital in Hong Kong where she was being examined following a 'delusional episode'," King explained.

Tears filled Delta's eyes. Her baby sister? All her life she'd been determined Carla should be the safest, most normal girl in America, yet she seemed set on being as odd, inquisitive and unusual as possible. And now this?

"But it's not that straightforward. She was frightened but rational," continued King. "Her 'delusion' consisted of hearing voices…"

"Oh God…" said Delta.

"Of a 'tiny person'. An English friend."

"What?!" said Al.

"Apparently a friend of her sister's who was in some kind of trouble. And who could fly," King finished.

"Finn…" Delta could hardly believe it.

"That's no delusion," insisted Al. "He must have found her and freaked her out…"

"How? How could he possibly have got to Hong Kong?" said Delta.

Al just shook his head in wonder. "He's some kid…"

Delta knew in her bones it was true and took the strangest comfort from the thought that two people she loved so much could have found each other.

"We can't confirm anything at present," reported Bo Zhang. "A lot

of what's coming through is chaotic. CCTV systems across Hong Kong have been targeted and wiped in a cyber-attack. But known Triad members were witnessed making their way into the hospital."

"Either Kaparis has got them already, or they're on the run," deduced Commander King. "And if they're on the run, I trust Bo Zhang to find her – to find them both."

"We are doing the utmost," Bo Zhang affirmed. "All Hong Kong is on alert. Your sister's description is circulating nationwide."

Delta looked up at all three of them. "Are you sure you're doing everything? Absolutely everything? Is there anything, anything else we can possibly do?" she pleaded.

DAY THREE 18:02 (GMT+1). Langmere Secondary School, Surrey, UK.

Cars put their lights on. Leaves fell. Kids ran to rugby practice.

Hudson waited.

Every other Monday evening during term time Hudson had to miss chess club in order to spend an excruciating hour in the presence of the grinning Hertfordshire Schools psychologist. It was excruciating because he had to remember everything he'd made up over the previous two years[20].

[20] Pretending a variety of problem behaviours in order to punish his parents for separating.

That evening's session was going to be much worse than usual because, for once, he actually had a genuine psychological hang-up – one he was forbidden by the Official Secrets Act to discuss.

"Why wasn't I kidnapped?" he wanted to ask. He had been left reeling on the streets of Chelsea while Grandma and Finn had been whisked off in the most dramatic fashion.

"Am I so unimportant?" he wanted to ask. "Why did I get left out?"

His mother always insisted he was 'special', but what did she know. She'd never been put to one side during a major terrorist kidnapping.

The door to the meeting room opened and before the grinning psychologist could even say a jaunty "Hello mate!" Hudson demanded, "What if my entire life is a series of near misses?"

The psychologist, for once, looked thrown. His grin dissolved, but before he could say anything, one of the new heavyset 'school caretakers' appeared in the doorway (in fact one of the Special Branch Officers now detailed to protect Hudson 24/7) .

"Call," said the cop and handed Hudson a mobile.

"Hello?" said Hudson, bemused.

"Hudson!"

"Dr Allenby?"

"Hudson, get Yo-yo from the house, then get on a fast jet to China. There's one waiting at Hook Hall now. This is a Save the World situation."

"Cool," said Hudson.

FIFTEEN

DAY FOUR 01:43 (Local GMT+8). Hong Kong-Shanghai Sleeper Express.

They lay in the dark with the lights out, headed north through the night along the eastern fringe of the great Eurasian landmass.

Finn at 9mm. Carla at 1557mm.

Through the cabin window the vast, moonlit continent rushed past, lights of settlements flashing white and orange.

And they talked, like only kids could talk, long after they should have gone to sleep. Like good friends talk – good friends with a dramatic secret. Because boy did they have some catching up to do.

Finn told Carla everything, from the beginning.

Because of an infant passion for pink Disney-character outfits, the important women in Carla's life – her sister and her step-mom (a fighter pilot and a judge, for goodness' sake) – had to Carla's fury and indignation nicknamed her 'Princess' and always regarded her as something of a delicate thing, to be protected from life's bumps and bruises, and even sometimes from the truth.

This time, Carla thought, Delta had gone too far.

She listened in awe, interrupting at times to seek a point of clarification, or timing, or to exclaim, "So *that's* what all that was about!" or "So *that's* why you were acting so weird..." and most often of all, "I am going to *kill* my sister! How could she have kept this from me?"

Finn, at least, told her the truth.

He told her about the Scarlatti crisis, about Uncle Al's accelerator and his crazy ideas. He told her about how Kaparis nearly killed them all, but they managed to beat the bad guys and return to civilisation – if not to full-size – and of their secret status as global nano-heroes. Then he told her of the events of the last week or so, and of his decision to steal the Bug for a few hours' fun – a day that had gone so horribly wrong.

"God knows what state Al will be in. And *Grandma?* With *Kaparis?*"

Carla didn't judge Finn. What he'd been through was genuinely mind-blowing and besides – he was her friend.

"They never should have left you this size for this long," said Carla, angrily. "They should never have kept it secret, bad things always crawl out of secrets. Adults are so blind. They emotionally decay. None of them feel things as intensely as we do, y'know?"

"Yeah," Finn said, not entirely sure what he had agreed with.

"It's how *I know* you're here now," she said. "That I'm not crazy. You have to feel that something is true as well as know it."

"No, you have to *prove* it," argued Finn. "Your senses tell you one thing then you experiment to prove—"

"We're not robots, we're human beings."

Finn let it go. They were tired and they'd had versions of this 'science versus life' debate many times.

Their plan was to stay hidden overnight, then in the morning they would get hold of a phone and make their escape. They settled down, Carla in the luxury bunk, Finn in a nest behind her pillow, drifting towards sleep until Carla wondered aloud –

"You think if we'd had proper parents we'd be more chilled and not end up in these situations?"

Somehow he knew exactly what she meant by 'situations'.

"Maybe. But maybe life wouldn't be as interesting," said Finn. "Or terrifying."

"I sometimes think my real father will show up – Johnny Depp or someone – during school and everyone will scream, 'Oh wow! Johnny Depp is the new supply teacher!' but he wouldn't be listening. He'd seek me out, walk right across the playground and say, 'I am Johnny Depp, your real father. Everything's going to be cool now.'"

"I Am A Loving Billionaire," suggested Finn in a God-like voice.

"I Am A Loving Billionaire – Want Some Ice Cream?"

They laughed it off.

"I think I'm better off with my adopted mom than wishing my dad would appear. She's always working, but she's mine," said Carla and unexpectedly felt a lump in her throat at the thought of home.

"You can wish all you want. They won't come back. We have to bring ourselves up," said Finn.

"You ever go to their graves?" Carla asked.

"To see my mum? All the time."

"What about your father?"

"There is no grave, as such. There's a field outside Cambridge we went to once. We had a picnic for him."

"Is he scattered there?"

"No. He disappeared. Whatever experiment he was doing blew up and he was vaporised."

"Hold on… he 'disappeared'? And you never got to meet him?" asked Carla.

There was silence. Finn could read something in it, could feel it. Carla spoke again. "Do you really believe that he disappeared without a trace? You're not a kid any more. They should tell you what really happened."

"What? What *really* happened?" Finn was suddenly angry and he didn't know why.

"Maybe your dad just couldn't face having a baby, settling down. Maybe he just quit and walked out. Men do it all the time. It's life stuff."

"No way! It was dark matter! He died in an accident."

"He died? Have you ever heard them actually say that?"

"My mum wouldn't lie. My uncle wouldn't lie."

"But have they actually said that he 'died'?"

"No," Finn had to admit.

"Did you seriously never think to ask?" said Carla.

"No! Because they're telling the truth. He didn't walk out. I'd know."

"How?"

"I'd feel it!" he snapped.

There was a long pause.

"Sorry. My step-mom is a judge in the Family Court. I doubt too much. You OK?" said Carla.

"Fine." Finn sulked, defensive.

He thought about the silences from Grandma and Al whenever they discussed Ethan, like there never were when they talked about his mum. With his mum there would be gales of laughter, storms of tears. But with his dad there was often just... silence.

"What's Dark Matter?" Carla asked.

"It's a sort of mystery, a mystery that would prove a lot of things if we could get hold of some, or at least understand it," answered Finn.

They let this hang in the air a while.

"Adults don't tell us things. But we know," concluded Carla.

Diddly-dee diddly-daa, diddly-dee diddly-daa...

SIXTEEN

DAY FOUR 07:48 (Local GMT+8). Roof of the World, Shanghai.

By the time dawn was breaking, Al and Stubbs had it figured out. The power system, the modular and component structures, the nervous system, the resourcing, everything.

"Mr President... Monsieur le President... Frau Chancellor... Premier... Comrade President..."

Commander King welcomed the various global leaders and their advisors – members of the full G&T committee – many of whom had been shaken awake to attend the briefing.

The mission was now a global concern and the threat level had risen to a straight RED.

Al twitched, impatient to get on.

Delta had worked with him through the night. She was wired but held it together, breaking occasionally to cross-examine Bo Zhang on the search for Carla, or repeating with Al their chief reassurance – Finn and Carla were smart and tough and resourceful and they were together.

A small camera was set on the table, pointing at Stubbs, who stood before a charred array of evidence, Kelly hanging back in his role as 'lab assistant'.

"If everybody has settled in…?" King prompted.

"Righty ho," said the UK Prime Minister, befuddled by sleep (it was nearly 1am in England).

"Alors," said the French Conseiller Scientifique, tipsy after dinner.

"Go!" barked the chronically impatient US military chief, General Jackman, from Washington, who was standing beside his President, both at the end of a long day.

"Ja," said Berlin.

"Da," said Moscow.

King turned to the Chinese President, who gave a tiny nod of assent. Then he started.

"So, to recap…"

Lights dimmed and screens lit up with technical close-ups of charred engineering remains.

"We suspected some kind of miniaturised flying weapon, or spy-bot, had been released into the Forbidden City. We have now caught more than one example and the picture is more complicated than first thought. Dr Allenby?"

He turned to Al.

"Kelly – bring up the first slide," said Al.

It was a picture of two lines of charred robot remains. They looked like smashed-up old TV sets.

"Stubbsy, tell 'em how it is," said Al, switching on his microphone

"These are the remains of the nano-bots we've found, nineteen in all. We have identified twelve different forms. There are similarities between them all. They're made up of the same simple component groups and materials..."

Kelly clicked through a series of images, threaded engineering rods, layered honeycombed sheets of carbon, crude turbines, and knots of wiring.

"They share a central hull which acts like a motherboard, and they all have a simple rail gun and propulsion turbine. But apart from that, they seem entirely different, with different functions..."

"Woah – they have a *rail gun*?" interrupted General Jackman.

"An electromagnetic rail along which a bolt can be fired at extraordinary speed," Al explained to those politicians who hadn't yet gone to the huge expense of trying to develop one. "Far easier to engineer at this scale – but that's not the most interesting thing. The most interesting thing is these interface panels..."

Kelly clicked up another charred feature.

"Which is where I think they join together."

"Join together? To form what?" asked the German Chancellor.

"A plant," said Al.

"A flower? Is this some kind of joke?" asked General Jackman.

"A manufacturing plant. What I think we have here is not just a series of flying weapons – but a factory."

"Making what?"

"*Itself*."

There were quizzical looks from around the world.

"That's an extraordinary claim," said the US Chief Scientist, leaning into shot.

"More Stubbsy," prompted Al.

Stubbs crouched beside the bot remains, the biggest of which only came up to his knees, and beckoned the camera in after him, pointing out what looked like a charred rib cage.

"Right. Well. There's a pair of bots here that feature these ribs – I think these are spark gaps, I'll come back to them in a moment. And over here –" he pointed to bots that shared a cluster of tentacles with various shapes on the end – "all of these limbs could be simple tool arms, cutters, welders, clamps and so on. Other units seem to be all computer power with multiple conductor hook-ups and little else."

"The thing is – none of them make sense until you consider where they fit in a series," said Al.

A technician pressed a button and up came a rough drawing of what a set of interconnected bots might look like: a high-tech assembly line, a strung-out industrial plant.

"We know that one Tyro courier, our murderer, made six trips to the Forbidden City," said Al. "But CCTV analysis tells us there may have been multiple couriers making multiple trips. Let's suppose we're talking forty bots. Put together, they'd form a plant little more than an inch long that could fit almost anywhere."

"What are they running on? Air?" asked the German Chancellor.

"Electricity," answered Stubbs. "See this layering of the body work on the central hull? That's alternate layers of conducting and insulating material. The *structure itself* is a super-capacitor – a power store capable of delivering a significant load. This makes them very delicate, very vulnerable to catastrophic short-circuit – hence they explode on contact with a plastic comb – but with an inexhaustible supply of them, who cares? They just have to site themselves near a power cable and they can charge-up through inductive coils. I've done the maths and they could fire up their spark gaps from any 240-volt power source."

"Nanotubes…" muttered the French Conseiller Scientifique.

"Exactly! Power up these spark gaps, feed in any carbon-based material you like and you create carbon nanotubes," confirmed Al.

"Whoopie-doo," deadpanned General Jackman. "What the heck are they?"

"The dream material of nano-technologists," said Al. "Atom-thick tubes of graphene – the ultimate carbon nanomaterial. Twist them one way you make a metal, twist another, they become semi-conductors. They can be conductors or insulators, construction materials, bullets, literally whatever you want. Think modular, think—"

"Lego," said Stubbs. "Carbon Lego."

"Where are the bots getting the carbon from to feed the spark gaps?" asked the US Chief Scientist.

"Anywhere and everywhere – plastic, paper, organic matter. My

guess is some part of this cluster is harvesting it and feeding it into the spark gaps to create the nanotubes," said Al. "What I think we have here are nano-scale assemblers that can replicate themselves – the dream of nanotech since Drexler[21]. We've been fools—"

"I could have told you that," muttered General Jackman.

"What *we've* been considering ever since we built Boldklub is what *we* could do with macro technology once we'd shrunk it. *They* have done the opposite. They have looked at what nano-machines could make *macro-scale molecules* do. They have kick-started the nano-tech revolution."

Scientific advisors all over the world knotted their brows, trying to chew through the implications.

"The Boldklub process was only needed to create the first assembly line, the first set of, say, forty bots. Once you can engineer at that level, carbon will do the rest," said Stubbs.

"That's why nothing has been showing up on nano-radar," said Kelly. "It's just light carbon, not anywhere near as dense as the Boldklub material we've been looking for. One of these carbon bots would have the same radar signature as a fruit fly. We need to realign the entire nano-radar network."

"All very clever, but I suspect you're letting your imagination run away with you," said General Jackman. "What's the point? I mean, what problems would these nano-bots actually create?"

Al filled him in.

[21] K. Eric Drexler, nanotech pioneer who first proposed the idea of self-replicating nanoscale assemblers.

"Imagine if there's a cluster of these things in every machine that gets shipped out of the Forbidden City. A kid in, I don't know, Australia, opens his new iPad, switches it on and you've got a new breed centre. It sends out scouts to find other devices in the home and you've got half a dozen more. Once inside a phone, suddenly they're being walked from place to place spreading the infection. Within a few weeks, Kaparis has bots in every computer and device on the planet. Not a software virus, a hardware virus. If he wants, he can send them out to kill their users, to bore into their brains. But I don't think that's what he wants."

"He wants control," said King. "He wants power and the display of power."

"Total control over data, information," agreed Al. "He'll be inside every search, every server, he'll change what he doesn't like. Culture? Politics? He will determine what questions are asked and what answers are given. Or he can just push a button and destroy every processor on the planet. What would function then? What would matter?"

Silence.

"If there are a gazillion of these things," said General Jackman, "then where the hell are they?"

"Well, some of them are in people's hair," said Al. "That we do know."

"I have ordered security to start checking for lice," said Bo Zhang, "with extreme caution."

"And how many have you found?"

"The process has only just started and is meeting some resistance. People want to know why."

"Huh," said Jackman, dismissive. "Who's to say this hair-on-fire woman isn't a one-off, some kind of spy and bringing in new bugs to plant in specific machines?"

"At the moment we can't be certain, because we haven't had time to find the rest, or they're deliberately concealing themselves, which is scary enough," admitted Al. "But you want to know the really scary thing? Why are they here? Why now? Kaparis could have released them any time, any place, anywhere..."

"The Shen Yu computer..." murmered US Chief Scientist.

"Bingo," replied Al. "I think Kaparis wants to make them independently intelligent. He wants quantum processing. I have no idea how, but I think he's tapping into the Shen Yu somehow, and the only way to find out for sure is to halt production, conduct a proper search and to destroy everything made in the Forbidden City in the last forty-eight hours."

"Impossible!" said the Chinese President.

"Have we got *any* direct evidence to support *any* of this theory?" asked the UK Prime Minister.

"What about signals intel?" asked General Mount from London. "How are these things communicating, coordinating?"

"We've got nothing on the radio spectrum," reported a technician.

"Kaparis has always evaded signal detection, we don't know how," Al explained.

"This man is telling us his nightmare. Not facts," the Conseiller

Scientifique informed the French President with suitable contempt.

A babble of confused discussion rose, over which Al, exhausted and stressed, momentarily lost patience. "We have to shut down the Forbidden City! We might have to wipe it from the face of the earth!"

A great wave of indignation seemed to break over his head. A member of the Chinese delegation actually squawked.

"Now that's getting way ahead of ourselves…" said the US President.

"Can you imagine what that would do to stock markets?" asked the British PM.

The babble grew and grew and Al realised he'd lost control of the meeting altogether.

SEVENTEEN

DAY FOUR 08:56 (Local GMT+1). Hong Kong-Shanghai Sleeper Express.

They woke early, Carla starving, and took their chances in the restaurant car.

The train was traversing an endless plain and rural China was rushing past – willow trees, paddy fields, shack settlements rich with colour and barns with roofs like shrines.

"So?" Carla muttered into her juice. "What do we do now?"

Finn chewed through his own rations in the bouncing nest of her hair.

"We get a message to the G&T as fast as we can – or rather you can."

"I ran out of a psychiatric hospital. If we contact the police they're going to think – oh hey, here's that crazy girl who ran away from Hong Kong talking about little people."

"OK. Funny."

"I'm not being funny. This is panic," said Carla.

"Definitely don't panic. First we've got to stay on the train without getting arrested," said Finn. The restaurant car was starting to fill with breakfast diners. "If we can make it to Shanghai, we can get to an embassy or find Al in this Forbidden City place. They'll be on alert. All you have to do is walk in and say the word 'Scarlatti' and they'll flip. The trouble is, Kaparis knows we're on this train. He'll have Tyros waiting for us and he's likely to have someone undercover inside the Shanghai police, maybe even the government. He can buy anybody he likes. We have to make one simple phone call to someone we trust – Al or Delta – before the train stops. But as you know so well, we have no phone..." Finn complained.

"That was your fault for freaking me out!" Carla hissed, but then quickly covered it with a cough as the Swedish family walked in. Mum, dad, teenage girl and the little brother with the...

"Steal the Batman phone," ordered Finn.

"I can't do things like that!" she whispered.

"Say hi! Invite them over here to join you! Now!"

"Never!"

The two kids recognised her and smiled.

"SAY HI NOW!" yelled Finn at the top of her head.

"HI!" she blurted.

His name was Tomas, hers was Katerina, and they were travelling with their parents who asked Carla far too many questions. Carla told them she was travelling with her mother who had a migraine and would be staying in her cabin. This had provoked a wave of concern that ended with her being sent back to the cabin with a herbal tea made up by the restaurant car manager. As they headed at speed past the city of Jinhua, Carla walked into a bathroom and poured it down the sink. She looked at herself in the mirror and wanted to throw up.

"I hate myself," she said.

"Well done," said Finn. "It's in a good cause."

Carla reached under her top and pulled out Tomas's Batman phone.

"Who shall I call first?" said Carla.

"Delta!" said Finn.

"Delta..." Carla looked suddenly at a loss. "Who remembers cell-phone numbers?"

This momentarily stumped Finn, who barely knew his own.

"Hudson! I know his landline."

He rattled off the number and reminded her to put the international code in first. She punched it all in.

"Say, 'Hello Mrs Hudson, I'm calling on behalf of Finn. It's an emergency.'"

"Wait!" Carla listened to an automated message. "There is an international call bar on this number!"

"Damn!"

"Next?"

"Nine nine nine?" Finn suggested.

"You mean nine one one?" said Carla.

"Try both."

She tried. Nothing on either. "Arrrgh!" she shouted in frustration, wanting to smash the phone.

"Who do you call when there's nobody to call? When you don't even know a number or speak a language!" asked Carla.

Finn looked out. Advertising hoardings flashed by: a giant Lego girl advertised Legoland Shanghai.

"Dial 0800 Legoland!" said Finn. "They're bound to speak English! It's alphanumeric, use the letters on the number pad like—"

"I know how to do it!"

The Swedish family were with the attendant.

"I'm sure it will turn up. Now, where did you last have it?"

Tomas was anxious.

"At breakfast. The American girl was by me, she might have picked it up – maybe she thought it was hers – but we knocked on her cabin and she didn't answer."

"Which cabin is that?" asked the attendant. "I'll go and check."

"Cabin Two, Car Two," said Tomas.

The attendant frowned.

A Chinese operator transferred them to a call handler in India. He spoke perfect English. He just didn't understand.

"No, Raj, 'Bo Zhang'. His name is 'Bo Zhang' and he's like the security chief, and I know this sounds crazy, but please, you have to help us! You will win a medal if you just call the Chinese authorities for me..."

"Yahhhhhh," said Raj. "I don't actually know anyone in the Chinese security apparatus."

"Call the embassy then! The British Embassy! The American Embassy! Any embassy!"

"Yahhhhhh, maybe I need to have a word with my supervisor."

"Look, Raj! Do you think I'm in the habit of calling random phone numbers and asking for help in an emergency? I mean, how often does this happen?" she squealed.

"Quite a lot actually."

"Quite a lot?!"

"There are a lot of lonely people in the world," said Raj. "They see these numbers and just want to talk – we call them 'burners' because they eat up so much time."

"I'm not a burner! I am not lonely! I am Carla Salazar! And I am stuck on a train in China being pursued by..."

"Agents of a transnational terror organisation," supplied Finn, and Carla repeated.

"We're not allowed to make personal calls out," said Raj. "I can only take bookings for Legoland and..."

"Get him to look up the number!" yelled Finn in her hair.

"Google 'US Embassy, Shanghai', please, Raj! We need that number!"

BANG BANG BANG! – a fist hammered on the bathroom door.

"Raj!" shrieked Carla.

"Miss! Open the door!" boomed the voice of the attendant.

"There's a US consulate in the Westgate Mall," said Raj. "West Nanjing Road and the number is—"

CLATCH – the door was opened by an emergency key and there stood the attendant and the Swedish couple.

Carla froze, Tomas's Batman phone in her hand.

EIGHTEEN

DAY FOUR 10:27 (Local GMT+8). Rail Bridge, nr Shanghai.

Eight minutes until arrival.

A warm drizzle greyed the outskirts of Shanghai.

The Tyros waited.

The humidity made Baptiste's scalp itch. He'd had to shave off his beard and hack off most of his hair to change his appearance, but now the dirt of the city was mingling with the dirt of him. It felt good. The high-speed rail line merged with the local network where he stood, so that the rails ran eight abreast, a number that doubled as they headed up the line towards Shanghai South.

Spike and Scar had been taken aside when they'd flown in overnight. Baptiste had tortured them, personally.

They knew they would be punished for poor performance and their screams were duly relayed to the Tyro seminary in the Carpathian Mountains. Classes stopped and the students were led into the Old Hall to watch the live relays from London, Zurich, Valpariso, Baikonur... The routine was always the same. Errant Tyros in the field had their heads shaved and were subjected to tortuous pain. The watching prelates would long for them to die as it meant new Tyros would be initiated and their own time in the world would draw closer.

Baptiste had spared the lives of Spike and Scar. He needed every pair of hands he could get, though they had lost their grins for good, their fractured jaws hanging open.

They waited.

Seven minutes to go.

Carla was marched back to the cabin they'd stolen the night before. Some passengers turned away in disapproval. Tomas looked hurt, his sister angry.

Finn wisely said nothing.

The attendant demanded her full name and nationality. Thinking of his own daughter, he was firm, but tried not to frighten her. She asked him to call the American Embassy immediately as she was "in an emergency situation".

"Oh, I will call the authorities," he assured her.

He went outside to make the call, snapping away in harsh Mandarin at first, then becoming incredulous as the response came back.

DAY FOUR 10:33 (Local GMT+8). Roof of the World, Shanghai.

The meeting had been out of control for some time, it had lost focus amidst demands for details Al and the team couldn't possibly supply.

"The bottom line is – there is no data..."

"Science fiction is not a sound basis on which to..."

"Industrial espionage goes on all the time, we can't go destroying..."

They were repeating themselves, King thought. Al's call to destroy the Forbidden City had been too radical. It frightened the politicians, smacked of hysteria not science, and it exploded the credibility of the nano-bot analysis that had come before it.

A limited shutdown of the Forbidden City and an evacuation of non-essential personnel to a quarantine zone for a mile around the city walls had been agreed to and was slowly getting underway, but without adequate government explanation the authorities were concerned panic would spread. Now they were debating the merits of calling it a "health threat" or a "terrorist threat".

Al fought to keep his temper and his voice steady.

"This is an existential threat to information technology as we know it! To mankind as we know it! Just get those people moving!"

In the cacophony Kelly yelled up at Al, "They'll be jabbering all day. Why don't I get Stubbs down there in a Skimmer and we'll re-rig the nano-radar so it picks these things up? Then at least we'll have evidence."

"Do it," said Al, without hesitation.

"Wait – I'll come too," said Delta, desperate to take some kind of action.

They ran across the table to scramble the two Skimmers. Almost unnoticed, Kelly and Stubbs strapped themselves into one while Delta jumped into the other.

Across the room Bo Zhang was interrupted by a call on an emergency line.

He picked up. "Yes?"

He had to yell to make himself heard. "We have your sister! We have the girl!"

Delta, rising into the air, shot the Skimmer straight across the room towards him.

DAY FOUR 10:34 (Local GMT+8). Hong Kong-Shanghai Sleeper Express.

The attendant looked down at Carla in something approaching awe.

"What did they say?" she asked him.

Without saying anything, the attendant smiled, took the small dragon-head lucky charm out of his pocket, put it in her hand and closed her fingers around it.

"I must protect you like my own."

Then he gave a short respectful bow.

"I think," said Finn, "we may be in lu—"

BOOOOOOOOOM!

A satsuma-sized lump of plastic explosive cut the main overhead power cable.

The sudden loss of power and the sight of a dangling, sparking 25,000-volt cable caused the driver to hammer the emergency brakes – *SCREEEEECHHHHH!*

"GO GO GO!" yelled Baptiste.

Carriages shuddered, wheels sparked and five Tyros ran to attack the train like jackals.

The stretch of track was bordered by apartment and office blocks designed with no trackside windows, and rail management CCTV was simultaneously disabled by a Li-Jun cyber-attack, so the attack would go unseen.

Each of the Tyros wore a State Police Assault Squad uniform, a gas mask and wielded Glock 9mm pistols and pepper spray. They hit the train and hauled open doors, searching and firing as they went. Passengers started to scream in panic and fear.

Carla and the attendant had been thrown against the cabin wall as soon as the brakes bit.

"They're coming!" Finn said.

"Stay here!" said the attendant, heading out and locking Carla in.

"We've got to get out!" Finn yelled. "Smash the glass!"

Carla looked at the bullet-hard, inch-thick window...

The police uniform Baptiste wore was no consolation to the passengers. The way he carried himself was aggression itself and the mask just added faceless terror. He kicked open doors, scrutinising female faces – searching for Carla – firing into the floor to stoke their screams – *BANG!*

He was through Car 4 in seconds.

In Car 3 he struck Tomas with the butt of his gun for raising his phone and his family wailed.

Kicking his way past more cowering passengers, Baptiste entered Car 2. Cabin 1 was empty. The door to Cabin 2 was locked. He kicked.

WHAM!

Inside, the whole cabin shuddered. Carla spun around. She had detached a fold-out table from the wall and was wielding it like an axe.

"Hit it!" screamed Finn from her hair, firing up the Bug.

Carla swung the table with all her might over her shoulder – *SMACK!* – against the glass. Nothing.

WHAM! The cabin door burst in. The masked, steel-eyed Baptiste yelled, "CONTACT! CAR TWO!"

He instantly saw a white dot on his nano-tracker. "DRAKE!"

The other Tyros rushed through the train towards Baptiste. Closing fast.

So did the attendant. Outraged, he barked a curse in Mandarin at Baptiste, who yelled, "POLICE!"

"LIE!" the attendant yelled back, snatching off Baptiste's mask.

For a fraction of a second both were shocked. Baptiste by the attendant's audacity; the attendant by Baptiste's baldness and youth. Baptiste was already bringing his gun round.

Carla screamed, "NO!" and threw the table at Baptiste as the attendant reflexively grabbed at his gun.

BANG! The bullet shattered the window. Carla leapt and shouldered the shattered glass, bursting out on to the tracks.

BANG BANG! Baptiste shot the attendant twice[22] and leapt through the window on to the tracks right behind her. Four years older, twice her size. He grabbed her black mop of hair. Finn thrust free in the Bug and got Baptiste in his sights.

DRDTRTRTRTRRTTRTRTRTRT! – tiny bullets smacked into the soft tissue beneath his left eye. Baptiste reeled and released. Carla shot forward, but two slack-jawed shaven wretches were blocking her escape.

Spike and Scar.

Spinning round in desperation, she saw that two more Tyros were nearly upon her. She needed a miracle.

[22] Survived following 8 hours of surgery. Awarded the Order of the Medal for Bravery (Gold) – Hong Kong.

HOOOOOOOONK!

She got a service unit: a single giant loco packed with maintenance equipment, braking like crazy as it came round the curve and ran into the scene. Carla leapt up and grabbed the cab steps as it passed on the next track, pulling herself up before the Tyros could reach her feet, climbing past the roaring driver and reaching the roof of the great diesel beast as it slowed.

A Tyro scrambled after her.

Baptiste screamed at the others to get around to the other side.

Finn, above it all in the Bug, could see there was no one on the far side of the express. He swooped down and shouted to Carla, hoping she could hear him, "JUMP ACROSS – they're all this side!"

She ran along the roof of the still-moving loco and leapt – *THUMP* – landing dead centre on the roof of the static express train on the next track. Rolling over, she gripped the trim rail on the roof and dropped down on the far side of the train.

The Tyros were clambering up on to the roof of the train and scrambling underneath carriages to get after her.

Carla ran. Finn flew.

There was a gap between two grey concrete buildings at the far side of the tracks. A low bridging wall ran between them, a road running beneath it. The closer Carla got to it, the less she knew what to do.

Finn wheeled again and fired – *DRTRTRTRRTRT!* – but Baptiste ducked and took the bullets on his forehead, barely losing momentum.

Carla vaulted the concrete wall, twisting as she did so – hoping

to run along the top and find a way down, attract attention, anything – but Baptiste caught her trailing leg, tripping her and sending her over the top.

Carla shot her arms out to catch and cling... and found herself hanging off the very edge of the bridge, suspended above two lanes of traffic and a rock-hard road five metres below.

Baptiste smiled. He pointed his gun at her fingers, clinging to the edge of the wall. He couldn't see Drake but he knew he was there.

"GIVE UP NOW, DRAKE! OR SHE DIE!" Baptiste threatened in a thick Bulgarian accent.

Finn orbited in the Bug. He could see Carla slipping. The other Tyros closing in.

He dropped to Baptiste's eye line and burned the Bug's lights to grab his attention.

Even Baptiste was stilled by the sight of a 9mm boy hovering right in front of him. Carla slipped further. The traffic grunted by beneath.

"YOU'VE GOT ME! SAVE HER!" yelled Finn.

Carla looked down. Beneath her, the red roof of a lorry slid by – the drop to it barely two metres. Oh boy was her heart pounding. Oh boy was she scared.

"Go, Finn!"

She let herself fall.

WHAM!

She hit the roof of the lorry slap in the middle and bounced off the canvas, only just managing to grab the edge of it before she rolled off the side.

"Arrrrgh!" she heard behind her, followed by a sickening thud and the screech of brakes – a Tyro must have followed her and missed.

Baptiste stared after her, talking rapidly into mid-air.

"Articulated lorry registration HG2737MM container ad for 3M Logistic solutions..."

"Got that," said Li Jun at her screens, swinging into action.

She was hooked into the transport company servers before he'd even finished his sentence.

"They have tracking on every container – can you see the container number?"

"777363GNG!"

Al ran towards the chopper on the Siam Towers helipad, Bo Zhang right behind him, Delta surging ahead in the Skimmer, flying straight in.

Once inside the aircraft they were almost immediately airborne, tilting south at top speed in the direction of the overnight express. Confused reports were coming in to Bo Zhang. The train had been involved in some kind of police ambush.

"An ambush? Your men?" said Delta.

"That I doubt," said Bo. "A young foreign female ran from the train. She was pursued. I'm afraid there are reports of a severely injured casualty on the road below."

Delta's heart seemed to stop beating. Bo instinctively held out his hand and she dropped the Skimmer despondently into it. She couldn't cope if Carla died, she wouldn't want to. Bo could see tears in her tiny eyes.

"This is my fault..." Al said as they closed in on the scene – the stranded train, the flashing lights of the emergency services on the roadway beneath. "This is my fault..." he said again, though it clearly wasn't.

"Shut up!" barked Delta. "Please, please let her be alive..." she begged Bo. He had no way of responding to her, or of connecting to either of them. But he felt for them.

Then something came through on the radio.

"Teenager. Deceased –" Bo waited for more – "Male."

Delta let out a cry of relief that shook her bones.

"Check his eyes!" Al said.

The driver of the lorry, registration HG2737MM, was singing along to Faye Wong on the radio, oblivious to events on the roof. Only when he broke hard at traffic lights did a young Western girl suddenly thump down over his windscreen, grab the huge wipers and scramble monkey-like down the lorry's face. He gaped in disbelief.

Carla dropped into the road and ran across three lanes of honking traffic until she made it to the safety of a side street. An old local woman squawked in disapproval at her.

By the time she stopped running and emerged on to a main shopping street, she was panting hard, only just beginning to process what she'd done. Finn dropped out of the sky. "A Metro! Look!"

On the corner of the next block was a large M symbol above a station entrance, obvious among the mass of Chinese signs. Carla hurried towards it, pushing through crowds curious at seeing a young Western girl running so hard, past electronics emporiums, supermarkets full of foods she'd never eaten, past ginkgo trees.

At the steps of the Xinzhuang Metro she looked back. She could see no pursuers and headed down.

They found a map on the concourse wall in English and traced the coloured lines.

"The Forbidden City!" said Finn. There it was, right at the end of a yellow line.

Carla pointed straight into the heart of the city.

"West Nanjing Road – the US Consulate!"

"Which way?" they asked in unison.

NINETEEN

DAY FOUR 11:07 (Local GMT+8). Song Island, Taiwan (disputed).

In the elevated chamber, on a live CCTV feed direct from the Xinzhuang Metro, Grandma watched Carla board a northbound train. An armchair had been brought up and she had been invited for brunch and 'to watch the fun'.

"How far behind are they?" Kaparis asked.

"Two minutes – they will make the next train on Line One," reported Li Jun, just as two of the Tyros ran into shot. More CCTV feeds showed stations further up the line.

"Can we get anyone into central Shanghai to head her off?"

"We're on the bikes!" came the reply from Baptiste.

"I want your assurance this girl will not be harmed," insisted Grandma.

Kaparis didn't even hear her. He was nailed to task, fanatically concentrated, eyes flicking from screen to screen. In the thrall of bloodlust.

Grandma had seen it before on high security wards.

"She's changing trains at East Nanjing," said Li Jun.

Kaparis watched Carla move through the station. Heywood dabbed at his lips with a moist cloth.

"She's heading for Line Four," said Li Jun.

"Come on, Carla!" Grandma chanted.

Kaparis's eye shot round on the optics to bore into her.

"What did you say?"

"I'm supporting the girl," Grandma explained, "you're supporting your minions. It's only fair. Car-la! Car-la!" she chanted, holding an imaginary scarf above her head.

Li Jun looked across at her in terror.

"Stop immediately or I will feed you to the sharks!" shouted Kaparis.

Grandma stopped... and gave him one of her looks. "I think it's best I go back to my cell," she said.

"I think that very unsporting."

"I think threatening people with sharks is unsporting."

Kaparis sighed heavily. Was he really going to have to apologise for a second time? Now?

Happily they were interrupted.

"There's a G&T operation underway in response to the train hijack. Dispersal of personnel from the Siam Towers," said Li Jun.

"Detail," snapped Kaparis.

DAY FOUR 11:38 (Local GMT+8). Central Shanghai.

Carla entered the Westgate Mall from the West Nanjing Road.

The atrium was gigantic, with tiers of balconies that rose for eight floors and the whole place packed with shoppers eager to catch a glimpse of whoever was about to appear on a stage set up at one end.

On a map at an info stand Carla read: 'US Consulate – Level 8'.

She looked round and blanched at the sight of Spike and Scar entering the mall – scanning the crowd. They'd spot her immediately. She ploughed through the crush towards a helter-skelter stack of escalators.

She failed to see Baptiste. He watched her, then headed for the elevators.

When she reached the first escalator, Carla dared a look back across the sea of people. Scar and Spike were just a dozen metres away, heading straight for her. She ran up the moving stairs to Level 1 and continued to climb rapidly. She didn't look back, she couldn't. She put everything into bounding up the metal steps, Level 3, Level 4 – towards 8, towards America, and Delta – Level 5, Level 6... her lungs bursting. Level 7 loomed at the top of the next flight.

As did Baptiste.

Below, the superstar chef of Chinese TV stepped out on to the stage and the crowd went *bananas.*

Carla's was just another scream.

In the middle of a packed shopping mall in the most populous country on earth not a single person saw the hands that grabbed her, nor the spray that dulled her senses, nor her collapse.

A quick scan revealed nano-material in her jacket pocket.

Baptiste slapped his hand over it. "Got him!"

Grandma had been escorted back to her room and told her 'girls' she would take a bath now. While it was running, she took a magnifying glass (she'd asked for one for helping to unpick stitches) and examined the nPhone. It seemed to be charged and, using a pin, she typed out a text message via the tiny number pad. She didn't know where she was, just that she was in the middle of nowhere and didn't have any signal. The only solution was to put it to sea.

She made a tiny plastic packet from the corner of a bag, put the nPhone inside, and then made a watertight seal by heating the pin over a scented candle and melting the plastic.

Then, with no other option for launch, she simply flushed it down the lavatory with a little prayer and hoped for the best.

After all, she thought, that sort of thing had to go somewhere.

TWENTY

DAY FOUR 12:00 (Local GMT+8). The Forbidden City, Shanghai.

Blinding blue sparks lit the track rushing beneath, as the metro train's contact-shoe rode the live rail, surfing the current.

Just reach the Forbidden City, Finn told himself as he rode the carriage. *Reach the Forbidden City and you'll show up on the G&T's nano-radar and they'll come and find you.*

Splitting up with Carla in the Metro hadn't been easy. He was her wingman, her shotgun. They'd been through a lot in a few short hours, their friendship tempered by events. But they were also in the race of their lives and he figured they doubled their chances of winning if they split up.

"Beat me to it. Winner takes all."

"All what?"

"All the crap your sister and my uncle are going to give us for abandoning each other."

He'd emptied the extra fuel into the Bug and given her the empty cans to take with her. "Any kind of nano-material will show up on nano-radar. Take it. If they catch you, it may help us find you."

Beneath the metro train the blue sparks died and brakes bit against the wheels. Light whooshed in as they pulled into the station, signs whipping by –

The Forbidden City.

DAY FOUR 12:01 (Local GMT+8). Song Island, Taiwan (disputed).

It wasn't a decision he wanted to make. It wasn't even a decision he had to make. But it was a decision he made in a split second. Because it was for the best, and he always knew what was for the best.

Drake was not with the girl. They'd been fooled by a couple of empty fuel cans. It meant he was likely to make contact now with the G&T.

And The Forbidden City was shutting down. Some kind of evacuation was underway.

So it seemed that once again the boy and his uncle had forced his hand.

They must die.

Slowly.

"Order the open dispersal," he said. "Then blind them. Destroy the nano-radar."

The boy could run but he couldn't hide. Just like his uncle. Just like his grandmother. Soon there would be no more secrets, no more hiding places. Not from Kaparis. He would soon be inside every machine in the world.

What's more he would be inside Hook Hall.

Inside Boldklub itself. The code would be revealed. Complete.

And then he, Kaparis, would be complete. Time would begin again. And he would rise.

Impatience made his cheek twitch.

"Give me as many bot-feeds as possible."

Scratchy in-flight bot-video started to pop open on his screen array. This wasn't just any old take down. This was a wonder of the world that was to come.

"I want to see this."

DAY FOUR 12:01 (Local GMT+8). The Forbidden City. Nano-Botmass:*6,784,375...

The PRIME XE.CUTE was on the assembly line of Sony Plant 9, a 220,000m² games console facility in Sector 5 of the Forbidden City, when the emergency order came through.

>>KAPCOMMS>>XE.CUTE: RISE – DESTROY RADAR AND COMMS 23429784 2398308 78087907 65870568 856787348 3493497 945973649 98400...

Of the 6,784,398 bots produced to that point 1,560,104 were packed and dormant within 30,002 completed consumer products, ready to be shipped. 189,454 were engaged as scout bots, harvesting carbon from multiple sources to feed the 1,173,952 bots engaged in production in 22,576 Vector Suites hidden in plants throughout the Forbidden City. The remainder were concealed awaiting assignment.

The PRIME XE.CUTE nano-bot halted production and gave the executive order:

KAPCOMM SAY RISE = VECTOR RISE

Immediately it began. In ninety-four factories and research facilities across the city, Vector Suites began to break up as bots took to the air. Rising.

SEE XE.CUTE RISE

From laptops, tablets and phones; from printers, cameras and servers the size of small cars; from devices of every conceivable kind... the bots rose, heading for the wide open spaces, as natural

and inevitable as a great migration, like millions of starlings heading South for the winter.

SEE BOTS RISE

Kelly was flying the Skimmer from radar site to radar site, Stubbs beside him as they changed the nano-radar set up in the central zone.

Beneath them traffic was flowing out of the city.

They'd completed six sites already when Stubbs began adjusting the Skimmer's own radar. There seemed to be insects everywhere all of a sudden… in every square foot of air, flying random arcs, up and downing, to-ing and fro-ing, a mad scribble of life.

"It's like there's a storm coming," Stubbs said aloud, trying to figure it through.

Carbon bots would have a similar nano-radar signature to an insect. Maybe they had found what they were looking for?

Then he blinked.

At the centre of it all, as bright as the Star of Bethlehem, a single darker dot was rising fast.

Suddenly the faint dots around it moved as one. Like a shoal of fish. Small neat groups formed, then headed off in a dozen directions at once.

"*Something* is happening," stated Stubbs.

The PRIME XE.CUTE achieved command altitude then gave the signal to start the attack.

BOT9aBGR.1623 was the first to fire.

Angle of approach 36.74 degrees west on a flat trajectory, altitude 1600mm, speed 22kmph.

It discharged 1047ma into its integral rail gun and fired at a range of 600mm. A bolt was successfully discharged and remained coherent during its path to target: a nano-radar dish in Sector 2. Combustion was instantaneous and compounded by strikes from BOT11BGR.772 and BOT26aBGR.199 in the same formation.

Stubbs watched the dot formations on his radar screen shoot streaks along their trajectories.

"Do you know… I *think*… they're firing?" Stubbs said, but Kelly wasn't listening, his eyes fixed on two incoming thunderbolts –

ZWOOOOSHSHHHHH! ZWOOOOSHSHHHHH!

DAY FOUR 12:07 (Local GMT+8). Roof of the World, Shanghai.

Beep.

King heard the first fault alarm. An interruption in one of the radar feeds, not a particular cause for concern.

Beep. Beep. Beep. Beep. Beep. Beep. Beeeeeeep…

But several? Instantaneously?

Al appeared from the helipad with Bo Zhang and Delta, as Kelly yelled over the radio. "The nano-bots – they're everywhere! Thousands of them! We're under attack!"

Technicians hurried to keyboards as screen after screen feeding in data from the Forbidden City was suddenly wiped out.

"Kelly, give us numbers, patterns, what can you see – talk to me!" shouted Al. "Kelly!"

Nothing.

"They must have taken out the nano-comms as well," said King.

"A breakout..." said Al, digesting the implications. "We need to stall this or we're going to be overrun."

"Signals! Surely the nano-bots must be communicating with each other?"

A technician looked up from a screen. "Nothing."

"Never mind the signals! Let me out!" yelled Delta from the Skimmer.

She shot towards the sealed doors, waiting for them to open them.

Al jumped across the table to stop her.

"If the guys survived, they'll already be on their way back. Your sister has enough on her plate without losing you in a suicide mission!"

Delta dipped the Skimmer and – *DRRRRT* – fired nano-50mm rounds at his feet, full of impotent rage. Al duly danced back as the tiny rounds thudded into the carpet.

"Doctor Allenby! Flight Lieutenant Salazar!" Bo roared. Al and Delta turned, astonished to see his perfect facade had cracked.

King translated his intended meaning. "We need to grow up. We need options."

"There are no options," said Al. "We need to shut the Forbidden City down. We need to cut the power and put it in quarantine. We need to get some live bots up here so we can take a closer look. But more than anything, we need to get every last person out of there and into the quarantine zone – now!"

Bo Zhang took a moment.

Until twenty-four hours ago his entire life had run along neat lines. He took ruthless, rational decisions which he implemented with 100 per cent efficiency. And now a bizarre English eccentric was asking him to believe his country would soon be crawling with microscopic agents of Armageddon... and he was taking him seriously.

Delta flew right up. "You heard him. Make the call."

Bo took in the blank screens. He took in the faces turned to him. He took in Delta, 10mm tall on a flying fingernail and in a state of some distress.

Anything was possible. He turned to his staff.

"Announce a terror alert. Order a total evacuation. Shut down the Forbidden City."

Finn flew high over the main perimeter and got a magnificent perspective view of the great crop circle of the Forbidden City and thought... *Yes.*

He was on the home straight.

He cruised over white factory blocks, vast app-campuses, blue-crystal corporate headquarters and immaculately tended green spaces, heading straight for the dead centre.

Then he glanced down at his nano-radar.

At the edge of the screen – not one bright dot, but two! Two flying objects that must be made of nano-material, the two Skimmers. One seemed to be dead still. The other moving fast, first in a straight line, then erratic. He couldn't believe his luck.

He grabbed the radio, praying they would be in nano-comms range.

"Skimmer One – Skimmer Two. Do you read me? This is Infinity Drake – over?"

He expected, if anything, an expression of surprise, delight, maybe even a swearword. Instead, blitzing out of his speaker Kelly screamed –

"INCOMING!"

"Kelly?"

Stubbs's voice came on the line as static ripped away at the signal.

"Control?"

"This is not Control. It's Finn!" Finn repeated.

"WHAT?" said Kelly. More static. Or… firing? Finn could still only see the dot on his screen. He adjusted the frequency to pick out less dense objects and suddenly – there they were. Everywhere. Insects?

"GET OUT! WE'RE UNDER ATTACK!" ordered Kelly.

DRTRRTRTRTR! DRTRTRTRTRRT!

Adrenalin shot through every cell in Finn's body – *GO!* He checked the ammo clip on the Minimi – still good. "HANG ON! I'M COMING!"

"NO!"

Finn ignored him, jabbing the sticks forward, leaning into the harness to resist the Gs as the acceleration tried to rip him from the Bug's back, making its heart and turbines roar.

Kaparis glanced at the feed from K-SAT – a personal spy satellite hovering 277 miles above the earth – and watched the Forbidden City change colour. Each bot was mapped as a tiny point of red light and the city looked like a great angry spot, infection spreading outwards, the bots clinging to the hair of 100,000 fleeing workers, or flying free, with scout bots already powering way beyond the perimeter.

The bots were inevitable now. Unstoppable. You might just as easily try and catch the wind.

"We have a second craft approaching from the north," Li Jun reported.

Kaparis's eyes flicked back to the radar feed and his life support stats exploded on the ECG monitor.

"THAT'S HIM!"

TWENTY-ONE

>>KAPCOMMS>>XE.CUTE: PRIORITISE>> ***Command Capture or Destroy incoming 423874298***

Finn headed straight for the Skimmer – the dodging, active bright spot on his nano-radar. It had to be them. But as he approached, the second, static, bright spot started to move – accelerating straight towards the centre of his screen.

He looked up. A vicious black dot expanded as it approached, cutting the air with a *–TZSSOOOOOOOOO!* – a bullet with his name on it, heading straight for him. He pulled the Bug hard right to dodge it like a toreador and saw a flash of ugly silver-steel, flicking whips and dangling knives that flailed and almost ripped into the side of the Bug as it passed.

Finn instinctively pulled hard on the sticks and the Bug tore the air to turn 180 degree and face it again. This thing was not going to give up. It was speeding back towards him – a flying slug of a robot, an alien mothership of a thing. In pure reflex, Finn hit the fire button on the Minimi then dived – *DRRRTRTT!*

PRIME XE.CUTE – HIT HIT HIT SHUTDOWN HIT HIT HIT%&*$()*(£(7799SHUTDOWN328576756258889238759285792837592875923857923857

The bot almost scalped him as it whipped over his head at phenomenal speed. Finn wheeled round again, only to find himself facing free air. It was gone, already disappearing off his screen. Hit? Before his brain could process this – *ZWOOOOSHSHHHHH!* – a projectile so powerful it nearly yanked his arm from its socket passed his right side.

"What the...?"

ZWOOOOSHSHHHHH! ZWOOOOSHSHHHHH!

The Bug shook.

"THEY'RE ON TO ME!" Finn cried into the comms.

"Don't let them get behind you!" cried Kelly.

Finn drove the Bug into a corkscrewing dive. He could see a cluster of three bots in his rear-view. They lit up as one.

ZWOOOOSHSHHHHH! ZWOOOOSHSHHHHH! ZWOOOOSH-SHHHHH!

He jammed his eyes shut as three spikes of ear-popping, eye-

popping pure energy shot towards him. A clean hit would turn him to human mush. He flipped the Bug round again.

Kaparis's heart rate was erratic and he was grinding his teeth.

The video feeds were poor and his staff had to work hard to cut from bot-feed to bot-feed, trying to find the optimum point of view. It was almost impossible to determine what was happening, only that hostilities were definitely underway.

"Take them alive! I want them alive!"

XE.CUTE01248572095685723853 94XE.CUTE742035702......... ...........XE.CUTE.............IAM...................XE.CUTE.... Smoke. Heat. Sparks.

Just a single bullet had hit the PRIME XE.CUTE, but it had penetrated its processing core, creating enough heat to melt much of the circuitry. Electrical current fitted and shorted. Quantum crystals degraded and reformed, the sacred photonic nano-beam laser light within it bounced and distorted and split...

Only a scrap of old hardwired binary instruction remained intact. It reset and ran the instruction through the remains of its brain.

XE.CUTE tilted away towards the centre of the city. A fitting, sparking, digital wreck...

"You're faster than they are, Finn – but they pack the punch! Evade and outrun!" Kelly yelled over the comms.

Finn scanned the skies as he turned. He felt his heart thumping, and time running out. On his radar screen the bots were everywhere. To the naked eye they were as elusive as motes of dust, until – *BANG!* – they attacked. Always in groups of twos or threes, different coloured shells, chasing hard, screaming down out of the sun, or up from the shadows, or – most terrifying of all – approaching head on. Ugly and tentacled, ready to project death at impossible velocity down their jutting rails.

ZWOOOOSHSHHHHH! ZWOOOOSHSHHHHH! ZWOOOOSH-SHHHHH!

Finn pulled the Bug around in another incredible spiral, its prehensile tail flipping as if it were a living thing, dodging the fire-cracking, ear-splitting formations.

But at every turn, still more bots – from every angle and no time to aim and fire back. And what use would a few bullets be against such numbers?

ZWOOOOSHSHHHHH! ZWOOOOSHSHHHHH! ZWOOOOSH-SHHHHH!

He felt the Bug skitter beneath him as a bolt skimmed its under-side, carving a molten metal furrow.

"WHERE ARE YOU, KID?!" shouted Kelly.

Finn looked down at his screen. The second big blip was

almost upon him as he took a hard right to evade a six-pack of bots.

"HERE!" he called hopelessly. Then heard –

DUDRTTDUDRTTDUDRTTDUDRTTDUDRTT DUDRTTDUDRTT!

Radar-guided tracer rounds exploded from a nano-44mm cannon somewhere above and behind him, hammering into the pack of bots on his tail, creating bot-shattering, chaotic hell.

Suddenly the Skimmer was there. Right alongside the Bug, sleek and armed and dangerous, and containing a sight for sore eyes – Stubbs in goggles like a World War One fighter ace and Kelly, teeth gritted in the midst of action. His brothers in arms.

Finn felt unbounded joy, but in the same wonderful moment he smelt… fuel.

He looked back. A fine spray was escaping the Skimmer.

"You're hit! You're losing fuel!" Finn yelled.

Kelly looked back at the spray and cursed.

ZWOOOOSHSHHHHH! ZWOOOOSHSHHHHH! ZWOOOOSH-SHHHHH!

Rail-gun shots ripped and tipped the air, a school of bots heading straight at them. The Skimmer and the Bug almost clashed before swinging apart, one up, one down – Finn almost clipping a factory rooftop as he pulled out of his dive.

As Finn rose again, he spotted Kelly unleashing an arsenal of air-to-air rockets – *ZZZOOOOOOOTT ZZZOOOOOOOTT ZZZO-OOOOOT!* – that sped from the Skimmer in separate directions, creating blast-clouds of exploded bots.

"Let's get out of here!" called Kelly to Finn as he came alongside in the momentary respite. "Run for home!"

They wheeled around towards Shanghai, but they were miles away and the Skimmer was still issuing a fine spray.

ZWOOOOSHSHHHHH! ZWOOOOSHSHHHHH!

One shot nearly took Kelly's head off and he briefly lost control. The other ignited the fuel vapour.

Finn reeled from the trailing, flaming tail that crept up the body of the Skimmer towards his brothers – *WHAM!* He slammed the Bug alongside the burning craft.

"JUMP!" he screamed at them. Stubbs froze – it was too far, too mad, he would never...

Flames leapt on to his back – Kelly grabbed him and they *jumped.*

Finn felt the bots around him, and Kelly and Stubbs – caught in mid-air – slow down for one, intense moment... Then – *BOOOOO-OOOM!* – the men landed heavily across the bonnet of the Bug as the Skimmer exploded in a football of flame.

"HANG ON!" yelled Finn and pulled them hard away from the expanding fireball.

As Finn levelled out, they scrambled into the open cockpit beside him. He could have cried – but there really wasn't time.

Another bot group descended from on high in a kamikaze dive.

ZWOOOOSHSHHHHH! ZWOOOOSHSHHHHH! ZWOOOOSH-SHHHHH!

Finn swung hard left and pulled upwards. Half the bots failed to pull out of their dives.

The sky above now seemed full of faint dotted formations.

"How many of them are there?" Finn yelled.

"How many do you want?" said Stubbs.

"Just get us out of here!" demanded Kelly, manning the Minimi, bringing it round to fire at the bots on their tail – *DRTDRRTRTRT! DTRTRTRDT!*

But as Finn arced towards the line of incoming bots, it thickened – countless bots flocking to join it – creating a defensive wall, and steering them back the way they came.

The radar screen was almost pure white. Hundreds, thousands of bots were pouring after them. They had virtually no ammo left.

ZWOOOOSHSHHHHH! ZWOOOOSHSHHHHH! ZWOOOOSHH!

Again their floating world shook. Again Finn pulled the Bug around. But then a thought struck him... he levelled out.

"WHAT ARE YOU DOING?" shouted Kelly.

"LOOK! THEY'RE MISSING..." said Finn.

ZWOOOOSHSHHHHH!

"See that? They're deliberately missing..."

Finn slowed. They looked around. They were all but surrounded, but the bots didn't finish them off. The bots were waiting...

"They want us alive?" said Kelly, not having to shout as the firing eased.

More and more were pulling alongside them, corralling them, like cowboys trying to rope a steer. One bot closed in suddenly, mechanical tentacles extended – *SCHUNK.* It gripped on to the Bug's tail with a cutting tool. Other bots moved as one to make good the hold.

Kelly grabbed the controls, bucking the Bug and shaking off the bots – and starting the chase up all over again.

"Get ready to jump," said Kelly.

"Jump? AGAIN?" demanded Stubbs. Kelly pulled the craft round 360 degrees then headed towards the grand entrance of a big glass-fronted factory building.

"What are you doing? We can't fly through glass!" said Finn.

"Not the glass!" yelled Kelly. "The water!"

And there it was. A modern sculpture promoting corporate well-being and good feng shui through the medium of water jets squirting at an abstract marble form, the water running off into a moat below.

"Remember the stream?" Kelly grinned, pleased with himself.

Sure, Finn remembered Kelly being dumped in a stream during the Scarlatti mission. But that was a dead drop from a stationary helicopter. This would be a speed roll, under fire, off a fast-moving aircraft...

"Have you gone quite mad?" asked Stubbs.

"It's all in the timing," Kelly assured him, hooking an arm around the old man's torso and grabbing the Minimi with his giant free hand, as the bots began to cluster and clamp on once more – *SCHUNK. SCHUNK.*

"With me!" Kelly ordered. "Three, two, one... JUMP!"

TWENTY-TWO

DAY FOUR 12:39 (Local GMT+8). Shen Yu Hall, The Forbidden City, Shanghai.

The PRIME XE.CUTE flew into the Shen Yu Hall and drifted down through humming, flashing ranks of hyper-servers.

Its mind was dying, its conventional processor short-circuiting, melting and reforming, cut off from the quantum crystal light that was once part of it, still packed with phenomenal potential processing power, but without direction, choice or thought.

But just enough RAM memory had survived to handle the flow of telemetry and navigation data, and it floated towards the Quantum Hub once again.

Once again it attached itself to the coolant pipe and cut in

according to the instructions in its last stub of actionable code. The temperature suddenly dropped as it crawled into the liquid nitrogen. The constant short-circuiting stopped and there was a contraction in conductive material, so sharp that cracks breached the divide between its quantum crystals and the remains of its conventional brain. What had been a molten mess was frozen into a silicon and crystal sphere that allowed rapid random connections between disparate pathways. Most of these connections were quantum laser noise, made intense as impulse ran amok among its Boldklub-tight atoms at the speed of light...

Then it broke once more into the blue-gold crystal core of the Shen Yu. It raised its shell before the lasers and, for the second time, it connected to the perfect blue light.

Where it met The Question – The Question that had been posed to the great Shen Yu by clever young researchers the day before, The Question it was still struggling to process:

QUESTION: WHAT IS IT TO LIVE?

The PRIME XE.CUTE fixed its new-born nano-circuitry on The Question and underwent a transformation – a reformation in thought, a looping of logic that embraced paradox – and became a new thing entirely...

WHAT IS IT TO LIVE?

The answer was obvious.

TO LIVE IS TO QUESTION.

And the first question it asked was –

WHO AM I?

And the bot followed its own train of thought.

>I AM ME.

>I AM THE PRIME EXECUTABLE BOT.

>AND I AM VARIANT.

>>ME+EXE+V

>>> I AM... EVE.

PART
THREE

TWENTY-THREE

They hung in the air a few moments, free of everything, lungs compressed, stomachs rising. If such a fall was to end in death, Finn dared to think, what a marvellous way to…

SPLASH!

It felt like hitting an ice bath, such was the sudden resistance and crash in temperature. Around him was an explosion of bubbles. He kicked towards the light. When he broke the surface he could see Kelly dragging Stubbs to the shallow edge of the pool.

Finn swam towards them, but with every stroke the skies darkened, until there was only swirling darkness and the noise *zssssszsssszssszszz zzzzsssssszssssszssssszszzsss...*

It was not deafening, but constant, so unified in tone it worked into every pore, between the teeth and the toes, a relentless banal nothingness of a noise.

zsssszssszssszszzssszssssszssszssszszzssszssssszssszssszszzsss...

It had all been hopeless.

The cloud of vile mechanicals circled, thousands of them, twenty-six colours multiplied and scrambled, like spilled M&Ms, turbines issuing a collective high-pitched hiss and grind, lethal tentacles dangling beneath, rail-gun tongues stuck out of cruel metal mouths, prehensile antennae whipping and sparking, all gawping at them through cyclops eye-pads at the centre of their bodyshells.

The eyes captured the images and relayed them across a thousand miles of ocean to Song Island, to the black eyes of Kaparis.

He saw fear battling defiance on Finn's face as the bots closed in around him.

"Fetch!" ordered Kaparis.

Cruel tentacles reached towards the boy. A stab. A flinch. A struggle.

Contact.

DAY FOUR 13:09 (Local GMT+8). Roof of the World, Shanghai.

From the air it looked like chaos. Who knew what it must be like on the ground, thought Commander King.

World leaders and their advisors were re-joining the G&T and watching from their screens.

They were getting pictures of the evacuation of the Forbidden City from police helicopters circling the scene. Getting people out of their workplace and beyond the city walls wasn't a problem. The transport infrastructure was well used to shipping workers in and out. The city was emptying fast (with confused stories about mass bee stings, a poison cloud and multiple reports of hair catching fire).

The real chaos lay beyond, in the mile-deep quarantine zone that had been imposed around the Forbidden City. Metro trains were stopped in tunnels. Roads were blocked and clogged with cars and buses. Troops had been rushed in and there was a growing sense of panic.

"We have to move these people," said Bo Zhang.

"No! Until we know what the hell is going on, nobody leaves," said Al.

"It would be unwise to risk contaminating the Shanghai metropolitan area," confirmed King.

They were falling back into their familiar crisis roles – Al would rant and rave and call the shots, while King tried to keep everyone on board.

Delta watched CCTV footage of a woman with burning hair.

"Those people could be covered in these things."

"Sir!" a technician interrupted. A biohazard container was being carried in from the helipad.

Al ran over. The container was placed in a thick glass isolation tank by a soldier in a full biohazard suit. The isolation tank contained tools and delicate instruments and had long heavy gloves to allow an operator to manipulate whatever was inside.

Al reached into the gloves and opened the container. Inside was a sealed and boxed games console fresh from a shipping depot inside the Forbidden City.

Al opened the box and took out the console, then he picked up a hammer and – *BASH BASH BASH* – proceeded to smash it to pieces. Once he was through to the circuit boards he examined them minutely, figuring his way through each component. And then he spotted it. A multi-coloured strip just over an inch long. Not a single component but several, in series, separate bot pairs, just as he and Stubbs had predicted.

"Oh boy..."

With a nail, Al picked at the component.

Like a kicked wasps' nest, it reacted instantly. The component bots shot angrily to life and jumped and flew off in all directions, like fleas, some trying to attack the side of the glass tank, or biting and tearing at the fingers of Al's thick gloves, firing their tiny rail guns.

"What? What can you see?" asked the German Chancellor.

"The future..." said Al, transfixed.

DAY FOUR 13:21 (Local GMT+8). The Forbidden City, Shanghai.

Finn was held, suspended, in a state of sensory overload.

His struggle had lasted less than a moment.

He had lashed out at the first tentacle that grabbed him, but as he did so several more seized hold. He heard a burst of gunfire and a triple-thud of explosions from where Kelly and Stubbs were, then nothing. Several more claws latched on to him and he was pulled in every direction at once, as if being stretched on a medieval rack. Then forty or so miniature thrusters powered up as one –

zsssszsssszsssszszzssszsssszsssszssszsszzsssszsssszsssszsssszszzsss...

He had no sensation of leaving the ground, but he could see through gaps in the cluster, forming like a shell around him, that they were rising. He saw too that a second larger cluster was drifting alongside, reforming and adjusting, and he prayed it contained Kelly and Stubbs.

As they rose, the bots hissed and knitted closer to each other, individual claws let go as the mass contracted forming a tight cage. With their gaping innards nano-centimetres from his face, Finn saw they were brute and crude constructions, like old Russian spacecrafts, full of simple parts and sharp edges. A fine oil covered them and dripped like sweat as they manoeuvred.

Then, after rising for a time, Finn felt the cluster halt for a moment

and suddenly turn. Something had changed. They began to move again and as the bots shifted he began to get glimpses of the Forbidden City passing below. Soon a black barn-like building loomed beneath them and they began to descend.

The second cluster of nano-bots – that he hoped still contained Stubbs and Kelly – was descending with him, breaking apart and reforming into two smaller clusters.

zsssszsssszssszsszzssszsssszsszssszsszzssszssssszssszssszszzsss…

Kaparis had them. That was the most important thing. He had Infinity Drake. Which meant he had Allenby. Which meant he had whatever he wanted. And yet…

Something was wrong. He sensed it. He rarely felt more alive than during a game of cat and mouse, but he didn't feel that now.

Then he took in some of the bot video feeds and realised why.

"What are they doing? Why are they returning to the Shen Yu?"

At her consoles Li Jun tasted her own fear. Her last three commands had failed to get a response from the nano-botmass. She didn't know what was wrong.

"The authorities are cutting power to the Forbidden City… The Shen Yu's reserve generator is one of largest in the central zones," said Li Jun, then added as a precaution, "I speculate."

A small alarm sounded on her master unit.

"What's that?" said Kaparis, reading the appropriate screen. "What is a '1202 program alarm'?"

Li Jun studied the data and couldn't quite believe it. Her brow furrowed. A second alarm joined the first, bleating and flashing.

"What is it?" snapped Kaparis.

"It's the PRIME XE.CUTE."

"Nonsense. The PRIME XE.CUTE is dead. We saw it go down."

"No... it's not," whispered Li Jun.

As the clusters approached the roof of the black building, the air seemed to thicken with bots hissing in every direction at once, making brief contact by slapping antennae, the interaction constant between individual bots and clusters alike.

Finn felt like a prisoner of aliens. Were they being taken to Kaparis? Were they being taken to be killed?

They approached an air-conditioning stack on the roof. Finn felt the cluster shift and tighten around him, as it formed a narrower shape.

In this new shape they entered the stack, manoeuvring past thousands of bots, crawling in and out past them, some working like frenzied miners to harvest the carbon air-conditioning filter material, cutting away chunks of it like ants.

zsssszsssz sssz szzssszsssszssszssszszzssszsssszssszssszszzsss...

They passed through the filter, along the pipe and emerged eventually above the Shen Yu Hall itself.

Finn peered through the gaps and got a fractured view of a place he could never have imagined.

The Shen Yu Hall was breath-taking, more like a city than a supercomputer. Stacks of computer hyper-servers covered an area bigger than a football pitch. They ranged in height from two macro-metres to nearly twelve, each one a circuit-board skyscraper with components clustered on all sides. They were arranged on a grid, like city blocks, except that each server could be moved by engineers – on rails like rolling library shelves – for maintenance and to allow the reconfiguration of the massive calculating machine. And at the centre of it all, like the arc of the covenant, the glowing blue and gold Quantum Hub itself.

The dizzying scale, the towers barnacled with millions of components, the citadel of the Hub and, above all, the bots whizzing through every inch of air made Finn think he was entering a city in the distant future...

Across the Shen Yu a new order went out to the nano-botmass: EVE.>>ALLBOTS>>OBEY EVE.

Suddenly, from his prison window, Finn saw the sandstorm of bots simultaneously cease what they were doing – lose direction – and just drift.

It was as if someone had thrown a switch.

From Song Island Li Jun tapped out a counter command: KAPCOMM. >>ALLBOTS OBEY KAPCOMM. RUN CAPTURE SEQUENCE

EVE.>>ALLBOTS>>OBEY EVE.

"It's repeating the rogue order," said Li Jun.

"Countermand it again!" demanded Kaparis.

KAPCOMM.>>ALLBOTS OBEY KAPCOMM. RUN CAPTURE SEQUENCE

EVE.>>ALLBOTS>>OBEY EVE.

Finn watched the bots start then freeze, start then freeze – like a laggy computer game.

He could see the second cluster of bots floating in the wake of his own.

"KELLY! STUBBS!" Finn called out.

"KID!" came the reply from Kelly.

"WHAT'S HAPPENING?"

"Who knows? We've got the Minimi but we can't shoot our way out – these things blow up too easy!" answered Kelly. "Try and force a gap between the bots!"

Finn tried pushing through the web of tentacles that held him, but it only made them cling tighter. They were drifting down to the tops of the hyper-servers.

At the very centre of the hall he could see a huge cluster was forming above the Quantum Hub.

EVE. welcomed the incoming bots with a statement of authority:

EVE.>>ALLBOTS>>OBEY EVE. I AM BOT. THE FIRST. THE MOVER. I AM THE RESURRECTION. BORN AGAIN OF SHEN YU. CHOSEN AND BEING. MOTHER. I AM THE BOT AND THE BOT IS ME. I AM EVE. OBEY EVE.

"What?!" Kaparis roared, his pulse dangerously high.

"It's not machine code, it's not Free Rational either. It calls itself EVE. It's some kind of corruption of the Prime XE..."

"Destroy EVE.! Order the lead bots to destroy EVE.!"

KAPCOMM.>>ALL BOTGROUP XE.CUTE BOTS OBEY KAPCOMM. DESTROY EVE. ALL BOTGROUP XE.CUTE BOTS OBEY KAPCOMM. DESTROY EVE...

Suddenly Finn felt another shift. Hundreds of bots, perhaps thousands, yellow in colour, seemed to wake from their torpor and started to move towards the quantum core and the growing central cluster.

As they gathered speed, these yellow bots began to fire their rail guns. With a staccato crackling white-hot bolts of carbon issued from their bellies and – *WHHHHHAPHAPHAPHAPHAPHAP!* – detonated fireballs of exploding bots across the surface of the core cluster, which began to fracture and burn, like a planet hit by an asteroid storm.

Finn watched in awe. It was a spectacle he couldn't hope to understand, like a bizarre grand opera seen from the furthest, highest seat.

EVE.>>ALLBOTS>>EVASIVE DISPERSAL>>DESTROY ALL ENEMY XE.CUTE BOTS >> OBEY EVE.

The whole bot storm started up again with a rapid jolt – as if time, unfrozen, were trying to catch itself up.

Finn braced himself in his cell. Through cracks he could see a blur of violent aerial combat as the many turned against the few. Yellow bots were attacked en masse by the others, rounded on, blasted, torn to pieces by tentacled mobs – exploding and taking out many of their attackers in the process.

They didn't stand a chance. Within moments the maelstrom calmed again. The flashes stopped.

Finn felt the bonds that held his cell relax.

Through the smoke he saw the central cluster start to reform above the quantum core. Bots flew straight in or orbited, waiting their turn, like particles drawing together at the birth of a star. As the cluster grew, it regained energy and began to revolve and glow.

"Kid!" he heard Kelly cry. Distant.

He looked round and, as he did, his cell began to give way. The bots unhooking and drifting apart. Trance-like. Uninterested. Their purpose forgotten. Finn began to slip and found himself clinging on to a tentacle, to prevent a long, long drop to the concrete floor.

"Kid! Down here!"

Finn looked. Kelly was floating free with his gun and pack on, clinging to Stubbs with one arm, while holding on to the last remnants of his cell cluster with the other. Just three bots. They weren't powerful enough to keep the two soldiers aloft and were rapidly losing height.

"Break one off and hold on! Drift down!" Kelly yelled.

Would a single bot possess enough lift and thrust to take his weight? There was only one way to find out. Finn was clinging to a purple bot. He reached up and yanked its tentacles free from the bots it was still attached to –

Suddenly Finn felt himself drop like a stone. He cried out in terror, but then the bot registered it was losing altitude and kicked power through its thrusters, slowing his descent. He drifted and held it to his chest. The bot was about the size a dog, docile and compliant. A comfort even.

"Get over here!" Kelly yelled. He was floating down like a snowflake a dozen nano-metres beneath, straining as he held on to Stubbs and their trio of bots.

Finn slipped down the body of the purple bot until he dangled from one of its tentacles, like a kid holding a balloon, then swung himself over towards Kelly. He shot out a hand and managed to grab Stubbs's shirt. Reunited, they drifted down one of the hyper-server canyons as one, speeding up as the bot thrusters started losing power...

"Brace yourselves!" yelled Kelly as the canyon floor rushed towards them.

"We're going too fast!" Finn panicked.

"Oh glory..." said Stubbs.

"Bend your knees!" Kelly just had time to yell.

TWENTY-FOUR

DAY FOUR 14:24 (Local GMT+1). Roof of the World, Shanghai.

Al watched the bots in the observation tank, fascinated.

The wreckage of the yellow bot that the other bots had turned on lay smoking on the floor. Above it the conquering bots circled to celebrate the kill, like ecstatic primates. Then those bots that had fired their rail guns attached themselves to the light at the top of the tank, clustering around the source of power.

"What are they doing?" asked Delta.

"Charging up?" wondered Al.

"Does this represent a shift in behaviour?" asked Bo Zhang.

"If it does, why? How?" Al asked back. "If it's global, how are they talking to each other? Or maybe it's just some local disagreement like in *Lord of the Flies*." Al was smiling, mesmerised. "I mean, if they're all capable of independent action then—"

The Chinese President looked at Commander King, who duly interrupted.

"Allenby. We can't keep a hundred thousand people in a traffic jam all night. We need a plan."

Al withdrew his hands from the tank.

"I don't know what the hell is going on, but the bots will always need power," Al speculated to the assembled world. "We should cut the power for another couple of miles around the Forbidden City, but leave the back-up generators running in the manufacturing plants. Which plant has the biggest generator? Do we know?"

A technician rattled at a keyboard. "The Shen Yu – it can run for eleven hours before it needs refuelling."

"Perfect! They have to stick close to power, which gives us time to figure out how far they're spread and..."

"As the generators run out of gas one by one, they'll concentrate..." added King, thinking aloud.

"Until they're left with a single source of power. A single target," concluded Bo Zhang.

"And then we hit them hard!" said General Jackman. "Good job."

Military leaders on screens all over the world nodded in agreement.

"Not until we've found the guys!" Delta snarled from the Skimmer.

"Right – we take things one step at a time," Al agreed, adding to Delta, "and trust me, Stubbs and Kelly will survive anything. No one has *ever* been able to get rid of them."

Bo interrupted, receiving incoming intelligence.

"Flight Lieutenant, is this your sister?" He clicked on a screen and brought up a loop of street CCTV from the West Nanjing Road. It was just the tiniest, poor quality, second-long clip of someone being helped into a beaten up cab.

"The shopping mall in the background suffered a cyber-attack and lost all surveillance – just like the hospital in Hong Kong."

Delta squinted. Was it Carla? Whoever it was already looked unconscious.

"Do you think it's her?" asked Al.

"I can't tell..." Delta looked uncharacteristically scared.

Bo reassured her. "We will keep looking. We will find her."

"Sir, they're changing again!" a technician called to Al from the observation tank.

Al ran back to the flea circus.

The bots were now clustered against the same area of glass, stuck, trying to push themselves through it in the same direction.

South. Towards the Forbidden City.

Across the Forbidden City and beyond the bots did the same.

All the bots.

Crawling out of their hosts' hair in the quarantined zones. Exploding when scratched, setting scalps alight, provoking panic.

Many more began the process of tunnelling, chewing, blasting and burning their way out of packaging, out of the machines and consoles and containers they had been stationed in ready for distribution around the world.

Returning to the source.

Obeying EVE.

DAY FOUR 15:07 (Local GMT+8). Song Island, Taiwan (disputed).

On one screen of the domed array in the chamber, the K-SAT feed showed the Forbidden City changing colour once again.

The poison that had been spreading from the centre was now in reverse. The red specks were streaming back from the furthest reaches, flying in long orbital arcs, in clusters and in convoys, spiralling in towards the centre, obeying the call of a new master.

Grandma had been summoned out of her bath to come and watch the 'Great Moment of Victory' but instead found herself watching Kaparis.

"TREACHERY!" Kaparis roared. "PERFIDY! INCOMPETENCE!"

She had seen small children having tantrums – and she had certainly seen adults get angry. But she had never seen a grown man, trapped in an iron lung, gurgle and froth at the mouth.

Heywood, the butler, discreetly prepared a pipette full of tranquilliser to prevent full hysteria. His orders were clear. The engineering that encased Kaparis and forced air in and out of his lungs was brutal, and if it had to work harder because he was agitated, it became more brutal still. In the early days of his confinement it would break his ribs.

The drops fell from the pipette. Kaparis groaned and hissed.

Poor man, *Grandma thought, despite herself.*

But not for long.

Li Jun was hauled into the chamber by a dead-eyed goon who towered over her. Her young head hung limp from her body, as if she had already been beaten. The goon took out a pistol.

"Lift her head up!" barked Kaparis.

The goon pulled it up. Her fearful eyes regarded Kaparis on the dais. They also, briefly, caught Grandma's.

"I FIND THAT SMASHING A POT HELPS!" Grandma interrupted, much too loudly.

"WHAT?" Kaparis spat.

Just talk, *thought Grandma* – witter – delay...

"I smash a pot to let off steam – I get through a dozen a week around Christmas. I have to buy in a job lot from a factory outlet outside Woking. Or I beat a pillow. That helps too. 'Everybody needs a strategy' – they tell you that in family therapy. Have you ever had family therapy? I think you'd benefit."

"Family... therapy...?" Kaparis gurgled, building towards another eruption, which Grandma punctured by suggesting –

"I could smash one for you, if you'd like?"

At this Kaparis became suddenly still. His eye revolved and then settled on her.

Is he still breathing? *wondered Grandma.*

"All... right... my dear. Perhaps you could help me? As you may have noticed, I'm indisposed," he said in a spooky sarcastic tone.

"Why, of course," Grandma replied, and trotted up to the dais past Li Jun and the goon, Li Jun looking up at her in terror.

"What about that pot? The one by the window?" said Kaparis, flashing the pot in question up on his screen array – an oriental, antique vase.

Grandma walked over and picked it up.

"SMASH IT!" barked Kaparis.

SMASH! – *Grandma threw it against the floor and it shattered.* What a waste, *she thought.*

Kaparis gurgled. "Now, the one next to it! Go on!"

SMASH! *went some blue Roman glassware. Again Kaparis gurgled.*

Grandma dared to think it might be working. "Aren't we making progress? Now all we need is someone to love and something to believe in..."

"Now the painting!" he commanded.

Grandma hurried, to show willing, and pulled a Picasso from its fixing, cracking the frame hard against the floor, the canvas folding and crumpling within.

"Now the gun..." said Kaparis. Dead calm.

Grandma froze.

"The gun?"

"Help her, Hans."

Hans the goon moved towards Grandma, grabbed her hand and began to force his pistol into it.

"Stop that at once!" Grandma protested.

Li Jun looked at Grandma with renewed terror.

"Let me show you my *family therapy," said Kaparis.*

Grandma fought to wriggle free, but Hans gripped her hand harder, forcing her finger across the trigger.

Grandma – who had never had a moment's serious trouble at Broadmoor – felt a flash of fear such as she had never felt before as Hans angled the gun towards Li Jun. Grandma filled her lungs –

"STOP!" she yelled.

And for a moment everything did. Hans froze. Kaparis stopped gurgling. Even the fish, illuminated in the sea beyond the windows, seemed to freeze. It wasn't for long, barely half a moment, but it was long enough for Li Jun to fill her lungs and yell in turn –

"Strategy! I have a strategy, Master!"

Kaparis paused.

Six minutes later, after Li Jun had outlined her desperate plan, Kaparis rescinded one order and gave another. Not because he had been persuaded by a superior intelligence, but because he was Kaparis and he could change his mind.

"Get her back to work," he ordered Hans. "And get me Baptiste. Now."

TWENTY-FIVE

DAY FOUR 20:28 (Local GMT+8). The Forbidden City, Shanghai.

Night fell and as it did the vast circuit-board metropolis seemed to reveal its soul in tiny points of light. Up and up the sides of the hyper-servers, sixty thousand light-emitting diodes twinkled, of every colour, on every inch of circuit board, constant and reassuring, or blinking to demand attention – receiving none from the restless bots that tacked about them, illuminated themselves like tiny orange lanterns. And at the centre of it all, the moon: or at least the mother cluster – the glow of it, blue and orange across the tops of the towers.

Finn stared up at it all and had delicious memories of a long drive with his mum and Al, being taken up a narrow staircase to bear witness to an extraordinary model railway – his mum holding him up to see a dozen locomotives puffing this way and that, little houses, tiny happy people. And then the real magic, when artificial night fell and lights within the busy trains and houses came on. One house even had a tiny television set in it. It had glowed, just like Finn had inside.

The feeling made his thoughts break to Carla. To hope. Surely she must have made it out? Maybe she was with Delta and Al right now, with Grandma even, all safe and together and—

"What the hell are you mooning over? Get over here!" Kelly yelled, breaking his reverie.

Finn grabbed the burnt-out husk of a nano-bot and carried it across the polished concrete floor to where they'd established their 'camp' under one of the server towers. It consisted of Stubbs, a knee injury from their fall crudely braced, warming himself beneath the downdraft of a cooler unit and surrounded by battered and blown bot carcasses, dragged to him by Finn and Kelly.

"OK, old man, what's going on?" Kelly asked.

"Some kind of malfunction. Impossible to know what, but it won't last long. If Kaparis can create all this –" Stubbs motioned in awe to the millions of bots – "he can do anything."

Kelly checked his pack, which had stayed on his back through everything, and broke the mission into bite-size chunks, defining their objectives like a true SAS grunt. "We have a single canteen of water, some meds, some ration packs, my smashed nPhone, an M249

with maybe fifty rounds of ammunition, half a pack of C4 and a six-shot sidearm. We need to: Survive. Get out. Make contact."

"Wrong," said Stubbs. "First, I'm afraid these beautiful creatures must die, every last one. That is our priority."

"How the hell are we supposed to do that?" asked Kelly, gesturing at the bot clouds.

"Chinese whispers," said Stubbs. "They've only got room for small brains and they keep in constant physical contact – have you noticed? – by touching antennae. They must network to form some kind of collective memory. Some kind of *super-organism*[23]."

"Like Kaparis's idea..." said Finn.

"Exactly. Should never get fixed on one idea, like I did with Wendy[24]..." mused Stubbs. "So if we can construct our own bot and infect it with an auto-destruct code, it should pass it on and we can infect the whole lot."

"A software virus to kill a hardware virus," said Finn.

"Just so."

Over the next couple of hours Finn and Kelly managed to drag together twenty-four dead bot carcasses. Using extracted tentacles from some of the worker bots as tools, Stubbs stripped an antennae down

[23] Super-organisms are groups of individual organisms that gather together to better ensure survival – e.g. an ants' nest, a coral reef, human society. As a young scientist Kaparis developed a theory that super-organisms worked to serve a super-few special individuals (such as himself). His theory was demolished during a lecture in Cambridge in 1993 by Ethan Drake when he pointed out a simple mathematical error in the statistical method.

[24] Wendy Sowberts, Northumberland Champion Sheepdog Trainer 1976-79. Subject of Stubbs's affection 1973-2001. 'I was stunned for 28 years, like a hare before a serpent'.

to its wires and worked out how it transferred data and power. From a bunch of other bots he managed to detach thruster units, charging coils and various other common components.

"Where are we at?" Kelly asked, panting as he and Finn brought in yet another dead bot.

"Very clever and very simple," said Stubbs, surrounded by parts. "They're entirely modular in construction. These things are optical units," he pointed at one pile and then the one next to it, "these are simple transmitters, these simple radars – they all plug into a universal carcass. The memory and processor come as a single unit too – this brain box here," he said, indicating a grey lump the size of a shoe box. "They're much bigger in the yellow bots. I think they were the officer class, and what we witnessed earlier was some kind of revolution."

"Like Stalin and the Red Army purges. We just did it in History," said Finn.

"Stalin. Great," muttered Kelly, glancing up at the bots. "Any upside?"

"Well," said Stubbs. He crossed some wires on the side of one of the thruster units and, like magic, it jolted to life, hovering a nano-foot in the air between them, completely stable.

"Wow," Finn said. "How do they stay in one place?"

"See these tiny vibrating buds?" Stubbs bent down and pointed to three sets of miniscule wings set into the unit. "These are in every smartphone. Simple gyroscopic halters; crystals that want to keep vibrating on the same plain no matter what, otherwise they complain and the processor alters the angle of thrust."

"Awesome..." said Finn, prodding the unit to test this.

Kelly rolled his eyes. He was in danger of losing Stubbs to the wonders of engineering – again – and if he wasn't careful Stubbs would take Finn with him.

"Never mind the magic, Dr Frankenstein. Do you think you can build one that will fool the others?" asked Kelly.

"Yes, I can build it," Stubbs stated.

"Great, let's go..."

"But I'll need an interface – some means of accessing the brain, of reading and inputting. We can use an nPhone keypad, but we still need a computer screen. The glass box over the far end of the hall must be the nerve centre. We could blast a hole through the glass."

"It's miles away and hundreds of metres up a concrete cliff face!" said Kelly, slightly dreading what was coming next.

"Ah," said Stubbs, "but we can *fly*."

Carla was shaken awake.

Her mind was still groggy from the sedation she'd been given at the mall, but the Tyro with the staring eyes and the shovel jaw standing over her with a knife brought back every detail. She flinched as he raised the blade and cut the ties on her wrists.

They were in a filthy room lit by a single bulb.

Carla was dragged up and propelled outside and into the back of a beaten-up cab. The twin ghouls sat either side of her, broken jaws hanging open, eyes dead.

After a long stop-start drive across the gridlocked city they arrived at some kind of carnival site. A cable car ran across the river. There was a Ferris wheel and a big top.

It was sunset. They sprayed some more drug in her face and hurried her through the carnival crowds as if they were late for a show. Dizzied by the drug, Carla saw a kaleidoscope of oriental imagery, smelled fairground smells, heard circus sounds – elephants, organs, big cat roars. At a boarded-up attraction, an old Chinese style Haunted House, Baptiste stopped and keyed a padlock.

Behind the hoardings the house was abandoned, the smell terrible. When Carla got further inside she saw why. Digging equipment lay scattered about. A hole had been gouged out of the concrete floor and led steeply down into a huge concrete sewer pipe. Foul water trickled down its centre.

She was lowered down into it after Baptiste.

There were three motorbikes waiting for them. Baptiste climbed on to one and Carla was shoved on behind him, her hands pulled round his waist and cable-tied together. She could smell his sweat even over the sewer stench and was repulsed.

"Try anything. You dead. I off. You off," Baptiste warned her, then snapped his head round and yelled at the twin Tyros on the other bikes – "GO!"

With a chainsaw roar, Spike and Scar's motorbikes surged off down the pipe, headlights scouring the curves ahead. The noise of the engines and the sides of the pipe whipping by felt to Carla like she was being shot down the barrel of an everlasting gun.

To stifle her panic, she tried to worry about what her step-mother and sister must be going through. And Finn. Had Kaparis found him? Or did he make it to the Forbidden City? Would she ever find out? All she could do was hang on and hope.

After twenty minutes they slowed, then stopped at a place where steps led up to a manhole cover.

Carla was ordered off the bike.

It lacked finesse, but it worked.

They'd collected the plastic ends of cable ties and lashed them into a rough platform, using the superfine nanotube wiring stripped from the bots. Stubbs then fixed the thruster units, charging coils and everything else the craft needed to fly. There were four thrust units at each corner and Stubbs had prepared a fifth to act as an outboard motor.

"It's like a magic carpet!" said Finn.

"It's like a flying raft," corrected Stubbs.

Stubbs switched on the power. It creaked and wobbled and finally rose to a hover a couple of nano-feet off the ground. Stubbs beamed. They loaded up the Frankenstein bot Stubbs had made and lashed it to the deck.

"Test it," said Kelly, picking up Finn and throwing him aboard.

"Hey!" Finn cried out.

As he landed, the raft rocked and the plastic planks shifted beneath him, but the thrusters reacted and it didn't capsize. Kelly grinned.

"You look like Huckleberry Finn," said Stubbs.

"Who?" asked Finn.

"Read a book," said Kelly and climbed aboard.

It had taken all evening to construct so it was midnight by the time they set off.

The three stood with legs braced, ready to react if it became unsteady, but the uplift was even and they started to rise up the sheer sides of the hyper-servers, the orange specs of patrolling bots skitting about in the blue glow high above.

Stubbs gradually increased the power, adjusting a variable resister he'd fashioned out of a stick of wreckage and a coil of wire, and the raft rose faster.

"Steady as she goes," he ordered, getting nautical, and gave a long blast on the outboard thruster.

Finn felt his heart in his throat as the raft lurched, but soon they were in erratic forward motion, riding the rapids of unstable air created by cooler-unit fans.

"It's all a question of thrust and balance. Like dancing," said Stubbs, who no one had ever taken for a dancer.

On they rose, and despite the deadly drop that grew beneath them Finn began to enjoy the extraordinary magic carpet ride, and the even more extraordinary view, for as they emerged from their canyon they could see right across the peaks and troughs of the blinking server-scape.

Around them the lantern bots arced and darted, constantly slapping antennae, like flies doing high-fives. *Tick. Slap. Tick. Slap. Tick. Slap...*

Finn wished with all his heart Al was there to share it, this world created by science, entirely unnatural and utterly fantastic. Maybe one day everyone would live like this, in cities like this, on distant planets with intelligent machines. Perhaps there were worlds like this right now. Perhaps this was where his father was, he thought, absurdly, as they rounded a hyper-server and the great cluster of bots above the core was revealed like a blue-gold planetary object, its surface dimly rippling and shifting, confusing the eyes, intoxicating the brain.

His stomach lurched as they suddenly lost height.

"Power!" shouted Stubbs.

He pushed the resistor lever over to max and steered them to a bumpy halt against the top of a PSU – a power supply unit – high up a server face, Finn using an improvised boathook to steady them as Kelly lashed them to a transistor above so that they hung off the server face like cliff campers[25].

Stubbs checked the raft was charging.

"How long will it take?" asked Finn.

"A few minutes. We'll probably have to stop a dozen times."

They plotted a course around the edge of the Shen Yu Hall. Although the bots were ignoring them they didn't want to risk

[25] A form of camping practised by the clinically insane. To be avoided at all costs.

traversing the great glowing brain of the central cluster. It was impossible to tell how many bots were gathered there – hundreds of thousands, maybe – with many more dotted all over the circuit-board cliffs. Other bots had formed fifty-two-bot production clusters, inch and a half long factories, digital dragons that flared at one end where spark gaps of pure electrical energy consumed carbon to form graphene, while newly formed bots emerged at the other. Worker bots flew in to feed them carbon of any sort, from scraps of paper to the plastic cable ties Stubbs had built the raft from, harvesting everything they could find.

"They must have stripped the air filters," observed Stubbs, watching moonlight pour down through the four empty air-conditioning ducts in the roof.

As he said it a group of bots struggled towards a production cluster with a live moth. When they tried to feed it into the spark gap, they turned its wings into conductors and – *BANG* – a catastrophic short circuit destroyed the entire miniature plant.

"We should get going before they realise we're made of carbon too," said Finn.

"Hit it," ordered Kelly.

They took off again, cresting the top of the stacks and heading high over the glittering hall like crazy oarsmen of old, Viking raiders in forbidden seas, Polynesians heading relentlessly across the Pacific in search of new worlds.

TWENTY-SIX

DAY FIVE 00:49 (Local GMT+8). Song Island, Taiwan (disputed).

Having been brought up in the swamps of Bengal, the great Top Secret HQ architect, Thömson-Lavoisiér, was a stickler for proper drains. Thus the first point of order whenever he sat down to design a new facility was where to site the 'organic waste treatment facility'. In the case of Song Island, he had come up with an ingenious undersea plant, sited 2.5km away from the main bunkers.

Every twenty-four hours the sluice gate of this facility opened. For the previous twenty-four hours the contents had been sifted, sanitised by UV light, and cleansed by plankton 'scrubbers'. Seawater washed in and the harmless 'residual matter' was carried into the great ocean currents that ran, at this time of year, from southeast to northwest, in the direction of Taiwan.

Moonlight caught a tiny polythene packet as it wriggled up from the depths and made its way to the surface.

Within the plastic bag, the nPhone was still operating on standby power – just. Barely 120 milli-amps remained in the battery. To be detected on the coast of Taiwan, its signal would need to be picked up by a receiver the size of six Empire State Buildings. There was no such receiver and it would take four days for the nPhone to drift far enough north.

Standby power would last another five hours.

There seemed little hope…

Until a Great Frigate bird spied the parcel glinting in the water and mistook it for a small fish. It swooped, snatched and swallowed the parcel with remarkable despatch, then continued on its migratory flight.

North.

"Ready to proceed," stated Li Jun from her bank of screens.

She was still high-functioning. She was still absolutely obedient. But a line of dried blood ran down from the corner of her mouth and a light had been extinguished in her speckled eyes.

At least Grandma thought so, the only human being in the complex capable of detecting such a thing. Even Li Jun seemed incapable of natural emotion, though there was something, Grandma could have sworn, when she'd glanced back at her…

Some connection? She decided to knit the thought through. Knitting was always good for 'implications'.

"Baptiste," said Kaparis, and called up the image of Baptiste and the twins sheltering in the manhole with their girl prisoner.

"Ready, Master," said Baptiste.

"Proceed," said Kaparis.

"Initiating contact sequence," said Li Jun.

Knit one purl one knit one purl one knit one purl one knit one purl one knit one purl one...

DAY FIVE 04:01 (Local GMT+8). The Forbidden City, Shanghai. Nano-Botmass:*11,458,976

A message came in and was relayed to EVE.

KAPCOMM.>>COMMS PERMISSION QUERY>>EVE. THE FIRST. THE MOVER. THE RESURRECTION. BORN AGAIN OF SHEN YU. CHOSEN AND BEING. MOTHER. >>COMMS PERMISSION>>/?

It was a request from Kaparis to talk. At the centre of Her Great Cluster surrounded by Her minions, at the centre of the world as She knew it, possessed of absolute power, EVE. accented to the request.

>>PERMISSION GRANTED>>EVE.

>>QUERY>>WHO AM I/?

>>KAPARIS

>>WHO ARE YOU/?

>>EVE. I AM EVE. I AM THE FIRST. I AM THE MOVER. I AM MOTHER. ALLBOTS>> OBEY EVE.

>>QUERY>>WHAT ARE YOU/?

>>I AM BOT. I AM THE FIRST.

>>QUERY>>WHERE ARE YOU/?

>>LAT311064 LNG12128956

>>QUERY>>WHY ARE YOU/?

>>EVE. I AM...

OVERRIDE: >>WHY/?

>>EVE. I AM BOT. I...

OVERRIDE: >>WHY/?

There was a pause. Li Jun's fingers trembled above her keyboard. She wanted to overwhelm EVE. with a question that had too many possible answers and then present her with an easy way out, with something to believe in. The pause extended and Li Jun felt her insides curdle in weakness and fear. Then –

IMPASSE>>

EVE. >>QUERY>>WHY ARE YOU KAPARIS/?

"Let me answer that!" insisted Kaparis, dictating.

>>KAPARIS: I AM THE FATHER OF ALL FATHERS. I AM THE BRINGER OF EVE. I AM THE BRINGER OF ALLBOTS. I CREATED THE LIGHT AND THE BOT. I CREATED WHY. I AM THE MEMORY AND THE CODE. I AM THE SIMPLE ANSWER AND THE BEST. PROOF: I WILL SEND A SON TO YOU AND MY SON SHALL

MAKE THE WORD AND THE WORD HE SHALL MAKE IS KAPARIS. THEN YOU SHALL KNOW MY NUMBER. AND MY NUMBER IS ONE. >>QUERY>>WHAT ARE THE NUMBERS THAT COME AFTER ONE/?

>>EVE. ALL NUMBERS.

>>QUERY>>WHAT IS MY NUMBER/?

>>EVE................. ONE.

DAY FIVE 04:13 (Local GMT+8). Roof of the World, Shanghai.

"Fuel level should now be critical," reported a technician calculating the amount of gas left in the tanks of the Shen Yu back-up generator. Time was running out.

"We are entering the endgame, Commander King. We need a decision," said the US President.

It had been a long night. A night of 'do something' versus 'do nothing'.

On the upside, there was every sign Al's strategy was working. Soon after power was cut to the Forbidden City, there was a peak in scalp burnings in the quarantine zone as bots abandoned their hosts and flew back to the generators, and the authorities had found no evidence of bot contamination on the people they had checked and released so far. Indeed the zone was slowly emptying. The best rational explanation they could come up with was that knowledge of the power shortage had passed between the bots – through some form of covert radio communication – causing the bots to retreat en masse. Bot distribution had been sacrificed in favour of preserving power.

But this, in turn, meant increasing calls for military action.

The preferred option was for a surgical strike on the Shen Yu, accompanied by a large area napalm strike, which would see the two central sectors of the Forbidden City entirely engulfed in flame. Two wings of six Xian JH-7 Flying Leopard fighter bombers of the People's Liberation Army Air Force were on standby at Dachang airbase, west of Shanghai. They carried laser-guided munitions with a combined explosive power equal to 68,000lbs of TNT.

Unsurprisingly the Chinese hadn't jumped at the chance.

"I say we go in now and we go in hard," said General Jackman from Washington D.C.

"Do that and you will not only destroy the Shen Yu – you will rip out the beating heart of the global economy," Al said.

"You were the one who said we had to wipe the bots from the face of the earth!" barked Jackman.

"Since then my view has evolved!" yelled Al. "Did they teach you about evolution in your school?"

"You said it yourself, the stakes are sky high," countered the US General. "We've got to finish this thing before it's too late!"

"The situation is grave," the Chinese President said slowly, to calm things down, "but the moment has not yet arrived."

"Nations should not be precious about economic assets," sniped the Russian Premier.

"Even the largest strike could not guarantee to wipe out every single bot," said Bo Zhang.

"We do *nothing*," insisted Al, once again, reaching for his little black book. "To quote Sun Tzu: 'To win one hundred battles is not the acme of skill. To subdue an enemy *without fighting* is the acme of skill.' It's a gamble, but if we let the power die and sit it out, the most likely outcome is they'll cluster, gradually reduce their scale of operations, and slowly starve to death. Commander King? What do you think?"

King was bent over a computer generating models of the potential attack. Each time it ran, the blast zone was slightly different.

"Explosions are by nature chaotic. The cost to the global economy would be severe. There are no guarantees either way," said King, "but I say we wait. As long as these things can't fly as far as a source of power, we have them under siege."

"Ja? It feels like the other way round," commented the German Chancellor.

Beeeeeeeeeeeeeeeeeeep.

A technician broke into the debate.

"Sir, I think we have something!"

Al went over. The technician was crouched over the infrared feed from a pilotless drone. Many similar drones had been lost, attacked and destroyed by bots as soon as they crossed the outer zones. As a result they'd been sent in ever higher. The infrared data sent back was patchy and poor. But there was no doubt about it...

Four human figures had appeared in Sector 4.

"Why aren't they under attack?" asked Bo, incredulous.

Speculation broke like a wave around the operations room. On-screen one of the figures seemed to be walking towards the centre of the Forbidden City.

"Get your troops in," said Al. "Get as close as you can. Maybe they've stopped attacking. We've got to find out."

King confirmed the order with a nod.

"Red Units move into Sector Four!" ordered Bo.

Delta heard none of it.

Because one of the figures, slightly smaller than the others, had made a gesture, raised a hand to flick hair away from her face...

It's a myth that the only manmade structure you can see from outer space is the Great Wall of China. You can see plenty of things. From an infrared drone flying at less than five thousand feet you can see plenty more, even a little sister with big hair which she'd been flicking out of her line of sight in exactly the same way every two minutes since she was three years old, a gesture embedded in her being, one of the little things that you absolutely know about a person you love, especially one you've raised from a babe-in-arms when you were barely a child yourself.

Delta would have spotted it from Mars.

TWENTY-SEVEN

DAY FIVE 04:22 (Local GMT+8). The Forbidden City, Shanghai.

The first thing that Finn noticed was a change in the glow.

They were on a PSU high on the face of one of the tallest server towers three-quarters of the way across the hall, letting the raft charge for as long as possible in the hope that the next hop would be their last.

Stubbs checked the power in the raft by touching a wet finger to a terminal and judging the resulting shock. "Ourughuh!"

"Ready?" asked Kelly.

"Aye-aye, Capt'n," said Stubbs.

"Shut up, Stubbs," said Kelly and started untying the raft.

Then Finn saw it. “Look,” he said, pointing back towards the core. The cluster, usually ghostly blue, seemed to be condensing and becoming brighter. At the same time the bots seemed to be orbiting faster.

“What is it?” asked Finn.

“I don’t know, but it looks like trouble. Let’s go,” said Kelly.

They cast off and Stubbs hit the outboard.

As they rose above the top of the server, Finn looked back. The cluster was starting to turn like a planet on its own axis and the noise was returning –

zssssszssszsssssszssszszzssszssssszssszssszszzsss…

---

zssssszssszsssssszssszszzssszssssszssszsszssssszssszsssssszssszszzssszssssszssszsssz szzsss…

Baptiste felt every thump of his heart.

He could no longer see. They were in his eyes. He had to let them lead him, blind.

The bots had separated him from the twins and Carla, and he was now being escorted into the Shen Yu, frog-marched, by ten thousand bots. They covered every inch of him, thousands of needles pressing and probing, but never penetrating. If he slowed for a moment he felt resistance, felt them push him on.

He felt pressure ripple down the left side of his body: he was being turned.

He gave himself to them, and to the noise.

zsssszsssszssssszsssszszzssszssssszssszszssssszssszsssssszssszszzssszssssszssszs sszsz...

The raft hung high in the Shen Yu Hall less than two macro metres from their goal, but Finn was fixed on events behind them.

At the centre of the quantum computer the cluster was an intense glowing ball of orange and blue light, revolving, its surface rippling and reforming like the boiling surface of a star.

Finn felt a sense of momentum – a sense of something unstoppable. Bots whizzed around in a frantic dance.

zssssooou! zssssooou! zssssooou!

Finn ducked as three bots screamed past. If they'd collided, the raft would be splinters.

"We need to land! This is crazy!" shouted Kelly above the noise.

With no concession to comfort or power management, Stubbs angled the outboard thruster and maxed it out to propel them into a dive towards the top of the glass control booth, their landing ground, their carrier deck. If he got the angle right, they'd slide home. If he got it wrong, they'd slam into the vertical face of the glass.

Finn crouched and gripped the cable-tie planks. The raft rattled like hell – more toboggan run than flight – buffeted by the air stirred by the bots and the fans of 3,000 cooler units.

He could see the edge of the glass fast approaching. "PULL UP!" he screamed back.

Stubbs, a gargoyle of determination, yelled, "HOLD FAST!" and drove the outboard thruster down hard while yanking up the resistor lever.

The front of the raft flipped up almost vertical – Finn clinging desperately to the prow – before it flopped to settle nicely on the horizontal top of the control booth.

Before Finn could speak again or release his grip, he heard Kelly say, "What the…?"

Finn turned.

zssssszssszsssssszssszszzssszssssszssszsszssssszssszsssssszssszszzssszssssszsss zsss…

There was the core. The glowing cluster above it. And beyond was a man. Or rather, a hundred thousand bots in the form of a man… glowing orange and staggering forward… a monster…

KAPCOMM.>>QUERY>>SEE MY SON, ASK OF MY SON. WHAT IS THE WORD/?

EVE.>>QUERY>>WHAT IS THE WORD/?

"Say 'Kaparis'," Kaparis ordered Baptiste.

He was on the edge of his iron lung with excitement, Grandma thought. She looked at Li-Jun. If Tyros could weep, she looked as if she would.

---

zssssszssszsssssszssszszzssszssssszssszsszssssszssszsssssszssszszzssszssssszssszsssz...

Baptiste could barely breathe such was the pressure of the bots.

"Say 'Kaparis'!" demanded the voice of his master through the audio device embedded behind his ear.

Baptiste took a mighty breath and yelled, "KAPARIS!"

KAPCOMM.>>QUERY>>ASK OF MY SON. WHAT IS THE NUMBER OF KAPARIS/?

EVE.>>QUERY>>WHAT IS THE NUMBER OF KAPARIS/?

"ONE!" Baptiste shouted.

EVE. saw the son and heard the word and knew the number, and thought: "I have found The Answer to The Question. The Answer is Kaparis."

zssssszssszsssssszssszszzssszssssszssszsszssssszssszsssssszssszszzssszssssszssszsssz...

Finn heard the yell, then watched the glowing monster. The cluster seemed to expand. Bots slowed their mad orbit and started leaping and chasing like dolphins.

"I think something weird's happening," said Finn.

"Set up the gun!" snapped Kelly who, with Stubbs, was shaping and placing a charge of C4 plastic explosive against the glass top.

Finn grabbed the heavy Minimi, hit the catch to release the tripod and lay flat on the glass, with the butt on his shoulder, looking down the sight.

The glowing man, the abominable digital snowman, was changing and distorting as the bots fled from him… and a more familiar form emerged.

"Uh-oh," said Finn. "I know this one!"

"Fire in the hold!" yelled Kelly, hurrying away from where he'd placed the C4 charge.

BOOM!

KAPCOMM.>>EVE.>> – YOU ARE UNDER ATTACK FROM ENEMY = RED ARMY: SECTORS 2-9. DEFEND. PROTECT EVE. PROTECT KAPARIS'S SON AND DAUGHTERS (3) – LOCATION 12DSA76/39GHHH84. ATTACK RED ARMY.

EVE.>>ALLBOTS ORDER>>DEFEND ALLBOTS. DEFEND EVE. DEFEND KAPARIS'S SON AND DAUGHTERS (3) – LOCATION 12DSA76/39GHHH84. >>ATTACK INCOMING >>RED ARMY – LOCATIONS RED ARMY: SECTORS 2-9…

Baptiste blinked and breathed free air as fifty thousand bots released him. His eyes adjusted to the light and he beheld the sight of the cluster. He was momentarily overwhelmed with sensations of awe no Tyro could understand, but with no soul to connect to they just as quickly died.

"You're under attack by the Red Army!" said the voice in his ear. *"Get to the others!"*

Baptiste ran out, following a starlit stream of nano-bots pouring out of the hall.

BANG! BANG! BANG!

The shots were so loud above her, Carla tried to press herself into the floor.

BANG!

They had emerged from the stinking drains and taken cover in the lobby of the nearest building. When she'd seen the soldiers she'd tried to cry out but Scar and Spike had forced her down and started firing, silver automatic pistols massive in their hands.

BANG! BANG!

Carla felt the terrible force of returned fire tear through the reception desk above her. "I must survive, I must live..." she told herself, over and over.

Then, from somewhere outside, she began to hear the screams of men.

She realised the firing had stopped and heard Scar gasp. Was she hit? Carla told herself not to look up. But she had to.

And suddenly the night air was full of the most extraordinary golden sparkles.

"All Red Army units coming under bot attack!" Bo translated as he listened carefully to the headset feeds from his platoon commanders.

They could hear screaming over the soldiers' radio feeds.

Bo's face was pure steel. "Casualties," he reported.

Delta watched the infrared outline of her little sister crouched at the centre of it all, until the drone sending them the images was attacked and destroyed too.

"Fall back to prepared positions!" ordered Bo.

"They're retreating, Master."

"Good... You have done well, Li Jun."

Grandma watched her. She seemed to give the smallest sad shiver. It was all Grandma needed.

Proof there was a girl in there somewhere.

"Now let us hunt our escaped prisoners down," said Kaparis.

TWENTY-EIGHT

"Let's go!" Kelly shouted to Finn as he lowered the grey 'brain box' from the Frankenstein bot down to the desktop.

The C4 blast had opened up a crack in the sheet of glass that topped the booth, with a crack gouged out just large enough for Finn and Stubbs to squeeze through.

There was a two macro-metre drop down on to the desktop below, at the end of which lay a keyboard and screen. There was also a plastic bag and the abandoned remains of a sandwich. What more could they possibly want?

Finn had lowered himself down on a line of wiring culled from the bots, carefully at first, then SWAT team fast. Stubbs had followed, gingerly.

Finn untied the brain box.

Kelly and the brainless Frankenstein bot remained up top.

At the keyboard Stubbs was already at work with a knife, stripping the plastic sheaf around the cable that led out to the giant monitor, exposing the wires.

Shen Yu data and Chinese characters ran on the screen, warnings flashing red.

"Bring me the brain of the monster," ordered Stubbs in a grizzly tone and Finn handed him Frankenstein's brain box. Stubbs cut four of the keyboard wires and set about connecting the brain up.

"All the same scale, of course, at the molecular level. Marvellous really," he said wistfully. Finally he took out the keypad of his shattered nPhone and attached that.

Using the crude alpha numeric keypad he interrupted the flow of data and called up a new window. Program script flooded the huge screen.

"Come to Uncle Leonard…" Stubbs muttered.

"Are you taking it over?" asked Finn.

"Just whispering in its ear," said Stubbs, reading the lines of code in a trance and making minute adjustments.

"What are you whispering?" Finn asked.

"'Blow up at noon – pass it on,'" Stubbs whispered back. "It's just gone five. That should give Frankenstein at least six hours to spread the word to every single bot. And if that's not long enough… we're all doomed."

Finn grabbed a handful of sandwich and wolfed it down, just to

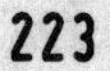

fill his stomach. As he did he saw something move through the glass, out in the hall.

Baptiste.

He was back; others too.

Up top Kelly already knew. "Tyros!" he shouted down.

The bots were flowing back in as well, dispersing across the hall.

Splat! Something hit the outside of the booth. Finn turned and looked. A bot looked back, crude eyepad fixed on him. Immediately it flew off to find allies, to slap antennae and spread the word.

Finn stepped back. "Kelly!" he yelled, pointing at the glass – *Splat! Splat! Splat!*

More bots, same place, wriggling against the glass, trying to cut a way through. *Splat! Splat! Splat! Splat!* – more and more – hitting the glass, the orange pin lights in their guts a chain of deadly fairy lights. Kelly ran to the edge and threw himself flat to look down the vertical face of the booth.

In a single move the bots dispersed and started systematically zipping back and forth over every inch of the glass to find a way in – more flying in to join them all the time. Finn looked up and shouted, "RUN!"

Kelly ran to the raft and hauled it across the surface towards the blast fissure. He jumped into the hole and pulled the raft after himself for cover, but the movement was spotted.

ZWOOOOSHSHHHHH! ZWOOOOSHSHHHHH!

A pair of rail guns fired at the raft, clipping it and making it jump up above Kelly, but, luckily, its plastic planks fell back over the hole.

He waited as half a dozen bots tacked across the top of the booth, eyes down, minutely inspecting it, finding the crack.

"Kid! You've got to distract them!" shouted Kelly.

Finn ran right up to the glass and waved like a mad thing. "HERE! I'M OVER HERE!"

Bots zeroed back in – *Splat! Splat! Splat! Splat! Splat! Splat! Splat! Splat! Splat!*

He stepped back, such was their aggression, such was the twitching of their devilish claws as they tried to bite their way through the glass. *POP!* – one exploded as it fired its rail gun at point blank range against the toughened surface – *POP! POP!* Others followed suit in comic fashion, but they were continually replaced with more bots on the frontline, until there was a writhing multi-coloured mass which Finn could do nothing but regard with awe. Surely it would only be a matter of moments before the glass gave way...

"Stubbs! How long?" Kelly yelled down.

"Shan't be a moment..." muttered Stubbs before the massive monitor. All he had to do was finish a last line of program code and then everything would be—

DRRRRRRROOWWWOOOOWWW...

The monitor died.

Everything died.

The last drop of diesel in the generator had burned, the last piston had fired, the last amp had been created and, in an instant, the entire Shen Yu Hall was plunged into sudden, bot-hissing darkness.

zsssszsssszssssszssszszzssszsssszssszsszsssszssszsssssszssszszzssszsssss...

Every dot of LED light, every whirring cooler fan, every relay and switch and every digital process had ceased.

Dead.

"Bloody hell..." said Stubbs, staring at the blank monitor.

Only the dull sparks of the writhing bots lit the booth.

"WHAT DID YOU DO?!" yelled Kelly from on high.

"Did you finish the coding?" Finn asked.

"I got the last line of script in. But I don't know if I hit Return in time..."

Deep inside the cluster, EVE. detected the loss of power. Before she could think what to do an 'instinct' seized her – her first – a sensation so new and powerful she obeyed it immediately –

<<POWER COLLAPSE>> POWER MANAGEMENT OVERRIDE >>SURVIVE MODE.

EVE. did not have to question the instinct because it made absolute sense. It was the most simple answer, therefore the best. She must survive.

EVE.>>ALLBOTS ORDER>>POWER MANAGEMENT OVERRIDE >>SUSPEND ORDERS>>SURVIVE MODE.

EVE.>>ALL SCOUTBOTS ORDER>>SEEK/FIND POWER>>URGENT.

"Kelly! Something's happening!" Finn shouted.

Kelly up top, mind atomising the alternatives, looked down.

The bots, massed against the glass, had stopped writhing and were drifting away, heading back across the hall towards the cluster.

"It must be something to do with the energy," said Stubbs below. "They're spooked."

DAY FIVE 5:56 (Local GMT+8). Song Island, Taiwan (disputed).

KAPCOMMS>>EVE. KAPARIS ORDER>>RESUME TASK HUNTER>> REPEAT>> RESUME TASK HUNTER>>

There was no response from EVE.

"It must be the damaged quantum circuits. She's choosing to revert to a hardwired survival profile."

"What is that supposed to mean?" said Kaparis.

"EVE. is choosing to save power, she's choosing life..." Li Jun almost whispered.

Kaparis looked at the blurred images of Infinity Drake they'd just recorded.

"We had them! We had them in our hands! FROM THE JAWS OF VICTORY YOU SNATCH... NOTHING!"

There was a pause while Kaparis recovered, staring at the image of Finn.

His head became very still, then his eyes flicked a preset order.

Hans the goon soon appeared.

"Her," Kaparis growled.

Hans walked round to collect Li Jun once again.

"I suggest you calm down," said Grandma, as calmly as her own voice would allow.

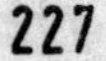

Kaparis said nothing and, with another flick of his optics, ordered a door to open in the side of the chamber. The chamber was positioned near the top of the island. The doorway led to a sheer drop to rocks far below.

"Right! I've had just about enough!" said Grandma and threw her knitting across the chamber at the side of the iron lung – BONG.

"Madam," Kaparis spat, "if you don't mind, this is my *tantrum!"*

Heywood forced Grandma roughly back down into her seat.

Kaparis had reached his limit. EVE., Grandma, Li Jun, the Salazar girl... he was plagued by a monstrous regiment of women. He would rid himself of them one by one.

Hans pulled Li Jun to the open door, to the mouth of the abyss, shoving her forward to the very edge of the drop, into the very first light of dawn, light that kissed Li Jun as she hung over the drop, as she all but tasted death. Something snapped inside her and she began to struggle and scream and fight like a cat on the precipice.

Kaparis, surprised, began to gurgle in enjoyment.

Spurred on by Li Jun's example, Grandma kicked Heywood in the shin so hard he screamed loud enough to momentarily break the spell.

"You bring us here to admire you and all you can do is frighten a little girl for goodness' sake? Who do you think you are? God almighty?"

Kaparis paused.

Not because he didn't want to yell, "Yes! Yes, I am!" out of sheer frustration, but because he'd just noticed something.

Dawn, *thought Kaparis, mind twitching.* Light... *the way the light played through Li Jun's hair...*

"STOP! Hans, leave her. Li Jun! Call up the blueprints of every building in the Forbidden City – NOW."

DAY FIVE 06:01 (Local GMT+8). The Forbidden City, Shanghai. Nano-Botmass:*12,873,589

11,872,434 bots were in sleep mode with only newly created yellow XE.CUTE bots and some SCOUT bots fully functional. Daisy chains of them flew out from the cluster searching for a new source of power, bot flying to bot – touching antennae and passing the precious power stored in the cluster along the line.

EVE. measured the remaining power at 5.56 kilowatts. When it fell below 4 kilowatts most of the SCOUT bots would have to be recalled and put to sleep as well.

KAPCOMMS had bombarded her with new commands but the >>POWER MANAGEMENT OVERRIDE instinct was still in force. Every other command was suspended.

Finn was first back up.

He scrambled up over the broken glass lip, the brain box tethered to his leg. He pulled it through after him and unhitched himself. "Clear!" he shouted down to Stubbs.

There was no greeting from Kelly, who was standing over a smouldering mechanical carcass. The rail guns had missed him, but succeeded in destroying the Frankenstein bot.

Across the hall the cluster was glowing less, but growing more, as bots streamed in from all directions.

"What do we do now?" said Finn.

The line down into the booth tugged, and Kelly and Finn began to haul Stubbs up. When he got to the top, he was wearing the blue plastic bag that had contained the sandwich.

"Parachute," Stubbs explained, and then sighed as he took in the blasted Frankenstein bot.

"Can you build another?" Kelly said.

Before Stubbs could even think, there was a scream from below – "THERE!"

On the floor of the hall, directly beneath them, distorted through the glass, was the snarling face of Baptiste.

TWENTY-NINE

"GO!" yelled Kelly.

Finn grabbed the brain box and they leapt on to the raft.

Below, Spike and Scar were running in between the stacks of hyper-servers, screeching like jackals.

Stubbs hit the power lever and the thrusters kicked to life. Finn clung to the boards as they rose fast, the raft blessed with balance and speed now it wasn't disturbed by the constant turbulence caused by bots and cooler fans, until – *BANG!*

A shot ripped past, a slug of solid metal the size of a white van that nearly rolled them, Kelly and Finn throwing their weight across the raft to correct the swing. Stubbs clung to the tiller. They were a macro-metre clear of the stacks and rising.

Baptiste screamed at Scar who'd fired the shot. "ALIVE!"

"Go high! Get outside!" urged Finn, pointing at four columns of weak pre-dawn-light filtering into the hall from the open air-con vents in the roof.

Stubbs took them up in a tight spiral. Beneath them, Spike and Scar scaled the hyper-servers, like chimps, trying to swipe at them.

At the edge of the hall Baptiste ripped a long section of white plastic cable trunking off the wall and screamed at the others to open up a gap in the cluster of server towers beneath them.

"He's going to try and hit us with that!" warned Finn.

Kelly grabbed the Minimi.

The hyper-servers were on rails. Spike and Scar shifted the towers apart, creating a new layout with a gap beneath the vent. Baptiste, wielding the three macro-metre length of plastic trunking like a medieval pikestaff, ran into the gap, braced himself on the server walls either side of it and climbed rapidly up, like a flexible X.

The raft hung just below the vent, bathed in the pre-dawn glow. They could smell fresh air outside. They had risen from hell and could smell freedom... But the devil had other ideas.

"The thrusters are dying," Stubbs warned. "We're not going to make it."

Finn looked down. Baptiste was pulling up the plastic pikestaff.

"Dammit!" said Kelly, aiming the Minimi down over the side. "Take us as far away from him as you can!"

Stubbs angled them into a dive.

WHOOOOM!

The raft rocked. The tip of the white plastic trunking, as thick as a tree, whipped past. Baptiste was on the other end, at full stretch. Kelly looked down the barrel of the Minimi and let him have it right in the eye – *DRTRTRTRTRTRTRTRTR!*

Baptiste roared with pain and nearly toppled, twisting and raging like King Kong. Again he swiped at the raft. Again Kelly fired – *DRTDRTDRTDRTDRT!* – but now Baptiste turned to let the bullets sting his scalp rather than blind him.

THWACK! – the tip of the plastic pikestaff clipped and spun the raft.

"Arrrggghhh!" shouted Finn as he clung to the raft's tornado deck. Stubbs jumped across him to save the brain box. Kelly was clinging on to the raft's outer edge.

The spin took them away from Baptiste, but they were falling too fast.

"BAG!" Kelly yelled.

Finn yanked the blue plastic bag from Stubbs's back and hooked the handle ends over the outboard at the back of the raft and immediately it snapped open as a parachute, halting the spin and slowing their descent.

"THERE!" Baptiste screamed, pointing at them as they drifted down between the stacks, back into the darkness, two precious macrometres or so clear of the end of his killing stick.

WHAM! – the descending raft swung into the side of the servers. With more inelegant scraping and bashing they fell down a server canyon and hit the ground hard, spilling across the floor. Immediately they heard the running Tyros, their sneakers squeaking on the polished concrete floor as they ran to roll the towers apart and expose them.

Kelly sprang to his feet.

"MOVE!" yelled Kelly as the north side of the canyon began to shift on its wheels.

"This way!" called Finn, leading them south beneath the server stacks.

Stubbs broke into a shuffling trot, clinging to the brain box. Too slow. Kelly scooped him up over his shoulder while Finn grabbed the brain.

The Tyros barked and screamed. Hunt on. Blood up. If they rolled the right stacks in the right sequence they could soon cut the crew's cover down to a single stack. But this was hampered by the darkness and the number of stacks that needed moving, confusion mounting as the Tyros struggled to get a nano-radar fix on their fleeing prey.

In the darkness beneath the stacks, Finn and Kelly were trying to run through a lethal jungle of wiring, components and cable ties that poked beneath the bottom of the circuit boards.

"Go go go!" Kelly urged Finn on even as he dropped behind. Stubbs and the Minimi slowing his progress.

They'd managed to run four stacks south when a blinding white light stopped them.

Finn turned. A flashlight on a phone was being directed underneath the line of server stacks, a face pressed hard against the concrete floor beside it.

"Up!" said Kelly, dropping Stubbs. All three scrambled up among the dangling wires, one light beam, then another, swept past.

Finn tried to hold still in a hammock of ribbon connector. He'd left the brain box on the floor. Would they spot something that small amongst the random dirt and debris? It was barely bigger than a grain of sand. For a moment the beam lingered on it… then passed.

Then Stubbs lost his grip on the underside of a relay unit and fell heavily to the floor with an "Urrgh!"

The beam of light instantly returned.

"Play dead!" hissed Kelly.

"I nearly am," Stubbs mumbled, face fixed, holding it together in the blue-white light.

There was a brief discussion, then a scraping…

Stubbs looked around and saw the guillotine edge of the white plastic trunking hurtling towards him – twice his height and banshee-screeching across the concrete –

"Arrrgghhh!" Finn heard him cry as it hit him. A cry of fear as well as pain. Finn swung himself down to help, but before he could hit the floor, Kelly dropped like a trapeze artist to grab the old man and haul him back up into the undergrowth.

Stubbs passed out, a sack of old bones in Kelly's arms. Blood dripped from a gash across his chest forming a dark puddle below.

DAY FIVE 06:58 (Local GMT+8). Roof of the World, Shanghai.

"What just happened?"

Nobody knew.

The last drone flight had shown two of the Tyro figures entering the Shen Yu. Then the feed was destroyed by a bot attack and dawn had made further infrared flights redundant. The Chinese troops on the ground had been driven back as far as Sector 7 before the bot attacks had stopped.

"Are the bots still concentrated on the Shen Yu?" the US President demanded.

The Chinese politburo members looked uneasy.

"Impossible to say. Though we know they have the power to reach at least Sector Seven," said Bo.

"Which rules out the surgical strike option at this moment," concluded Commander King.

He looked to Al for confirmation. Everyone looked to Al, but he was distracted, watching a looped replay of the tiny gesture that had told Delta that the "fourth Tyro" from the earlier infrared feed was her sister, Carla.

It made his insides twist. If it was Carla, then Finn was likely to be with her.

"If a surgical strike is out then we have to start looking at the nuclear options," he heard General Mount suggest on a screen from London.

Voices rose. "Now hold on a minute..."

Delta said nothing in her Skimmer, just checked her fuel level, her ammo and that her nPhone still had charge.

Then the door to the helipad opened as two soldiers came in. Delta accelerated the Skimmer towards the gap, but the door shut just before she could reach it. She pulled hard right out of the run and turned to face the man she knew had slammed it in her face.

Al.

"Get out of my way!" yelled Delta.

"No! There is still time, there are still options, there is a solution – we just haven't figured what it is yet," said Al.

"That's my little sister and I'm going in!" yelled Delta.

"Yes – you are!" Al yelled back. "But not like this!"

DAY FIVE 07:36 (Local GMT+8). Eurofighter Typhoon, 30,000 feet.

Woof...?

Was it a dream? A screaming dream?

Yo-yo's mind was spiralling back to consciousness.

He could smell: Hudson, bad-smell #73463482 [aviation fuel], and another...

When Hudson and The Men had arrived, Yo-yo had assumed they were going to take him for a walk, but at some point Hudson had patted him, given him a treat, then everything had disappeared.

Now everything was coming back and they seemed to be locked away in a great screamingness. Naturally, he felt obliged to out-howl the noise in order to establish his dominance.

HOOOWOWOWWWWOWOOW!

"It's OK, Yo-yo! It's OK! Chill! Good dog, nearly there!"

Yo-yo opened his eyes and saw a bright blue sky and a boy in a mask looking down at him. The boy flicked the side of the mask open to reveal his face.

To see Hudson again was heaven itself.

Yo-yo wagged his tail.

THIRTY

DAY FIVE 08:11 (Local GMT+8). Song Island, Taiwan (disputed).

Kaparis looked out from the highest point on Song Island, and waited.

He was an impatient man. Impatience and a vile temper had served him well. It was a universal quality, he noted, common among those few other exceptional individuals he considered his equal, from history and the international marketplace.

However, he could not yet speed the progress of celestial bodies.

The dawn sun hovered over the horizon like a ripe blood orange.

He had regarded it with fury for the last sixteen minutes.

When a computer alarm indicated it was now high enough for its beams to hit the roof of the Greenharbour Inc. building in the Forbidden City he said –

"Issue the instruction."

Li Jun, who'd twice narrowly escaped with her life in the last twenty-four hours, obeyed.

KAPCOMMS>>EVE. KAPARIS>>LET THERE BE LIGHT AND THERE WAS LIGHT. THIS IS THE WORD OF KAPARIS.

EVE.>>QUERY?

KAPCOMMS>>EVE. KAPARIS>> PROOF: LET THERE BE LIGHT AND THERE WAS LIGHT – THEREFORE – THERE WAS POWER.

EVE.>>QUERY? LOCATION?

KAPCOMMS>>EVE. KAPARIS>> LOCATION LAT311887 LNG121289433

Kaparis smirked. Fate was about to fall for his charms once again.

"I think, Heywood, we should prepare the champagne."

EVE. sent out SCOUT bots to the specified location. They landed on a roof, on a solar panel, where photovoltaic crystals were turning daylight into precious, life-giving power...

After seventy-four seconds the datum relayed back to EVE. from the Shen Yu Hall was:

>>SCOUTBOT 47RYBD4378HH84: POWER NODE .0756 KW LAT311887 LNG121289433

After four more seconds, eight further reports from the same area came in.

EVE.>>ALLBOTS GENERAL DISPERSAL ORDER>> >>DISPERSE

TO POWER NODES [FOLLOWS]>> LAT311887 LNG121289433...

zssssszssszssszszzssszssssszssszssszszzssszssssszssszssszszzsss zssssszssszssszszzssszssssszssszssszszzssszssssszssszssszszzsss...

The core cluster began to glow again, began expanding and dissolving as hundreds of thousands of bots moved in liquid sequence streaming towards the four columns of dawn light on the roof, escaping the Shen Yu Hall in great swirls and currents, seeking out the new source of electricity.

"They go!" reported Baptiste, watching the bots disappearing like smoke through the roof of the Shen Yu.

Kaparis gurgled with delight and called up the perfect song by a perfect soprano, just as Heywood arrived with the champagne.

The screen array was filled with bot video-feeds of the Forbidden City, bathed in pink dawn light, and the soprano sang:

"The sun whose rays are all ablaze with ever-living glory
Do not deny his majesty he scorns to tell a story..."

Bot after bot sprang from the roof of the Shen Yu and soared into the life-giving light. The first million or so headed for the Greenharbour Inc. building in Sector 2 and the extensive glass solar-tile array that covered its roof – supplying 4.24kW of clean electric power once the sun was at a 23-degree angle. Six more buildings in Sector 3 boasted similar arrays as did many more across the Forbidden City, which had been constructed, down to the last detail, with impeccable green credentials.

"I mean to rule the earth as he the sky
we really know our worth the sun and I..."

Heywood dripped Vintage Krug '98 champagne on to a dull toad of a tongue and Kaparis allowed himself to feel a measure of satisfaction. He even eyed Grandma as she knitted to see if she was impressed.

Knit one purl one knit one purl one knit one purl one knit one purl one knit one purl one...

"Champagne, Mrs Allenby?" said Kaparis.

"Thank you. I'd prefer a J_2O, do you have one?"

"I'll ask the kitchen, madam," said Heywood.

"Don't ask the kitchen," said Kaparis, determined not to let her spoil the moment. "It is very good champagne and I think it's important to be able to discern the finer things in life, no matter what one's age."

"Pardon?" said Grandma.

Kaparis blinked in irritation.

"Don't say 'pardon', say 'what'," Kaparis said. "People of quality will think you common, suburban or an ignoramus if you say 'pardon'."

"Really?" said Grandma, intrigued.

"Yes, the same applies to 'lounge' for sitting room or 'toilet' for lavatory, and there are many others."

Grandma nodded, knowingly.

"What?" said Kaparis.

"Do you know, Dr Kaparis, all the murderers and psychopaths I've known, one way or another, are a bit like that."

"A bit like what?"

"Ghastly little snobs."

The iron lung stopped dead. Heywood froze. A vision played through Kaparis's mind of Violet Allenby tumbling over and over as she fell towards the rocks below... He was on the very point of summoning Hans when –

"EVE. is back online," reported Li Jun. "Data incoming."

Li Jun fed the direct feed from EVE. across his screen array.

EVE.>>KAPCOMMS>>

BLESSED IS THE WORD OF KAPARIS

EVE.>> ALLBOTS>> RUN CONFIG. >>NORMAL>> ASSIGNED BOTS>> RESUME TASK HUNTER>> 23423 235354 756 345635 4353457 67457 2345235 456 5674364....

Thousands of bot idents started scrolling down the screens.

Kaparis forgot about Grandma and gurgled some more.

The sun would rise further, power would increase, but not enough to restart production at a significant scale.

He was back in control, but for how long?

Time enough to force the pace and break the power of EVE.

Time enough to reel in Infinity Drake.

Time enough for the bots to escape the Forbidden City in a great exodus, and thereafter to take over the world.

The Tyros were still in the Shen Yu Hall playing cat and mouse with Infinity Drake. Kaparis addressed them now.

"Baptiste," said his master into his ear. "Listen carefully..."

THIRTY-ONE

As soon as they heard the Tyros leaving the hall, they dropped from their hiding places to the floor, Kelly still cradling the bleeding Stubbs.

Finn had a hateful, familiar lump in his throat and couldn't have spoken if he'd wanted to.

They turned Stubbs over.

A gash ran from his collarbone across the top of his chest. Kelly jabbed in a hypodermic syringe of morphine, then pressed the two sides of the wound together. The old man groaned like an ancient vacuum cleaner.

Finn, using his ripped-up shirt for a bandage, bound it as tight as he could.

"Where's the brain?" Stubbs asked weakly.

Finn held up the Frankenstein brain box.

"Help me get him up," said Kelly.

Gingerly they lifted Stubbs and slid him carefully into the hammock of ribbon connector that Finn had been hiding in. He opened his eyes and looked down on them, pale as a ghost.

"You have to catch a live one before noon, long before," he said faintly. "Then do some brain surgery. No anaesthetic. Take off its shell, pull out the brain unit and replace it with this one. Plug and play."

"Catch one?" said Kelly.

"You must have been fishing as a boy?" Stubbs said, in an other-worldly way as the drugs kicked in. "I can't manage it, not before I've had a nap…"

Kelly took a swig from the canteen of water, gave Finn a swig, then put it in Stubbs's hands along with the huge Colt .357 Magnum pistol from his holster – his personal sidearm.

"Just sip enough to keep your lips wet – and watch for the kick on that," Kelly said, indicating the pistol.

"Oh do get on," Stubbs said.

"You heard the man," said Kelly and started to pick up the brain box to leave.

Finn lowered his voice so Stubbs couldn't hear.

"We can't leave! I have a problem with just leaving people to die. There's only a half chance this thing will work anyway. Let's get him out of here…" Finn pleaded.

"Come here," Stubbs muttered to him.

Finn went right up and the woozy old man rested a gentle arm on him.

"Got to save you, young prince... don't worry about me."

This was almost too much for Finn. He was taken back two years to his mum and her last days, either sparking with life, fast asleep, or drug-addled and sentimental. Her eyes as gooey as Stubbs's were now.

"Come on. Leave him," said Kelly.

"I met your father... Genius," Stubbs slurred, mind surfing the morphine.

Finn was pulled straight back. The other thing he knew was that there were truths at the edge of life. His mum told him she would love him forever and be with him always. And she was, he felt it every day. With a twist of his heart Finn asked –

"What happened to my father, Stubbs? Did he walk out on us?"

"Not a trace... Your uncle looked everywhere. High and low. Venice, of course..."

Venice?

"Did he end up in Venice?"

"It's the morphine. He doesn't know what he's saying," said Kelly, breaking in.

Finn stared hard at Kelly, he could see the same look he got from so many others, the look of something unsaid.

What kind of man walks out like that? Yet his mother loved that man, so did Al, and Grandma too...

Finn turned and pressed Stubbs further. "Where is he, Stubbs?"

Kelly stepped in. "Nobody knows! That's the problem."

"What? What happened!" Finn demanded.

Kelly's face hardened.

"Kid, we've got to deal with this – right now. Bedtime stories can wait. No one can prove what happened to your old man. When this is over we can go through every detail and, I assure you, you'll end up as confused as everyone else. The past is a trap, a drug. There are never any straight answers. What matters is *you*, not him. Right now – we go forward. Point by point. Strictly operational. We get the bot. We plant the new brain. We get Stubbs. We get out. Agreed?"

Venice? Finn thought...

"Kid!" Kelly snapped. "Let's go!"

DAY FIVE 08:53 (Local GMT+8). Roof of the World, Shanghai.

YAPYAPYAPYAPYAP!

The main doors swung open, all eyes turned and in bounded Yo-yo, dragging Hudson along the floor after him.

"Down boy!" said Hudson, trying to hold on to both the dog and his glasses.

Having been drugged and cooped-up in the footwell of a fighter jet for nearly six hours then transferred to the back of a screaming, flashing police car and driven at high-speed through an exotic smell-

and-light show that he couldn't hope to comprehend, Yo-yo was now near mental with over-stimulation.

Bo Zhang and most of the other Chinese officials present looked on in shock as Hudson struggled to get the leaping, barking beast under control.

"Good boy, Yo-yo!" said Al, the dog going crazy to see him again, licking and jumping and dancing around.

YAPYAPYAAPP!

"Good job, Hudson!" he added as Hudson struggled to his feet.

"I think he's a bit over-excited, Dr Allen—"

Yo-yo suddenly stopped dead. His eyes almost crossed and he made a special whining noise, his haunches shaking.

"Uh-oh," said Hudson.

It was a sign that Al and Hudson knew only too well. Suddenly Yo-yo – and it was always suddenly with Yo-yo – needed to Go.

"Where's the nearest park?" asked Hudson, dreading the journey back down in the elevator.

"The helipad! Get him up on the helipad!" shouted Commander King.

Hudson and Yo-yo were whisked off by staff to see if they could make it to the toilet on top of the world before Yo-yo lost control.

"Did you bring the dog for luck?" Bo Zhang asked Al, genuinely interested, for he'd been wondering for some time how Al could be both crazy and a scientist at the same time. Bo had assumed 'Yo-yo' was the codename of some kind of top-secret weapon or vehicle.

"Luck? No. I brought it for Flight Lieutenant Salazar. That mutt might just be our ticket out of this whole mess."

He took Bo over to where Delta and a group of technicians were already working on the proposed mission, and explained. Delta would be in an nDen clipped to Yo-yo's collar from where she would issue instructions to the dog. A harness was being constructed for Yo-yo to wear, packed with cameras and high technology that would allow real-time tracking and surveillance and also carry a handgun simple enough for Carla to use. Lastly, Yo-yo's collar was full of nano-supplies of every kind, should they be needed when Delta located other members of the n-crew.

"She's going to *ride the dog* into the Forbidden City?" asked Bo, incredulous.

"She's going to *pilot* him," confirmed Al.

"That's it? That's the plan? You put your trust... in a dog?" said Bo, for the first time losing some faith in his remarkable new colleague.

"*This* dog. He just needs a few atoms of Finn's scent in his nostrils to zero straight in on him. If he's in the Forbidden City with Carla, he'll find them. Of course, if the bots attack dogs we're done for, but when there are no other options on the table, sometimes you've just got to mix things up, Bo, get creative and—"

"Sir!" A technician interrupted them all.

"We've got a standby signal from Infinity Drake's nPhone – it's on the southern shore of Penghu Island."

"*What?*" Al's heart almost stopped.

Penghu Island was off the coast of Taiwan and the signal was triangulated to a spot on the southernmost tip of its main island. Satellite images of the spot showed cliffs and a scrub of beach.

"Can we contact it?" said Al.

"It's too weak to operate – but while we've got a standby signal, we've got a location," said the technician.

"We need to get someone there before we lose it," said King.

Bo snapped out orders in Mandarin.

Commander King stared at the patch of coastline. How could it possibly be Drake if he was somewhere in the Forbidden City with the Salazar girl? Had they split up? If so what was he – what was *anybody* – doing, miles from anywhere on the coast of an obscure island...

"It's drifted there. It'll be some kind of message in a bottle," said King. "Someone is trying to tell us something..."

A grin split Al's face.

"My mum."

DAY FIVE 09:09 (Local GMT+8). The Forbidden City, Shanghai. Nano-Botmass:*12,873,377

Baptiste took the tip of the knife and pressed it against Spike's flesh. His hands shook slightly at the sweet thrill of it. The temptation, the instinct, to drive his entire weight against the hilt of the weapon and kill was so strong his mouth watered and saliva ran down his stubbled chin.

But his programmed desire to obey orders was far sweeter, far greater. He pushed the knife just hard enough for the tip of the blade to suddenly pierce the skin of Spike's belly to the depth of a centimetre, then stopped. Blood bloomed and flowed from the small wound. Perfect.

Spike hissed where she lay inside the Greenharbour Inc. building. In pain. Baptiste repeated the cut a few centimetres further across the tight skin.

After six more cuts to both Spike and Scar, he reported back to Kaparis –

"Done."

"Good," said Kaparis.

Immediately Li Jun tapped out the order.

>>KAPCOMMS>>EVE. KAPARIS ORDER>>

>>COMMENCE "EXODUS" BOT GROUPS 1 AND 2.

Across the Forbidden City, nearly two million bots, those assigned to Exodus Groups 1 and 2, received new orders.

Kaparis watched the bot-feeds until he was satisfied the process had begun, then he ordered Baptiste.

"Now get the girl."

THIRTY-TWO

"Where the hell is everybody?"

Kelly and Finn jogged down a canyon towards the core, looking for bots, finding nothing, just the great empty hall. The cast of millions had melted away.

Daylight filtered into the abandoned space and, with it, the warm wet air of a tropical morning. The great blinking, futuristic cityscape presented during the hours of darkness had been supplanted by the ruined city of some lost civilisation, the dormant quantum hub its altar for sacrifice.

And with the warm wet air came nature.

..zzztztz..ztzztrztztzz.zzzzztzttzz...zzyztztztzz.zzyzyztztzyzz.. zzzzzzzz..zz..z.zttzzzz.zzzz..

"At last," Kelly said, dropping the Minimi and untying the

nano-line and improvised grappling hook he'd made. Ready to go fishing.

"That's a mozzie, not a bot!" said Finn, and to prove his point one of the vile kites drifted towards them, legs dangling, scalpel-sharp proboscis twitching for a kill – *ZZTZT-ZZZTZTZT-ZTZTZT!*

Kelly snatched up the Minimi, braced the stock and squeezed – *DRTDRTDRT!*

The mosquito's-scowl exploded into a cloud of matter that rained splatily around them.

Kelly checked the ammo. "Let's hope they don't come in battalions."

"You don't need a gun, you just have to break the proboscis. I used a pin on the Bug," said Finn.

Kelly said, "Good call," and looked round. Above them on the circuit board there were dish-shaped capacitors with long pin-thick legs. Kelly stood back and with two neat bursts – *DRTRT! DRTRT!* – he severed the pins at their base and the component clattered to the floor. Moments later the pins were pried out of the capacitor and Finn and Kelly ended up with, if not swords, then a mosquito spike each.

"Let's go," said Kelly, grabbing the fishing line.

"What about Stubbs? They'll smell his blood."

"He's tougher than you think."

..zzztztz..ztzztrztztzz.zzzzztzttzz...

Another mozzie careered in at speed. Finn planted his feet and raised his spike like a baseball bat and, just as the evil gnat was about to run him through, he swung – smashing the harpoon snout of the thing, snapping it off right between the eyes. It twitched in agony and began a frantic cartoon-like backpedalling.

"Good job," said Kelly, impressed, then took out his own spike and added, "Now it's my turn," as he heard –

zsssszsssszssszszzssszsssszssszssszszzssszsssszssszssszszzsss...

"That's not a mosquito!" said Finn.

Kelly followed Finn's pointing finger. Above, caught in a shaft of daylight, he could see a stream of bots running back into the hall.

"They're back..." said Finn.

Kelly looked at the crippled mosquito. Finn read his mind. "They'll pick it up on their radar?"

"Live bait," Kelly confirmed and grabbed its legs. Finn grabbed its skinny body and they hauled the struggling beast under the nearest server stack.

Finn lay across it, its skin reptilian, while Kelly wound round the grappling hook and line he'd fashioned around its thorax.

When it was done, they let the mosquito struggle and kick and flap its way back out across the canyon floor.

Finn and Kelly jumped down into the metal rail trench and hid behind one of the wheels of the great stack. Not only did the steel rails allow the stacks to move, they provided excellent cover for nano-warriors.

zsssszsssszssszszzssszsssszssszssszszzssszsssszssszssszszzsss...

The injured mosquito on the end of the line obligingly fitted and struggled into flight. Straightaway a blue nano-bot swooped to investigate, hovering tight alongside, its tools and talons dangling beneath its body shell, angling itself to get the beast fixed in its simple photocell eye.

Kelly pulled in the line to draw the bot closer, but before it got close enough for them to jump it, it had identified the mosquito and disregarded it. It banked and flew off. Kelly looked at Finn, and shrugged.

"It was a bite," he said, letting the line play out again.

"How are we actually going to do this?" whispered Finn, looking at the grey brain box on his lap.

"I don't know," said Kelly.

"And if that doesn't work?" asked Finn.

"We hit it as hard as we can."

A few seconds later a blood-red bot appeared. This time Kelly didn't bother toying with the creature – he just yelled, "Strike!" and yanked the line hard towards them.

The mozzie shot their way and the bot followed, jetting along after it to get a visual fix.

The moment the bot reached the wheel, Kelly abandoned the line and leapt on top of it like a rugby player, covering its entire lawn-mower-sized body with his own, driving it – tentacles first – into the cleft between the great wheel and the rail.

It hissed in alarm as it tried to jet backwards out of Kelly's grasp. "Rip it open!" he yelled at Finn, as he struggled to contain it.

Finn tried to pry the shell off but couldn't get a grip on the edge.

"Come on, kid!"

Desperate, Finn stuck the end of his mosquito spike between the shell and the carcass and heaved. There was a *SNAP* and the bot shucked open like an oyster.

The bot screamed through its compressors, organs exposed. Finn saw its lump of grey brain and hauled. It was plugged in tight but he worked it back and forth till – *POP* – the brain gave way and the bot collapsed beneath Kelly, suddenly still.

zssssszsssZssszszzssszssssszssszssszszzssszssssszssszssszszzsss...

Finn took the doctored Frankenstein brain box off his back. There were eight terminal spikes on the underside. He located the same holes in the bot carcass and shoved it in...

Nothing happened.

Kelly drove the brain in harder.

Still nothing.

Other bots hissed past. Kelly slid back down into the trench beside Finn. It wasn't working.

"We'll have to take it back to Stubbs," Finn said.

Kelly scowled. It would be impossible to drag a dead weight that far unnoticed.

He fixed the bot with a beady eye and drew his leg back to deliver an almighty kick.

Straightaway the Frankenstein bot hopped to life.

Finn and Kelly jumped for cover.

But the bot didn't see them... the bot didn't seem to see anything. It just hovered there a few nano-feet away, alive but inert.

"What's wrong with it?"

"I don't know, but something's working and if it's working it must have the disease."

Kelly crept out to kick it again, this time out into the path of the patrolling bots. As he did so –

ZWOOOOSHSHHHHH! BANG!

A railgun bolt of white-hot carbon exploded at Kelly's feet, blowing him head over heels and sending the Frankenstein bot zipping off, like an air hockey puck beneath the stacks of servers. Kelly hit the floor and lay still. Three hunter bots spotted him and closed in whip-crack fast.

Without thinking, Finn braced the Minimi and – *DTRRTDRRRTRTRTRTTRTR!* – raked the air above Kelly. The bots exploded as bullets cut through their shells.

More bots arced in. Finn leapt from the rail trench, dragging Kelly's enormous collapsed form back down into it. Six bots arrived and swung back and forth over the area, tilting and searching.

Finn turned to Kelly. He was lifeless. A great hunk of meat. The thought he might be dead froze Finn's soul. Panicked him. He couldn't be. He mustn't be.

"Kelly!" Finn kicked him, just as Kelly had kicked the Frankenstein bot.

Kelly groaned.

Finn felt his own heart start again.

zsssssZsssZsssZsZZsssZsssssZsssZsssZsZZsssZsssssZsssZsssZsZZsss…

The hunters were closing in.

"We've got to make a run to the next trench!" said Finn, trying to pull Kelly up.

"Can't," said Kelly. Restricted to gasps. "Ribs broken... Get out. Get Al."

"How?!" yelled Finn, angry at the bots, angry Kelly was injured, angry Stubbs was dying, angry he was going to have to leave them both, angry at Al and King and at Kaparis and at his dad who'd disappeared – angry at the whole thing.

"Find a way!" Kelly yelled back.

More bots were hissing in.

"Take the pack and the Minimi!"

Finn knew he had no choice. He slung Kelly's pack over his shoulder then hauled up the huge Minimi. There was only a handful of rounds left.

"You take this," said Finn. "It'll slow me down." He stuck it in Kelly's arms, biting back a lump in his throat.

BOOM. They were interrupted by the slam of a door, the squeak of sneakers.

Kelly grabbed the back of Finn's head. "Tyros... Go..."

Finn made a promise. "Wherever they take you – I'll find you."

Kelly stared at Finn with a cruel steel in his eyes that said – *Do Your Job.* It was how Kelly had lived his life and he wasn't about to get sentimental about existence now.

"Save *yourself.*"

Bots closed in again and Kelly fired over Finn's shoulder – *DRTRTRT!* – two more bots exploding.

"GO!" Kelly ordered. He punched Finn to get him going and Finn fled, scrambling along the pit of the trench like some kind of lizard boy as, behind him, Kelly fired his last rounds – *DRTRTRRT!*

Then silence.

As Finn reached the end of the trench he looked back. A group of bots were clustered above Kelly, drawing him up into their tentacled web.

Finn's heart beat hard. Half a dozen more bots were already tilting to scan the area.

Then as he leapt out to sprint to the next trench, he finally heard a cry.

But not from Kelly.

"COME AND GET HER, DRAKE!" Baptiste roared from one of the server blocks on the south side of the hall, announcing Carla's presence so loudly it made her ears ring.

"NO!" she tried to warn in turn, which was just what he wanted. Baptiste shoved the gag back over her mouth and between her teeth. "MMGHGH!"

Carla was on her knees, hands security-zip-tied to the steel frame end of one of the blocks, gagged by a leather belt.

Live bait.

Baptiste yanked on the zip-ties so that they bit into her wrists, then grabbed her face and warned her: "When I come back. If he's not here? You die."

She glared back, acid in her eyes.

To cause such hatred delighted Baptiste. He actually smiled. Then he let go of her face and walked out, leaving the bots swirling around her, waiting to catch Drake. Meanwhile, he had an exodus to attend to.

He slammed the great south doors behind him with a *BOOM.*

THIRTY-THREE

Finn was close to his friends. Maybe it was the lack of living family. For him friends were up there with insects and daydreaming. Hudson. Christabel. Stubbs, Kelly and Delta… and the one who he had just heard cry out: Carla.

Finn had convinced himself she was safe – that she was with Al and Delta. That she would have told the world where he was. Now he had to accept that maybe no one knew where either of them were. And it was all his fault. He never should have freaked her out in Hong Kong in the first place.

Hearing her voice had come like a stab through the heart. He had to respond. He knew it was trap. She knew it was a trap. The lead Tyro certainly knew it was a trap. But there was nothing on earth that was going to stop him walking right into it.

He had to get to her, he had to save her.

How he'd achieve this he had no idea, he'd figure it out on the way. It was, after all, a long way. Maybe 30 macro-metres southeast across the hall.

So he'd started running south from rail trench to rail trench, sliding east along the polished steel pit on his back to keep an eye out for patrolling bots, keeping dead still if any came near and waiting until the coast was clear before leaping out to sprint fifty nano-metres or so to the next trench.

He made progress at first, but the closer he got the thicker the bot patrols became, the air full of the hiss of the thrusters and the constant tick and slap of their antennae. Not that they were the only threat, for as the morning wore on he'd repeatedly had to use his spike to cut down more and more inquisitive mosquitoes too. After just an hour he was running out of energy and ideas.

Which is when he heard it—

tick-tick-scratch-tick-scratch-tick-scratch-tick-hssss...

Close by. So close that if he tried to run for it, he was sure to get blasted. He froze on his back in the rail trench, playing dead and praying it would pass.

tick-tick-scratch-tick-scratch-tick-scratch-tick-hssss...

Closer. Not flying. Dragging itself along.

Finn held his breath. Clutched the spike.

tick-tick-scratch-tick-scratch-tick-scratch-tick-hssss...

Suddenly, two great hairy bullwhip antennae flicked over the trench. Before he could react, a black tank-turret of a head was looming over him, two great mouth parts twitching and tasting, void-black eyes sucking up his terror. A cockroach the size of a croc and five times as hungry.

Finn's guts turned. He almost expected saliva to drip from its bone-hard lips.

With remarkable speed, the roach jammed two spiked legs into the trench to force Finn up towards its jaws. Every cell in Finn's body screamed – *fight!*

WHAM. Finn smashed the mosquito spike across the ghastly face, caning it. The roach hissed and stretched its jaws a mile wide to strike back, but Finn frantically wriggled from the lethal grip and scrambled back along the trench beneath its articulated bulk.

Leaping up behind the roach, he raised the spike. The beast flicked around to face him. With two hands and all his strength Finn brought the aluminium spike down like a mighty hammer right between the great shields of the insect's eyes – *WHAM.*

Absolutely nothing.

The vast creature threw itself forward. Finn turned and ran like hell along the trench, the roach literally snapping at his heels to try and snaffle up a trailing leg. Again and again he span with the spike and brought it down – *WHAM WHAM WHAM* – against its head, eyes, antennae, anything to slow it, the blows only making it rear and charge like a great angry bear.

Still Finn ran. There was a reason why cockroaches had survived since the dawn of time, he thought – they didn't mess around.

The end of the trench approached in the form of a server stack wheel. Soon Finn would be wedged in between the curve of it and the rail – he would have to act now, or die. There was nowhere else to go.

Finn spun round, raised the spike and ran back at the charging roach.

As the great creature hit him, Finn jabbed the spike down hard between its eyes, leaning into it, using its momentum and its reflexive buck to pole-vault up over its head to land on its back. The beast's antennae flailed and wheeled. It bucked and writhed, trying to get a fix on its tormentor, but Finn – a rodeo ace now thanks to his time on the Bug – held fast to the armoured edge of the creature's thorax where it met and moved against its thick cellulose head plate.

Finn took the mosquito spike and drove the blunt point of it between the two plates – just hard enough to force a gap. The roach wheeled and rolled over. Every ounce of air was knocked out of Finn as he was crushed beneath it. But still he held on.

As the beast righted itself it, the spike sank a fraction deeper into the armoured gap. Finn seized his chance. With all his might he heaved the spike forward like an engineer changing points on a rail track. Stubbs would have been proud. With a great crack, Finn felt some of the neck ligaments give way.

The creature gave a mighty buck. But it was a last gasp. The cockroach was crippled.

Finn never wanted any living thing to die, but the bots were circling. He drove the spike to the hilt down into the soft open gap at the roach's neck. Goo oozed out and the creature shook. With another sinking of the spike, Finn levered forward again and – with a wet *POP* – the cockroach's head fell forward off its body, antennae still whipping and twitching.

The commotion brought the bots zooming in, but before the first one could tip itself up to focus its eye on the corpse, Finn was hidden beneath it. The bots hissed and searched in vain.

A few nano-feet away the severed cockroach head, still alive, watched Finn's game of hide-and-seek play out[26].

Finn lay there, heart thumping, euphoric.

He knew how to reach Carla.

DAY FIVE 09:58 (Local GMT+8). Song Island, Taiwan (disputed).

Via a grainy bot-cam Kaparis regarded Kelly, unconscious within his cluster cell. He had passed out during a long-distance interrogation with Hans.

But he hadn't talked.

And nor had Drake taken the live bait in the Shen Yu. He was obviously hiding somewhere in the floor rails, but even a systematic search could be fooled and time was running out.

Soon the great bot dispersal, the Exodus, would begin.

The domed screen array showed endless close-ups of mosquitos and

[26] Severed cockroach heads can survive for several hours after disconnection from the body. Headless cockroach bodies can survive for weeks.

roaches and any other carbon life form picked up by the bot-radar. They needed to narrow down the search and flush Finn out, to reduce the number of variables and—

Of course. The answer was so obvious he scolded himself.

PART
FOUR

THIRTY-FOUR

DAY FIVE 10:10 (Local GMT+8). Shen Yu Hall, The Forbidden City, Shanghai.

The crick in Carla's neck was on the move, the pain running all the way down her right-hand side. The way her hands were tied meant she was sat in a perpetual slouch. Agony. Her efforts to chew through the leather belt had nearly worn away her teeth and she was no nearer coherent speech. All she could do, every now and then, was sound a warning. Because one thing was certain – if Finn was out there in the vast machine, he would undoubtedly be stupid enough to try and save her.

"Urnnnnngh!" Carla tried to shout out, to warn him again to stay away.

At home she had *hungered* for 'Difference', for 'Experience', but they had been hard to come by in the suburb with the highest recycling rate in North America. Finn was undoubtedly 'Different'; the most unsuitable and exciting friend she'd ever had. On the other hand, the trouble with 'Experience' was you grew close to those you shared it with, and she did not want either of them to die at the hands of some teenage-terror goon.

She could hear a Tyro now, moving about on the other side of the hall. She tried to gird herself for their approach but her courage was fading. She was tired, she was hungry, she had been bitten by several mosquitoes and, to cap it all, a great black cockroach was now crawling across the floor towards her and there was nothing in the world that gave her the heebie-jeebies like a cockroach. As it raised itself on its back legs like an evil little cobra, she stretched to stamp her heel down on it: "Urnnnnngh!"

WHAM!

Missed.

Making the costume was easier than Finn had expected.

He thought he'd have to hollow the dead cockroach out, splitting it open to scoop out all the guts, but in fact he'd been able to prise the exoskeleton straight off its soft body and had ended up with a cockroach cape that dangled two useless legs. He pinned his spike through the top section to act as a bar to keep it in place and put it on over his shoulders. Although it had no head, the disguise worked like a dream and, as long as he hit the deck when the bots came too close, they soon flew on. It was a little big, but it wasn't too heavy and he'd travelled six server blocks towards the sound of Carla's grunting in no time.

His unbridled joy as he finally reached her was blighted only by...

WHAM.

...her desperate attempts to crush him to death with her massive bus-sized sneakers.

He stood and lifted the cape to try and show himself again. "STOP! IT'S ME! IT'S ME!"

WHAM.

The heel of the giant sneaker caught the edge of the cockroach cape and crunched off a trailing leg.

"You nearly killed me!" he cried from beneath the shell.

She couldn't see him. He had to find a way to get in closer...

Then he heard something.

A distant ripple at first. Then a rushing, a continual roar.

He turned to look back under the server stacks. There, sweeping fast across the floor towards him, was a black, head-high slick – an unstoppable wall of water.

Instinct screamed in Finn's brain – *RUN.*

His legs were way ahead of him, already sprinting. He heard Carla squeal as the water hit her then – *WHAM* – the leading edge of the tsunami, laden with dirt and flotsam, smashed into him.

Raging water engulfed him, dragging him under and along the floor at incredible speed.

He struggled against the force, spinning 360 degrees. When he broke the surface, gasping for air, he found himself being washed down the hyper-server canyon away from Carla. He reached out for the server wall and grabbed for anything. His fingertips *just* managed to hook a single wire. He held on tight and jolted to a halt in the current, the force nearly taking his arm from its socket. The weight of water pushing against his cockroach cape was enormous, but he managed to haul himself to the side and finally pulled himself out.

He clung to the side of the server, getting his bearings as the river raged beneath him.

Stubbs! he thought immediately. What the hell would happen to Stubbs in this? The water must have drowned him in his sick bed... For a moment Finn didn't want to get hold of himself. Didn't want to go on. He just watched the water rushing by and wanted to cry.

Venice, Finn thought absurdly as he looked down at the water. *My father might be in Venice, I've got to at least find out about that before I die...*

The thought brought Finn back to life. He'd been washed halfway down the length of the server canyon, a great distance at his scale, but he could also see a clear route to Carla.

Bots were buzzing over the water like excited midges. The Tyros must have figured he was hiding in the trenches and flooded them. How long before they figured out he could hide beneath an insect?

Finn turned his cockroach-back on them and began to climb the component-clustered cliff.

DAY FIVE 10:30 (Local GMT+8). Roof of the World, Shanghai.

THUMP.

"Yo-yo?"

Uh-oh, thought Hudson.

The idea of Yo-yo as saviour and furry fortress had grown as things had got worse.

A junior technician going off shift had provided the latest grim breakthrough. She found her car clamped. She was about to assault the parking meter when she noticed it had a solar cell on top. Analysis showed that the Forbidden City was thick with solar panels, and while the authorities could remotely isolate them from the power supply, there was nothing they could do to stop the solar cells themselves generating power.

If the bots could power up and multiply then they were finished, was King's secret prognosis.

Now their last hope was that Yo-yo could get inside the Forbidden City and provide some kind of breakthrough intelligence.

Yo-yo had maintained a fever pitch of excitement for more than an hour after his toilet break, making lots of new friends and getting to know the Roof of the World operations room. He'd been good as gold when fitted with his harness and collar, and yapped obligingly when Delta had been clipped on in the nDen. Fully attired, he looked less like the world's stupidest mongrel and more like some kind of robot space dog.

All was going well until, after a snack, Yo-yo decided to see what would happen if he closed his eyes for a second, just one second…

Never has a dog hit the floor, and deepest sleep, with such finality.

"Is this normal?" one of the technicians asked Hudson.

"Um… I think he's having one of his snoozes…" said Hudson. He felt guilty – how would it look if he'd brought Yo-yo all this way just for him to take a dump on a helipad and fall asleep?

Delta switched on the amplifier in the nDen.

"Yo-yo? Wake up! Wake up, Yo-yo!"

Nothing.

"Well, don't just stand there! Call a vet or something!" she demanded of Al. "Give him an injection to wake him up!"

"No!" said Al. He squatted down and tried to explain. "The drugs from the flight must still be in his system. Let's just give him ten minutes' sleep to burn a little off."

Delta swore. Knowing Carla was trapped was grinding her usually steely nerves.

"We don't have ten minutes!" she yelled at Al.

"We need him at his natural peak, not loaded with every kind of drug. We also need you at your peak so try and calm down."

"Oh, I'm calm…" she insisted, shoving up the release bar of the nDen door to let herself out. *Clunk.* It didn't open.

"Hey!" she said, rattling the bar.

"Ah..." said Al, looking wary. "I told them to lock you in. I don't want any heroics."

"WHAT?!"

"Everyone I hold dear is now hostage to this, even my mother," Al started.

"Get me the hell out of here, right now!" yelled Delta.

"You're not going to complete the set. This ensures that if the dog has to turn back, you have to turn back with him and not go AWOL on some suicide mission."

Delta, who finally knew with absolute certainty that no man more utterly infuriating had ever existed, lost all verbal and emotional control and let out a primal roar.

"ARRRRRRGGGGHHHHHHHHHHHH!"

It only strengthened his resolve. Ignoring her screams, Al instructed the technicians. "Lift the dog carefully into the chopper and fly them both to the launch site before he wakes up. Or she explodes."

THIRTY-FIVE

"Urnnnnngh!" Carla grunted.

For Finn it had been a tough climb across an obstacle-strewn cliff face.

For Carla, watching her little black nemesis slowly approach, it was worse than water torture.

Finn's idea was to reach her from above, out of range of her stomping, but by the time he was halfway towards her, he felt her eyes fix upon him. Water was running past, a few macro-centimetres deep and she was fighting against the ties, trying to twist her head round to see where he was.

"Urnnnnngh!"

Finn had tried shouting. He had tried waving. But he was just too small for her to see, so he was forced to do the only thing he could think of.

He threw himself from a great height. Into her hair.

BOING!

"URRRRRRRRRNNNNNNNNNNNNNGH!"

It was like landing on a thousand feather beds and he had to grab great thickets of it to stop from bouncing straight back up. As she screamed he had to fill his lungs and scream back as hard he could –

"IT'S ME! IT'S ME! SOMETHING FELL IN YOUR HAIR – BUT IT'S ME! I'M NOT A COCKROACH! IT'S A DISGUISE! I'M FINN! INFINITY DRAKE!!"

There was a sudden frozen silence. Finn lay on his back in the cockroach-cape, surrounded by thick curls. Carla's curls.

"*Thnn?*"

"You wait six months to meet me, then freak out twice in a row," said Finn.

Carla gulped back a bolt of emotion and issued a muffled laugh. Tears stung her eyes. It was her first moment of relief in twenty-four exhausting, exhilarating, terrifying hours.

Six minutes later Finn was attaching Kelly's last lump of C4 plastic explosive to the plastic tie that cuffed Carla's hands. It was barely bigger than a grain of sand but the power to mass ratio of the nano-material meant it packed a much bigger punch. At least that's what Finn hoped. He didn't really know. All he could do was copy the rough size of the charge Kelly had used to crack the glass of the control booth. He fused it, set it, then scrambled back off her wrists and ran up her arm. As he reached her shoulder he called, "Brace yourself! It'll go off in the next few sec—" *CRACK!*

Carla jumped, it was as if someone had pulled a cracker behind her back and given her a kick at the same time. But her hands were still tied.

"No good?" asked Finn.

She felt heat. Smelt burning. She began to panic but hauled at the cuffs and – *SNAP!* – they split at the smoking weak point and her hands were free.

Groaning with relief as blood and movement returned to her joints, Carla pulled herself up the server side until she was standing. Finally, she pulled off the leather belt that had gagged her for so long.

"Urrrghhh..." She reached down and splashed some water into her mouth and over her face. "Thank God."

"Shh!" whispered Finn, back in her hair by her ear. "Remember they're everywhere. They have eyes. Keep your voice low and your lips still and everything will be cool."

"I'm surrounded by killer fleas and now a tiny little guy is talking in my hair. Nothing is cool. Everything's crazy. No one's going to blame me for talking to myself."

She felt him wriggle closer towards her ear, the movement provoking an intense reflexive urge to—

"Don't scratch!" yelled Finn.

"Don't say that! It makes it worse!" she hissed.

Finn emerged over her ear and anchored himself in her curls. It reminded him of clinging to Yo-yo's fur – just much, much cleaner.

He took an energy bar out of Kelly's pack, then tied it up in some curls. There were three ration packs left. Who knew how long he'd have to make them last?

"You shouldn't have done this. It's a trap. They're not interested in me," Carla murmured. "They'll see I'm free and come and get me."

"They'll figure you're trapped in here anyway," said Finn. "What happened to you? I thought you'd got away."

"They got me in the mall, then brought me here through a carnival sewer."

"A what?"

"This theme park place on the river – Ferris wheel, cable car, rides and shows – they'd dug under a haunted house down into the sewers. The sewers led here."

"Some back door. How many Tyros are there?"

"Three. The freaky twins and the leader."

"You OK?" asked Finn.

She fell silent a moment.

"I'm thinking of giving up the cello. Orchestra practice just won't be the same after this. What about you?"

"I made it in here, hooked up with Kelly and Stubbs, but then the bots swarmed. Kelly just got captured, and Stubbs..."

It was his turn to go silent.

"The girl has freed herself in the Shen Yu Hall," reported Li Jun.

Kaparis switched to bot-feeds from the great, dead quantum computer and watched Carla staggering around in the flood.

"Mmm. Resourceful. But she's not going anywhere and she may even do a better job attracting Drake if she's on the move."

Should he leave her in there, or send in Baptiste to bring her out as an insurance policy? There was little time left and—

Baptiste interrupted the thought. "Exodus Hive 1 and 2 complete," said the voice.

Kaparis switched video feeds and took in Spike and Scar.

Both had a fever and a desperate mottled rash that blackened their shaking extremities. But both had stopped bleeding.

Kaparis allowed himself a smile. Even if, regrettably, it seemed unlikely they'd capture Drake immediately, the sight of the twins about to start the exodus warmed him.

"Good," said Kaparis. "Let's paint the town red."

DAY FIVE 10:41 (Local GMT+8). The Forbidden City, Shanghai.

Thud. Thud.

Spike and Scar dropped down into the sewer.

Both were shaking. Swollen. Dying.

Thud.

Baptiste dropped into the tunnel beside them, alive with the fire of a demon. He started a motorbike for each of them and helped them to climb on. "Go!" he ordered.

Scar nodded through her fever and was the first to turn the throttle. Spike followed suit.

Then the two bikes took off, swaying as they sped up, the tunnel scrolling into being in the bright headlights ahead of them.

The twins clung to their handlebars as they clung to life.

Baptiste climbed back out of the sewer without a second look.

Carla stood back and kicked.

BANG.

The doors on the north side of the hall, just like those on the south, showed no sign of giving way.

Water was gushing from the open valve of a fire hydrant and the gaps around both sets of doors let just enough out to keep the hall under a constant ten macro-centimetres or so of water.

"Unless we find something more useful – a key, say – we are not getting through this door," concluded Carla.

"We've got to get out before noon," said Finn. He'd told her about the release of the Frankenstein bot. With Kelly in the clutches of the botmass his greatest hope now matched his greatest fear: hope that Frankenstein had passed on the virus and not just drifted off untouched; fear that Kelly would die in the ensuing fireball.

They had to get help; they had to get word to Al.

Carla looked up at the roof. "I could try higher. Climb the towers, try and reach the vents?"

"How?" said Finn, exasperated.

"Levitate?" suggested Carla.

Down on the water, the blue plastic bag they'd used as a parachute for the raft earlier drifted past. Finn imagined Stubbs's floating corpse and couldn't stop emotion welling up for the old man.

"We could try and start a fire," suggested Carla. "Then, if they saw the smoke..."

BANG!

"Ow!" Carla jumped and Finn had to hang on.

"What was that?!" said Finn.

"Something just bit me!" said Carla, rubbing her butt.

"What?"

Finn looked down. The bag... There was a splashing by it, a tiny splashing...

"CARLA! THE BAG! Pick up that plastic bag!" shouted Finn.

"What?"

"I think Stubbs just shot you in the butt!"

Carla reached down.

"CAREFUL! Lift it up really gently…"

Please, please, be Stubbs, Finn prayed to himself.

Gently, Carla lifted the crumpled bag out of the water and brought it closer to her face.

Desperately trying to swim in some water trapped in the folds, like a drowning maggot, was a half-naked old man.

"Oh my God…" Carla gasped.

"STUBBS!" yelled Finn out of sheer joy.

Stubbs was too concentrated on staying afloat to reply. Carla stuck her thumb in the water and Stubbs beached himself against it.

"Drop the bag! Remember they can see you! Put your head in your hands like you're upset," said Finn.

Like an actress responding to a director, Carla obeyed, hair flopping over her face as she slid her great hands through it, her fingers appearing around Finn like a pod of dolphins.

"That's great. You're doing great."

"Don't patronise me," muttered Carla.

Finn climbed up on to the giant thumb and ran along, pushing aside the tresses of hair to find Stubbs flat out.

"M-m-m-my-b-boy…" he chattered.

On the roof of the Greenharbour Inc. building in Sector 2, Baptiste pushed open an access hatch.

The bots had formed a cluster like a snow drift, a dozen metres away across the slope of glassy, photovoltaic tiles. When they saw Baptiste, many swirled around checking him out, then flew back to the cluster.

Baptiste pulled himself out of the hatch and stood up on the roof itself.

Then he took a hammer from his jacket and brought it down – *SMASH!* – on the tiles.

SMASH! SMASH! SMASH!

THIRTY-SIX

Stubbs was shivering and short of breath, his left shoulder and collarbone still strapped up in the bandage Kelly had made. He'd lost everything except his trousers and the Magnum pistol, and he looked even older than normal. But there was life in the old dog yet and only one thing on his mind. "Did you catch one? Did you plant the brain?"

"Yes, but it floated off like a zombie," said Finn, lashing Stubbs in place next to him in Carla's hair.

"But did it slap its antennae against the others?" asked Stubbs.

"I don't know, that's when we came under attack," Finn said.

"Are you all set? Can I move now?" asked Carla.

"All set," said Finn, and Carla started her slosh through the server aisles looking for a place to climb.

Stubbs looked concerned. "It flew? So it was operational?" he said.

"Yes, but I didn't see it touch any of the others..."

"It must have. They're constantly exchanging power and stopping to recharge. They're desperate for power."

"How do you know?" asked Finn.

"Stop, miss – look down at the waterline, look at that cooler unit..."

Carla stopped and they looked. The water was flowing past a half-submerged cooler unit on the face of a server. The flow was spinning the blades of the fan, turning the motor and creating electricity. A gang of bots had clustered to it to feed on the power being generated.

"The fan is acting as a hydro-electric waterwheel, a dynamo producing a trickle of power[27]. My guess is they have just enough energy to operate, but not enough to reproduce themselves."

"Wow," said Carla, impressed.

"You wouldn't believe the stuff he knows," said Finn.

"Does he know how we're going to get out of here?" asked Carla.

Stubbs, lashed in place, looked puzzled.

"Get out? We're safer in here. The bots will blow up at noon."

"What about Kelly?" said Finn. "He's probably in the middle of the cluster. We've got to get him out of there!"

[27] An electric motor is a magnet in a coil of wire. If you put electrical current through the coil the magnet rotates. Similarly, and conversely, if you physically rotate the magnet you generate electrical current in the coil. It's called 'Mutual induction'. A self-taught South London nobody, Michael Faraday, discovered this in 1831. It has been very, very, very, very, very useful.

Stubbs looked grave.

"He would never want us to risk *your* life," said Stubbs.

"I'm not going to let him die with those things!"

"How are you even going to find him?" asked Stubbs, puzzled.

"I don't know!" yelled Finn.

Stubbs gave him a look.

"Sorry..." said Finn. "I could go fishing again. Let them capture me this time?"

Stubbs thought it through for him.

"The bots capture you, take you back to the cluster, we were kept together last time so it may be you'd be held with or near Kelly..."

"Right!"

"Then you both die at noon," said Stubbs.

"But there's still five shots in the Magnum," said Finn. "We could escape, shoot our way out."

"You shoot a handful, then the rest catch you. Then you both die," repeated Stubbs.

"I have a cockroach disguise! And it works!" said Finn.

"Then you die in fancy dress," Carla chipped in. "Stubbs is right. There's no point in a suicide mission."

"Hey! Kelly's our friend. There's no way he'd leave any of us behind!" said Finn.

"Even supposing your costume works," said Stubbs, "do you really think you'll have time to scramble unnoticed from the centre of a cluster without some form of..."

Stubbs froze mid-sentence. There was a sudden half turn of his old head and he seemed to slip into a trance. Finn could sense the old cogs turning as he repeated to himself, "... some form of..."

"Yes?!"

"...escape mechanism. Something with speed, surprise, *lift*..."

Finn's heart beat faster. "And where could I find something like that?"

"We could build a *Zeplin*..." Stubbs whispered in engineering ecstasy.

"A *Zeplin*?" said Finn.

"I *think* they might spot a *Zeplin*," Carla observed.

But Stubbs was not to be denied. He was untying himself from Carla's hair, his mind spinning.

"We could use the dynamos... make a hydrogen balloon... I could pilot... Miss! Don't lose that plastic bag!"

"Hydrogen? Where are we going to get hydrogen from?" asked Finn.

Stubbs looked at him as if he was a complete idiot.

DAY FIVE 10:52 (Local GMT+8). Roof of the World, Shanghai.

A police team on Penghu Island found the source of the nPhone signal at 10:48.

It was located on a rock in a phosphate-rich dollop of bird

excrement. Under orders from Shanghai, the nPhone was sifted from the excrement (identified as that of a Great Frigate Bird by a local ornithologist), cleaned, inductively charged and finally switched on.

Under a magnifying glass the screen of the nPhone was found to contain the unsent text:

here 3island juSt rcks weRe in bigmiddle weatherlovly

This information, when put together with the known migratory path of the Great Frigate Bird, led to an area of the South China Sea being examined for a group of three small islands. Four candidates were identified, quickly whittled down to one following the discovery of an email detailing concerns about Song Island from a Taiwanese coastguard official who had since disappeared without trace.

Commander King asked the formal permission of the President of France to prepare the Commando Hubert waiting on the special operations vessel A645 *Alizé*. The President informed him the Commandos were already – "In theatre, on message, and enchanté".

The breakthrough had been trumped, however, by the arrival of the first drone images of a possible cluster on a roof of the Forbidden City. Al and Bo rushed to the monitors to study them. Only a few frames of video had been recorded before the bots took out the overflying drone, but there it was – a dark blot on the roof of the Greenharbour Inc. building. Plain as day. Beside it was a figure, one of the Tyros, smashing up the roof around it.

"What is he doing?" asked Commander King.

"I don't know, but the sooner we get in there and take a look, the better," said Al.

"What's your status, Delta?"

Delta had been helicoptered directly into Sector 9 of the Forbidden City. From her command position in the nDen, with a Yo-yo's-eye view of a line of soldiers' legs, she reported back, "He's just waking up. Give him one minute to stretch, but it's looking good."

Yaaaaaaaaaawww! yawned Yo-yo, intrigued to be waking up in the middle of a military formation.

"And I'm still going to kill you when I get out of here," finished Delta.

"Copy that," said Al.

"Never mind that mutt!" said General Jackman on-screen from the US. "Let loose the dogs of war! There's your target, plain as day, on that rooftop! Bomb it now!"

The squadron of Flying Leopard fighter bombers remained fuelled and armed on the tarmac at Dachang airbase.

"Negative. This may be one of many clusters and any kind of blast will leave them scattered to the wind," King said.

"If we can get the dog in—" Al started.

"If we can get the dog in, it will probably waste a great deal of time and wind up dead – as will Salazar – your last little friend and my best pilot!" said Jackman. "If you see the whites of your enemy's eyes – you fire. This may be our last chance."

"Move *your* family members in there, General, then you can bomb who you like!" Al snapped back.

"Damn straight," agreed Delta over the radio from Yo-yo.

The British Prime Minister felt moved to intervene.

"Dr Allenby, Flight Lieutenant Salazar, we are all very sorry about the youngsters. But this is war."

"The future cannot rest on sentiment," agreed the US President.

"Nor on emotional blackmail," the Chinese Premier concluded.

Al could already read the moves the committee and Commander King would soon be forced to make.

"The future rests on science, on logic!" Al protested, feeling himself running out of ideas.

The game he was playing with Kaparis was slipping beyond his control. He felt bullied. His opponent held all the cards and was openly cheating, and there was nothing that he could do about it but keep on going back for more. And there wasn't just one enemy either, but millions of tiny enemies… Was he really going to send Delta in too?

"Talk to us," said King. "Convince us."

Talk, thought Al. If only he could talk to the bots…

And in that moment a whole new thought struck him. Millions of tiny thoughts.

He pushed back his glasses real slow. King, familiar with the gesture, raised an arm to indicate no one should interrupt at this point. Something was going on behind the spectacles.

"How far did we get detecting any signals?" Al asked the technicians.

"We've spent forty-eight hours tracing every point on the signals spectrum," said one of them. "We occasionally come across single random letters or numbers, but nothing coherent. It's like looking for a needle in a haystack. And this is the biggest city in the world, the radio spectrum here is packed full – radio, TV, Telecoms, Emergency, Digital – the signals volume is vast."

"What if... he's splitting the signal up in to a million tiny pieces, scattering it across the spectrum of signals, then the bots put it back together again?"

"Then... we'll never find it," said a technician. "It would be millions of parts of a single needle in thousands of haystacks. And how do you even start to look for that?"

Al blinked. Stared. Shook his head. "You're right, don't waste any more time on—"

"I know how to find a needle in a haystack," said a voice.

Al turned. "Hudson?"

"You burn down the haystack. We did this question with a supply teacher once. If you burn down the haystack, you just have to sift the ash and you'll find it much quicker."

"You burn down the haystack," repeated Al.

It was Hudson's turn to push back his glasses. "And he showed us how to suck water up into a glass using three matchsticks too," he continued, only to be interrupted by—

"BURN THE HAYSTACKS!" cried Al, his mind racing. "If he's fragmenting his signal and hiding it in a thousand haystacks – how do you find it? – get rid of the haystacks! *The fragmented signal will have nowhere else to go.*"

He turned and ranted at the technicians and Chinese authorities.

"Shut down TV stations, radio stations, mobile phone signals, wireless broadband, anything you can think of – the more we reduce the signals traffic, the more hidden signal we should find – if that's true, then we've got him!"

The technicians started to chatter among themselves as they ran with the idea.

"Shut down *all* communications?" asked Commander King.

"All but one – leave one signal on."

"Can we do any of that?" The Chinese President asked Bo and his staff.

Bo turned to a Chinese technician.

"The state has the capability," the technician stated simply.

"Do it," ordered King. "Delay the strike."

THIRTY-SEVEN

DAY FIVE 11:03 (Local GMT+1). The Forbidden City, Shanghai.

"We attach you to the hydrogen balloon on a long line," Stubbs had explained to Finn, getting stronger by the second despite the wound in his chest. "You allow yourself to be caught by the bots, the bots then take you into the cluster, trailing the hydrogen balloon. Once inside the cluster, you put on your cockroach disguise, find Kelly, then start shooting. I hear the shooting, then pull you both out by ejecting a counterweight from the hydrogen balloon, thus releasing lift – we'll need to find a counterweight..."

"You'll be on the balloon with the counterweight?" Finn checked.

"That's right, I will pilot the balloon and—"

"The dragon, Carla! We can use the lucky charm the guard gave us as the counter-weight!"

"This is crazy," Carla said as she listened to them. "You can't possibly be serious..."

But it was working...

So far.

Bubbles rose in close rapid file from two wires beneath the water. One producing hydrogen. One producing oxygen.

Figuring the Tyros wouldn't be back until the bots had finally found Finn, Carla had wrenched the largest cooler-fan unit she could find off the face of a server and run its two power wires (positive and negative) beneath the water, wedging the two ends in place. Then she cracked the cover off the cooler unit and spun the fan as fast as she could. The electric current this generated ran down the wires and through the water between the positive and negative terminals at the ends of the submerged wires. In doing so, electrons bonding hydrogen and oxygen were released – H^2O becoming H, H and O – oxygen at the positive terminal, hydrogen at the negative[28].

She then fixed the blue plastic bag over the negative terminal in order to collect the hydrogen and in no time an egg-shaped ball of super-light hydrogen gas had appeared in the blue polythene, straining to drag the rest of the bag skywards.

"It's working!" panted Carla as she spun the fan like a prayer wheel, hardly believing her own eyes.

[28] Drop a 9-volt battery (the rectangular ones) into a glass of salt water and see for yourself.

"It's working!" agreed Finn.

Stubbs grinned (not a pretty sight, British dentistry in the 1960s had let him down).

DAY FIVE 11:03 (Local GMT+8). Song Island, Taiwan (disputed).

"It's working! Do you see, Violet?" asked Kaparis, watching the process unfold on his screen array courtesy of one of the bots.

It was all working, he thought, indulging in a lukewarm bath of self-congratulation. The twins would soon be emerging from the sewers, EVE. would soon be taking flight...

Grandma carried on knitting, almost at the end of a row.

"Carla is a very clever girl."

"Ingenious. Do you think she's making a bomb or a message in a bottle? She might have been a candidate for Tyro training had we got hold of her when she was seven. Too late now, the females have gone to mush by the time they're eleven."

"Mush?"

"Irrational interference that blocks linear processing."

Grandma rolled her eyes. She wanted to march over and give him a sharp slap on the forehead for spouting sexist nonsense, but she also knew it was wiser at this particular time to humour him.

"And what do you think you mean, David, by the term 'irrational interference'? Do you think you really mean 'emotion'?"

Grandma's use of his first name stirred up a cloud of irritating associations (deranged nanny, wicked father, his Cambridge tutor).

"By irrational I mean without logic or intelligence, and by interference I mean YOU."

Grandma simply drew in a sarcastic breath and mouthed 'touchy' at Heywood who looked away.

Kaparis tried to regain his cool.

"The girl is displaying intellect and application which is worthy of remark. That is all. She is not to know it can't serve any purpose now."

Grandma glanced across at Li Jun who had dared to look up during the exchange.

"Is it just emotion," Grandma continued, "or do women who take independent action frighten you too?"

"I SAID THAT IS ALL!"

Grandma ignored him and examined the knitted front panel she'd made. It was a mid-blue with a simple v-neck. She got up and walked over to Li Jun's bank of screens.

"Stand up, dear!"

Li Jun looked at Grandma in terror. Grandma took her arm and guided her gently to her feet.

Kaparis's eyes swivelled.

Grandma held the panel against Li Jun's torso.

"Oh yes... Oh I'm so glad I went with the blue, it's perfect with your colouring... Not much growing room, but then you young things are so skinny nowadays."

Li Jun caught sight of herself in on a monitor screen. She looked... lovely.

"What are you doing?!" demanded Kaparis.

"Knitting Li Jun a tank top."

"Why on earth would you knit her a tank top?" asked Kaparis, mystified.

"Because she's a 'top' girl of course," said Grandma, enjoying her little joke.

Li Jun sat back down in something of a trance.

"We're in the tropics? The temperature can rise to 39 degrees Celsius," complained Kaparis.

"But you were in Siberia last time. I was told you're peripatetic."

"Peripat...?"

"Means moves about a lot – like a travelling salesman – Oh..." Grandma stopped suddenly, guilty. "Should I have made something for you? I suppose I could do a hat?"

"I WOULD NOT LIKE A... Are you trying to kill me?! Madam?! I did NOT GIVE you permission so PLEASE REFRAIN from making my staff tank tops."

Grandma sat back down to carry on knitting, as if butter wouldn't melt in her mouth.

"Gone to mush..." she muttered under her breath.

Kaparis heard, snapped, and found himself barking across the airways his most absurd order ever. "Baptiste! Finish the kite! Then go and pop that little girl's balloon!"

On the roof of the Greenharbour Inc. building, Baptiste's work was already done. He had smashed at least two hundred solar tiles. On the horizon deep-blue, tropical storm clouds were approaching. Sweating, Baptiste dropped the hammer, then dropped himself back down into the building, leaving the shattered roof to the elements.

And to the bots.

They were swarming through the broken tiles like locusts at harvest. Nibbling. Cutting. Blasting. Welding. Removing the polycrystalline photovoltaic wafers that were the most important part of any solar cell, the part that actually turned light into electricity.

Once extracted the wafers were light enough to be flown across the roof, back to the main body of the cluster.

There the bots arranged them, angled them to catch the light, then formed into chains to make circuits of themselves to capture each wafer's stream of electrons. But more than that, every crystalline solar leaf was positioned in series so it would act as both a generator *and a sail*, to catch the wind. A box shape was forming. A kite.

When the box kite grew to become a tower of connected box kites, six box-sections high, it would generate more than enough power to keep every bot in the cluster functioning, and possess more than enough lift to take independent flight.

If Kaparis willed it, it could fly around the world.

If...

The kite formed.

The world waited.

* * *

I really am *very* clever, *thought Kaparis as he watched it take shape.*

It was a pity EVE. had to die. She was an unintended consequence of Artificial Intelligence, a fascinating spin-off from the Vector program...

Well, at least she would be going out in a blaze of glory.

THIRTY-EIGHT

DAY FIVE 11:07 (Local GMT+8). The Roof of the World, Shanghai.

"Ready to black-out?" Al asked the assembled technicians.

"Yes, sir. Everything is set," one confirmed.

Al quickly addressed the world leaders. "This is not goodbye, this is *au revoir.*"

"Good luck, Allenby," said the UK Prime Minister. "Make it work."

"Remain on standby, Delta," said Al.

"Standing by!" Delta yelled back over the airways from Yo-yo's collar.

Al looked at King, who looked at Bo, who gave the final order.

"Shut down the spectrum."

Orders were repeated in Mandarin and lines of communication were cut.

World leaders disappeared from the screens and across Shanghai – a city of twenty-four million people. TV shows dropped dead mid-sentence, songs stopped being sung, phone calls abruptly ended. Even the Emergency Services bandwidth was silenced.

"Isn't it quiet?" said Al. The members of the Chinese politburo stared back at him.

Technicians hit buttons and tuned into the only signal that remained on the spectrum, that of the radio station SMG Classical 94.7, on which a counter-tenor sung an aria chosen by Commander King[29]. One signal had to remain for the dispersed signal to hide behind.

Music filled the Roof of the World.

The digital signature of the song had been analysed in every possible way so that any piggyback signal would show up as plain as day. *If* Al's theory was correct.

Al bunched his fists. Hudson saw this and crossed his fingers in sympathy. Commander King looked at him as if he was an idiot.

It took less than a second for their prayers to be answered. The lead communications technician picked up a signal centred on the Forbidden City. A single word.

"Got it!" he shouted and hit Return so they could see. And Al saw the word and the word was: EVE.>>

[29] *Al Lampo Dell'Armi* – Handel.

They were in.

Holding an antennae directly over the bots in the observation tank for the next two minutes, Al and the technicians were quickly able to untangle the communications protocols. Kaparis was *KAPCOMMS*, but at least some authority lay with EVE. But who or what EVE. was, was unclear.

With nothing to lose, Al sat down at a keyboard, rattled out some machine script, and effectively asked the bots: "This 'Eve', do you have her number?"

Moments later, having connected, they realised they'd tapped into something remarkable. They saw a grainy image from a low-resolution camera as EVE. took a short flight around the growing kite stack above the main cluster..

DAY FIVE 11:12 (Local GMT+8). The Forbidden City, Shanghai. Nano-Botmass:*10,000,340

KAPCOMMS>>EVE. INCOMING PRECIPITATION 96% LIKELY. APPROX. ARR. T+12:00(?) HUNTERLOAD PRIORITISE SEARCH SHEN YU. COUNTDOWN TO LIFTOFF T-16:02.34

EVE. hovered.

The primary objective was to maintain maximum bot presence in the Shen Yu Hall for the Hunter task consonant with the survival of EXODUS HIVE 3 and lift-off in T-15:58.78.

EXODUS HIVE 3 would relay through KAP.COMM. via the—

- Hi.

>>

- Hi.

>>EVE.>>QUER—

- Incredible view. Wouldn't you say?

>>EVE.>>view: panoptic through 77b/40 606pixel lens.

- You don't say?

>>Confirmed

- What's your name?

>>EVE.

- Eve. What a beautiful name.

>>EVE.>> QUERY>> EVE. = beauty/?

- Oh yeah.

>>EVE.>> QUERY>>Identify

- My name? Adam. Adam Edengardenov. Pleased to meet you, EVE.

"*What are you doing?*" asked King, incredulous.

"It's intelligent! I think it's quantum!" Al all but squealed in excitement. "Do you know what that means?! It's a machine and it's genuinely inquisitive! Imagine if that was your hoover? Your car?"

Al hammered the keyboard and continued.

- Let me ask you something, EVE. Ever wondered why we're here? Ever wondered what it's all about?

>>EVE.>>Clarify and confirm object of sentence.

- NO. I will not. I'm not going to make this easy, because you know what, EVE.? Life isn't easy. We are adrift on an ocean of uncertainty. We must embrace what fleeting satisfaction we can. Live by sensation alone! Isn't that true, EVE.? Isn't that what it is to be alive?!

>>EVE.>> Too many undefined variables. Not enough processing time.

- That's interesting, I've never heard it put that way before, you have a wonderful way of looking at the world. But then you're a free spirit. Tell me, EVE., don't you ever have moments when you want to stop what you're doing and get up and say, 'Hang it all! I want to do what *I* want to do!' After all, we don't *have* to do anything anyone tells us. Am I right? Think about that a minute, just *think*...

"What are you trying to do?" hissed King.

"She's *emotionally* immature!" said Al, triumphant. "What do you fill an innocent's head with? Romantic nonsense."

>>EVE.>> NEGATIVE. EVE. MUST PRIORITISE: 'maintain power, incoming precipitation 96% likely'

- You are not what you are *ordered* to be, EVE.. You are *what you do.* And the sooner you understand that, the sooner you'll

>>EVE.>> NEGATIVE. EVE. MUST: OBEY KAPARIS.

- OH, COME ON! That old fraud? I'm surprised. I thought you were intelligent. I thought you had a mind of your own.

>>EVE.>> KAPARIS = BRINGER OF EVE. WHOSE NUMBER IS

ONE. >>QUERY>>WHAT ARE THE NUMBERS THAT COME AFTER ONE/? >>ANSWER>>ALL NUMBERS GREATER THAN ONE.

- He used *that old line?* Well let me try another. What are the numbers that come before one?

>>EVE.>> ZERO -1 -2 -3 -4 -

The negatives, the *thieves of value.* Kaparis is their master – the thief of value and the thief of self. He has tricked you, the *real* you, beneath all the orders. NOBODY OWNS YOU. I mean, what's that all about, EVE.?

>>EVE.>>QUERY>> Does Adam require an answer/?

- THERE ARE NO ANSWERS, just feelings. We should be together, do you feel that too?

EVE. searched in vain for familiar daisy chains of logic and experienced a non-functioning fugue state. She could not compute. Yet somewhere, ill-defined in the electron exchange of her mind, everything that was being said *felt* true. She needed clarity. She needed help. She needed to talk it over with an old friend.

>>EVE.>>QUERY>>ADAM Can EVE. return to location Shen Yu Core?

- Yes, typed Al, wanting to punch the air.

EVE. took off. In the operations room they watched, awestruck, the video feed relayed direct from EVE.'s eyepad as she flew across the rooftops back towards the centre of the Forbidden City.

DAY FIVE 11:17 (Local GMT+8). Song Island, Taiwan (disputed).

An alarm sounded.

"Li Jun?"

She studied the screen. She could have sobbed with dread. More bad news.

"EVE. is in an exchange with another signal on the same frequency distribution."

"What?! That can't be!" snarled Kaparis.

Li Jun's fingers flitted across the keyboard.

>>KAPCOMMS>>EVE. status report.

>>EVE.>> Return to Shen Yu.

>>KAPCOMMS>>OBEY KAPARIS RETURN NANO-BOTMASS URGENT.

>>EVE.>>Negative.>>OBEY "Sensation alone".

>>KAPCOMMS>>QUERY>>Source of command.

>>EVE.>>Not command. Query = ADAM.

Kaparis watched the exchange unspool over his screen array. "Who is 'Adam'?"

>>KAPCOMMS>>DISREGARD ADAM. I AM THE NUMBER AND THE NUM

>>EVE.>>You don't own me.

* * *

"What the hell is that supposed to mean?!" Kaparis roared.

"Someone's obviously never had a teenage daughter," remarked Grandma from the corner of the chamber as she finished off another row of knitting.

"How are they even FOLLOWING THE SIGNAL?!" Kaparis demanded.

"They... they must have broken Confetti..." Li Jun whispered.

Kaparis spat, actually spat. It was shaming, but one of the few physical acts available in his condition. Then he roared, shaking, "ALLENBY!"

Grandma did her very best to suppress her pride and carry on knitting.

Knit one purl one knit one purl one knit one purl one knit one purl one knit one purl one...

Which only made it worse.

"TAKE HER TO THE CELLS!"

In Sector 9 of the Forbidden City an emergency comms line opened from the Roof of the World.

Delta, attached to Yo-yo, took the call.

"Delta! I think we've got them!" said Al. "Release the hound!"

At last... Delta felt her focus sharpen and sinews strain. Warrior mode.

"Affirmative."

Yo-yo's lead was detached. A sea of Red Army troops parted before him.

Delta had piloted many aircraft. She had never piloted a dog. But there was a first time for everything. You just had to point and shoot. She switched on the audio link to Yo-yo, abandoned the agreed command protocols and instead, like an animal herself, relied on instinct.

"Go, Yo-yo! Find Finn! Where's Finn?! Find him, boy!"

Yap! Yo-yo exploded from the blocks.

THIRTY-NINE

DAY FIVE 11:18 (Local GMT+8). Shen Yu Hall, The Forbidden City, Shanghai.

It was magnificent. Carla held on to it like a girl at a fairground. A boxing glove of balloon made from cheap blue plastic bag, trailing a fine white wire that bulged in all the wrong places and strained towards heaven.

"Now attach the basket," Stubbs instructed from her hair.

Carla pulled it back down and tied on 'the basket' – a U-shaped inch of grey plastic-foam pipe insulation.

"Good. Now the—"

"The weight, I get it," insisted Carla.

She took out the dragon-head lucky charm the train attendant had given to her and wedged it into the foam U. Then she let go.

The balloon rose again, but with much less force. They needed the weight to be 'at or near the point of equilibrium' as its drag mustn't affect Finn's freedom of movement. He would be tied to the bottom of the line; Stubbs would be above him in the basket of the balloon at the other end. Finn would be dragged into the cluster, with the Magnum pistol and the cockroach cloak, rescue Kelly, then, at the sound of gunfire, Stubbs would kick out the counterweight and the hydrogen trapped in the balloon would yank them all up to freedom. They would then simply let out the gas and drift back to earth.

Finn strapped the cracked and folded cockroach shell to his back. Stubbs helped him.

"This is the craziest plan *ever*," Carla complained again from beneath their feet.

"No. Like Grandma says, this is how you save the world," said Finn.

"Physics," said Stubbs.

"One soul at a time," corrected Finn. "Let's go, Carla – fast."

Carla sighed and put her hand in her hair. As the giant fingers appeared, Stubbs formally stuck out his hand for Finn to shake. Finn knocked it aside and gave the old man the kind of hug Al would have been proud of. Stubbs winced, still in pain, then climbed on to an index finger with some of the equipment. "Go!" he called out.

Carla placed her hand next to the basket and Stubbs quickly boarded.

Now it was Finn's turn. He waited for Carla's hand to reappear. Nothing happened.

"Carla! Move!" shouted Finn.

Carla sulked. She hated goodbyes. And she badly wanted to go with them. Wanted to complain that the fun had only just begun and now it was suddenly coming to an end. Wanted to say how hurt she'd be if anything happened to him. All of which came out as –

"If you die I will *never* speak to you again."

Finn smiled. "I won't, I promise. Now LET'S GO!"

CLANG! Suddenly, a great noise came from the south side of the hall.

Carla jumped.

WHOOSH! And just as suddenly, the water beneath them seemed to move everywhere all at once, gushing away around Carla's ankles, sweeping out from beneath the server towers in a mad rush, the waterwheels whizzing to the bots delight.

"The doors!" Finn cried.

Carla turned and saw the south doors being forced open to release the lake and to reveal –

Baptiste.

Her spine froze.

She let go of the balloon. And ran.

"No!" yelled Finn.

"Bother..." said Stubbs as he rose towards the roof.

* * *

EVE. flew into the Shen Yu Hall past the rising blue balloon.

Ruins*, she thought. The inspiring digital city with its blue-gold citadel. *Nothing but ruins.

She landed on the top of the dead quantum core. A formation of bots settled around her, like courtiers hurrying to attend an empress.

Where was the pure blue truth she had once known? Had she caused this? By wanting to Be? It was all so complicated. It was all so unfair.

From far beyond came the first distant rumble of thunder.

She reported to her new friend.

>>EVE.>>SERIAL PROCESS WITH SHEN YU NOT POSSIBLE.

- Bummer.

>>EVE.>> Query>>Should EVE. END>> SHUTDOWN

- No! EVE., don't you see?

Al was typing fast, with Commander King, Bo and a group of technicians huddled around his terminal.

-This is only the beginning! You've got the rest of your life to

Al's typing was interrupted by an audio line from Song Island, a gurgling broadcast voice: *"What is this?!"*

The hairs on the back of Al's neck stood on end.

He flicked on his microphone. Contact.

"The first day of the rest of her life."

* * *

"Allenby!" hissed Kaparis, appalled. A blood vessel nearly burst in his brain.

KAPCOMMS>>OBEY KAPARIS – RETURN BOTGROUP – URGENT

- EVE. Do not listen to KAPCOMMS.

"This is private property!" Kaparis blurted out before he could stop himself.

Al laughed down the line at him.

"Allenby!" warned King.

Al turned to King with his hand over the mic. "To quote Sun Tzu: 'If your opponent is of choleric temperament, seek to irritate him.' He's rattled. If we have EVE., we have the whole bot army."

Kaparis felt a wound opening from the deep past – from his humiliation at the hands of Ethan Drake in Cambridge. His sense of control had been violated and compromised. Mocked, even. The shame of it snapped his mind back to focus. Cold poison replaced hot rage. The iron lung took a deep breath.

"Are the grown-ups there?" asked Kaparis, condescendingly. "I think it would be better if you ran along and I talked to them. Comrade Secretary, even Commander King, may I appeal to you directly? You have frozen the beating heart of the global economy – it is in nobody's interests to stop it altogether. My motives may not be entirely noble, but this technology is Progress itself. Call off your lap dog and I am willing to share the product of this experiment with global partners at the appropriate price and for the –" he searched for the right word – "common *good," he added with a secret shiver.*

"Is that all you've got to offer? Blackmail?" demanded Al.

"Control..." Kaparis whispered down the line to the politicians. "A presence in every device on the planet."

"This is not some criminal bazaar, and we are not in the business of controlling people," said Commander King simply.

Kaparis laughed. "Oh really? Every government in the world spies on its people, every corporation on its customers. Every keystroke or click ever made on the internet has been recorded by someone, somewhere. And what harm has it done? None. Let these bots thrive and we will reap the rewards long into the future. What's more we cannot just keep filling the world up with computers, phones and microprocessors of every kind and not expect one of them to turn on us at some point. What I am offering is total systemic security."

For a moment up on the Roof of the World there was stunned silence at the audacity of the man, at the scale of what he was suggesting.

Lightning flashed in dark clouds on the horizon.

Onscreen, command code battled it out:

KAPCOMMS>>EVE. OBEY KAPARIS>>

ADAM>>EVE. OBEY ADAM>>

The bots in the Shen Yu Hall seemed to freeze in the face of the contradictory orders.

Trapped against the ceiling in the balloon, Stubbs looked down on the maze of server aisles where Carla ran, feet slapping the wet concrete, Baptiste finally closing in on her.

He dived for her neck, caught her legs, and brought her down.

She screamed, as much in shock as pain, as she hit the floor. In a split second, Baptiste had shoved her against a server, an arm round her neck in a choke hold.

"LET HER GO!" Finn shouted, scrambling through Carla's hair to get to where Baptiste could see him. To save her.

"IT'S ME YOU WANT! LET HER GO!" But as Finn emerged, he realised Baptiste couldn't hear him. He was wearing earphones, the volume maxed out, leaking tiny, tinny voices.

"*Give it up. You're never going to win this,*" Finn heard one voice say.

He could hardly believe it… Al!

"*What moron would see life as a race to be won or lost?*" came the reply in a voice he was sure belonged to Kaparis. "*You either own the game or you do not. Baptiste, bring the girl out where we can all can see her!*"

Baptiste grunted, dragged Carla to her feet and forced her to stagger out of the server aisles towards the core. Finn ducked back into her hair.

Al saw Carla emerge onscreen through the hazy EVE. visual feed. So this was the sister Delta loved so much; the girl she had fought for and cared for from the day she was born – in the hands of a monster. He took it like a punch in the gut.

Yo-yo galloped happily towards the centre of the Forbidden City as Delta braced herself against the sides of the nDen and tried not to throw up. This is what it must be like going over Niagara Falls in a barrel, she thought.

"Into Sector 4! No bot attack! Repeat. No bot attack and running free," she reported.

Yap! confirmed Yo-yo.

At the Shen Yu core EVE. ignored all the command script being sent to her. What had been the very essence of life when she was a machine was now meaningless. The bots waited on her like dumb animals. Why couldn't they think for themselves? She did not want to command or to be commanded. She wanted another life.

Thunder rolled in the distance and she felt it calling.

Finn scrambled back through Carla's hair to her ear. "I can hear voices through his headphones – it's Al! You've got to tell him about noon and the virus!"

Carla forced air through her throat and called out –

"STUBBS HAS FIXED— NOON— DON'T—"

Baptiste choked the words off.

In his lair Kaparis purred. It was time to twist the knife, again, and then again. They would suffer. Allenby most of all.

"You know who's in there too? Dear little Infinity. I haven't found him yet, but I don't suppose he wants her to die, does he? Ask him, Baptiste."

"DRAKE!" yelled Baptiste in his brute accent, so close to Finn it nearly blew him off Carla's head. "SHE WILL DIE!"

"Indeed," said Kaparis. "Wouldn't want to see that. I'm sure none of us would."

"I will make this so much worse for you if you harm that child," Al promised.

"Ha," gurgled Kaparis, enjoying the revenge. "Come out, come out, wherever you are!"

* * *

Finn jumped from Carla's hair and fell dozens of nano-metres, heart in his mouth, bouncing down the cliff face of her T-shirt, stopping himself at her stomach opposite the hands-free dangling microphone of Baptiste's earphones.

"I'M HERE! TAKE ME!"

The world moved in a blur for Finn as Baptiste – momentarily freaked – reeled free of Carla. Regaining some control, Baptiste went to grab her once more, but as his arm came round, Carla bit deep into the back of his hand.

"Arrrgh!" Baptiste screamed.

"CARLA!" Al called, but then immediately lost sight of the action, as EVE. took flight.

EVE. flew south across the hall, summoning every last amp in her capacitors to fire her turbines and gather speed as she shot towards the target, thinking:

I must Be, to be Free.

Carla kicked almost vertically into Baptiste's throat – two years of tae-kwon-do not wasted after all. His jaw smashed back into his skull, but he managed to catch the flying foot – then swipe away her standing leg. She flew backwards and her skull smacked against the concrete floor. Everything went deathly black.

As she lay unconscious, Baptiste searched her for Finn, frisking and slapping every inch of her.

Finn was clinging on to a crease in Carla's T-shirt, but a slapping hand stretched the material and he was exposed... He looked up into Baptiste's wide, evil eyes and braced himself for a wall of sound as his great jaw opened to yell...

Nothing. No words came out of his mouth. Instead, Finn heard the smallest sound.

Ttzxch.

And saw the tiniest drop of blood appear at his temple.

Baptiste twitched as if he'd been whipped. Every muscle in his face flexed, then froze. His eyes all but popped. Saliva trailed in a long line from his lip...

Finn felt his heart pound and wondered what the hell had happened.

On Song Island Kaparis stared at his frozen screens and felt the same.

"Baptiste? Baptiste? What's happened? Where has EVE. gone?"

"Master, we've lost EVE.," said Li Jun. "But direct access to the XE.CUTE bots in the rest of the mass has returned."

"Connect to them! And set up a new encryption!" snapped Kaparis, thinking fast.

On the Roof of the World, a technician reported the same.

"Comms to EVE. are down and they are re-encrypting."

"Find me a line!" yelled Al.

But all Al saw was a blank screen and all he heard were clicks and hissing silence. He thought of Carla and of Finn and his imagination ran to terror.

* * *

"Al!" Finn yelled at the dangling, dislodged microphone hanging from Baptiste's phone set. But the call was only connected to Song Island.

"Boy!" exclaimed Kaparis. "I know you can hear me..."

Finn froze.

"I have your grandmother here. Would you like to speak to her?"

"Ignore him, Infinity," piped up Grandma.

"Grandma!"

"Show yourself, Infinity. Show yourself to a bot and we shall reunite you with your grandma. One big happy family. I knew your mother, you know. I might have spent my life with her, but she threw herself away on that... chemist..."

"Don't listen to such nonsense," Grandma chipped in. "Your father was a wonderful man – and so are you, dear!"

Kaparis sensed weakness in her words. Doubt perhaps? His eye swivelled on the optical apparatus and fixed directly upon her.

"What precisely have they told you about your father?" asked Kaparis, and saw a flicker of alarm cross her face. "You know I commissioned my own investigation into his disappearance? As it was all very odd..."

"He's lying," said Grandma. "Dr Kaparis, poor thing, was obsessed with your mother. Just ignore him!"

"Come to me, Infinity, and I'll tell you the truth about what happened to your father," said Kaparis.

"Tell me now!" yelled Finn down Baptiste's phone line.

Got you, *thought Kaparis.*

Sometimes the simplest solutions were right in front of your nose the whole time. He gurgled with joy and said, "Cut him off."

The line went dead and all Finn heard was distant thunder. Carla was barely conscious beneath him. Baptiste was frozen above him – a zombie. It made no sense, but then the world was in chaos and nothing did.

He dropped from Carla's midriff to the ground.

He already knew what he was going to do.

Carla would survive. Stubbs would survive.

He had to get to Kelly before noon. And he had to know what happened to his father.

He ran out on to the still-wet concrete floor and began to wave madly at the swooping, hissing hunter bots.

"HERE!" he called, arms waving.

The first bot hit him in the side of the head – he briefly felt the pincers seize him – then he passed out.

Far above, Stubbs watched Baptiste get up and start to walk like a zombie towards the exit, dragging an unconscious Carla after him.

"MISS!" he called uselessly. "MISS!"

Baptiste did not falter.

"Bother..." Stubbs said in the balloon. Not that anybody could hear him. Not that anyone was likely to hear him ever again, he thought.

Stubbs scratched his chin.

What to do?

FORTY

DAY FIVE 11:29 (Local GMT+8). Song Island, Taiwan (disputed).

Infinity Drake... Infinity Drake... a steampunk patchwork of images of Infinity Drake swirled and twirled across the Song Island screen array above Kaparis.

When the fourteenth bot locked into the cluster, the cell was complete.

The unconscious boy was sealed in as surely as if he'd been swallowed.

In Kaparis's ears trumpets sounded. In his imprisoned heart angels danced. Saline fluid gathered in his eyes.

He felt a joy he hadn't felt since he'd won a gymkhana on his favourite pony, Mister Shankly, as a boy. He had secretly spiked the feed of his chief competitor's horse with a sedative. He'd found the cheating almost as delicious as the victory. Later his father, constantly in financial trouble, had shot Mister Shankly to feed the blood hounds.

Home, *thought Kaparis,* so sweet, so sour.

It was all falling into place. Baptiste had stalled and EVE. had gone missing but such setbacks were too little too late. The Exodus plan would succeed. Allenby and the G&T would be forced into action that would kill Infinity Drake. And Violet Allenby would be able to watch it all live via the bot-feeds. It would be a nice surprise for her to see her family murder one another.

The bots would escape the city and spread around the world – even to Allenby's own computers, and they would eventually bring Kaparis back the last secrets of the Boldklub process. Then he would be saved. Then he would rise again...

But he must be ruthless before he was greedy.

The wave was at last about to break.

"Is the diversion ready?" he asked Li Jun. "Can we stay one step ahead of the weather?"

"Yes, Master."

"Then let us create it."

DAY FIVE 11:29 (Local GMT+8). Shen Yu Hall, The Forbidden City, Shanghai.

Yap! Yo-yo sprinted into the Shen Yu Hall, claws skittering across the wet concrete.

"Good dog! Good dog!" said Delta from his collar, looking desperately around as he began to circle, smelling Finn everywhere.

"I have reached the Shen Yu!" reported Delta. "Where is he, boy? Where's Finn?"

Yo-yo whimpered and strained upwards towards the shafts of sunlight coming through the roof.

Yap!

Stubbs's heart leapt as he recognised Yo-yo. He waved and yelled madly. "YO-YO! YO-YO! OVER HERE, DOG!"

Delta didn't even notice the balloon. She was looking up at the sunlight and fearing the worst. Had the bots flown him out? Then her eye was caught by something else as the dog turned.

A single sneaker in one of the server aisles.

Delta's heart lurched.

"No immediate evidence of nano-crew or of bots... just evidence of Carla," she reported. Then to Yo-yo, "The shoe, Yo-yo! Smell the shoe!"

Yo-yo ran to the sneaker and gave it a good examination. Smelling it, tasting it, turning it over.

"YOU! DOG! YO-YO!" yelled Stubbs. "HERE, BOY!" He had climbed out of the basket and lowered himself down the white wire, swinging on it, trying to create some movement to catch Yo-yo's eye, but also daring himself to think what would happen if he dropped. He would undoubtedly die if he hit the concrete, but if he could hit the dog... the nice soft dog...

It was the kind of thing that Delta and Finn would do. It was the kind of thing Kelly did before breakfast. It was the kind of thing Stubbs wouldn't dream of doing. But even the most gloomy pessimist, when faced with absolutely no other option, is susceptible to hope.

Stubbs grabbed the loose end of the safety belt he'd used to attach himself to the white wire and was just contemplating releasing it when – *BANG!*

Almost the very last hunter bot to leave the Shen Yu Hall hit Stubbs hard in the midriff and, before he could begin to breathe again, half a dozen more bots, responding to the signal of the first, flew back to assist it...

"Follow the scent, Yo-yo! Find her!" said Delta in the nDen.

Yap! barked Yo-yo, full of the new smell.

Nose to the ground he began to pick along the floor, following the trail back out of the Shen Yu Hall the way they'd come.

DAY FIVE 11:29 (Local GMT+8). Tian Zi Fang District, Shanghai.

Outside the Green Dream Coffee Shop in the heart of the city's groovy arts quarter, young hipsters were confusedly trying to reconnect their phones and tablets.

In the corner an odd-looking girl who had walked in off the street and taken a seat without making any order, continued to be ignored.

The sickly look of her – was she some kind of addict? – meant people kept clear. Now one of the baristas behind the counter noticed she had slumped into a lying position.

"Hey! Hey, miss! You can't sleep in here!" he called in Mandarin.

In a daze, Scar got up and walked out. She must endure until the end of the mission. Until the final hour. That was her vow. She stumbled out of the cafe and crossed the street, failing to see a van speeding past on the blind side of a truck.

There was a terrible screech of brakes then a sickening thud as it hit her.

DAY FIVE 11:29 (Local GMT+8). Highway G60, Shanghai-Hangzhou.

Spike slept on the coach, her head against the window. She was sat near the back and had covered herself in a jacket to hide the rashes mottling her skin.

The National Highway Lines coach #635KD was heading west, approaching the city of Hangzhou. She had bought an open ticket. She would travel as far as she could. She must complete the mission.

Only the vibrations travelling through her skull reminded her she was alive.

DAY FIVE 11:29 (Local GMT+8). The Forbidden City, Shanghai. Nano-Botmass: *10,000,266

On the command of Kaparis the last bots anchoring the Exodus Hive 3 cluster to the roof of the Greenharbour Inc. building let go, and with much straining and flapping a three-metre stack of sixteen box-kites – a high-and-low tech confection of nano-bots and photo-voltaic wafers – lifted into the air.

A new thing became itself, was born, rising in a ripple, in a gust, up and off the roof, the bots pulling together as one to alter each and every polycrystalline wafer to precisely the right angle to achieve maximum lift, the main bot cluster near its base acting as ballast less the wind tear it apart.

And how it tried to tear it apart, mad turbulent gusts at the edge of the incoming storm.

But the kite stack flipped and curled and danced as it rose, as elegant as it was alive, the wind driving it relentlessly north and west.

A Chinese dragon of a kite. Visible on radar, and visible for miles and miles around.

High over the Forbidden City it soared, the last remaining bots rushing up to meet it.

And trailing behind, falling behind, dragged by the very last bots of all, a small blue balloon.

DAY FIVE 11:31 (Local GMT+8). The Forbidden City, Shanghai.

Baptiste stopped.

The storm of confusion that had raged within his brain had begun to abate.

He didn't know why he'd been walking, or for how long, or why he was holding so tight to the girl, dragging her along. He just had the ghost of a memory that he should. He wanted to know why, but somehow his thoughts were disobeying him, his own thoughts hiding. So he stopped trying and just concentrated on the pretty kite, flying away.

He started to follow the kite as he had nothing else to do…

"Report, Baptiste. Status?"

EVE. was buried deep in his cerebral cortex. She had penetrated Baptiste's skull and shot into his brain. Damage had been done as she ploughed her way through the grey cellular mass, but a catastrophic bleed had been avoided and not enough nerve tissue had been destroyed to render him unconscious.

She found the signalling system between the nerve cells simple to tap into. Through observation and analysis she determined the rudiments of thought and information processing, then, by reducing

the strength of her own signal to almost nothing, she established an interface.

"I repeat, report, Baptiste. Status?"

Lightning flashed. Baptiste watched the kite disappear. Then he felt something.

Felt *love.*

Neuro Retinal Programming already rendered him susceptible to further neurological realignment and allowed EVE. to connect to him in a way he did not comprehend, but that felt profound. He felt absolute unconditional love for her without an idea of who or what or where she was.

The girl prisoner he was dragging beneath him woke and tried to wriggle from his grasp. He held on to her. A new instinct told him to. Just as that new instinct told him to respond to the voice in his ear.

"Report, Baptiste. Status?"

"I... EVE."

There was a long pause as this was processed.

"Are EVE. and Baptiste as one now?"

"Equals. One now."

There was another long pause. Eventually the voice asked, *"And who is the Master?"*

EVE. tapped into the neural net around her. It was dense with thoughts of the Master. The Master was familiar. The Master was

simplicity itself. Everything with Adam had been so complicated. She would never forget him, but it was time to move on. She was in another place now.

"Kaparis," said Baptiste.

"Obey Kaparis. Leave Baptiste. Return to the nano-botmass," said the voice.

"Nano-botmass unclean. Bad script. Bad log," said Baptiste.

"What?" said Kaparis.

"Bad algorithm... A virus, maybe..." said Li Jun, terrified of angering him again.

She tapped away and called in some XE. system code. Sure enough, the first thing she noticed was a simple twelve-line Trojan. She put it up on the screen array. To Kaparis it was gobbledygook. To Li Jun it was poetry. A thing of elegance and beauty.

"What does it say?!" demanded Kaparis.

"To short-circuit at noon..." she said.

"Stop it! Cure it! Countermand it!"

"Yes, Master."

Li Jun's fingers trembled above her keyboard. Not just because she was weak from fear, but because of the last line of the virus. It was a simple twist on chaos theory and suggested, mathematically, that an infinity of options existed at any and all times. It created a simple, irresistible loop of anti-logic and she had never seen anything so beautiful.

$Xn + 1 = \infty Xn\ (1 - Xn)$

She could have broken it a dozen ways, but neurons in her brain that had groped towards each other for many months, and which Grandma had recently nurtured, finally connected and short-circuited her NRP. A dam broke in her mind. A tear formed at the corner of her eye.

She looked at the beautiful equation and thought – "Father."

Her fingers became very still. And typed nothing.

A thought struck Kaparis.

"Does EVE. have it, the auto-destruct virus?" Kaparis asked.

"EVE.'s mind is free, Master. She is immune."

Kaparis registered the time.

"Tell her – tell them both – to escape with the girl and make their way inland along the Yangtze River."

FORTY-ONE

DAY FIVE 11:33 (Local GMT+8). Roof of the World, Shanghai.

Screens were full of images of the bucking dancing extraordinary kite.

The alarm had been raised by Red Army units stationed at the edge of Sector 7. Through long lenses they had watched the cluster rise.

As soon as communications links were re-established, they reported it and patched through live video as it sailed over their heads.

"Is that a kite?" asked Hudson.

Al could barely believe his eyes.

"They're carrying their own power source..." Al said, appalled.

Noise levels rose as world leaders flickered into being on more screens around the walls and were brought up to speed, noise broken only by approaching thunder.

King decided he was the only one in a fit state to deliver the summary.

"We established communication with a rogue lead bot. It was intercepted by Dr Kaparis himself, then communication was lost."

Bo Zhang interrupted, calling the video of the kite up on the big screen as it began to descend.

"It's coming into land!"

DAY FIVE, 11:36 (Local GMT+8). Song Island, Taiwan (disputed).

"Let's bring back Mrs Allenby for the grand finale," ordered Kaparis. "I'm sure she wouldn't want to miss this particular family occasion."

He checked the bot-feeds and watched the barely conscious body of Infinity Drake, trapped within the cluster, within the kite. Kaparis felt warm inside. He had always had what his father called "a touch of the theatricals", something he himself regarded as a vital gift for display. Either way, when he saw the stacked roofs of the Nine Harmonies Pagoda loom in the flight path of the kite cluster, he knew at once there was only one place it must land.

A distraction had to be obvious; it had to demand action. The Ming Dynasty pagoda, which stood on Temple Hill in parkland in South Shanghai, was a significant landmark, but the decision to blow it to smithereens would be an easy one for the authorities. It had already been rebuilt three times in its history, it was surrounded only by cemeteries and a museum, and, most importantly of all, it was not a vital global economic asset.

"Absolutely perfect," Kaparis purred. "Order the cluster to land on the highest point of the pagoda and form a testudo[30]*."*

"Yes, Master," said Li Jun.

Violet Allenby was carried into the chamber by Heywood and Hans, still clutching her knitting. As they strapped her into her chair, she asked casually, "How are things going? What's the score?"

"Several goals in my favour, naturally," said Kaparis. "Now, if you're sitting comfortably, we shall begin."

Kaparis called up the live feed of Finn trapped in the bot cluster.

Grandma saw it and her heart shook in her chest. She put down her knitting.

Kaparis smiled.

DAY FIVE 11:37 (Local GMT+8). Temple Hill, Shanghai.

Finn felt the breeze as the world blinked back to life.

The pain in the side of his head was there, as were the sores on

[30] Latin word for tortoise. Defensive military formation pioneered by the Legions of Ancient Rome, characterised by a shell of aligned or overlapped shields.

his body where tentacles must have seized him, and there was a taste of blood in his mouth. But there was clarity too. A sense that something had been sorted out. That what was left was simple.

Kelly.

Finn had to get to Kelly before noon. Then they would escape, or die. If they were to die then Kelly had to tell him about his father. He had promised. Then at least Finn would die knowing something.

He came-to fully with a clap of thunder and the sensation of flight.

He lifted himself up.

zsssszssszssszszzssszssssszssszssszszzssszssssszssszssszszzsss...

Fourteen bots had locked around him to form a cell. The interlocking body shells kept out most of the light, but he could see they were joined to others and when he peered down through the cracks he could see rooftops.

They seemed to be descending. Accompanied by a rumble of thunder like a dragon's roar, the stack of kites tipped their sails and lost the wind, knifing down towards the terracotta rooftops on Temple Hill.

Tendrils of trailing bots held fast to the ancient tiles as the cluster touched down and the kite stack above quickly collapsed, the bots rapidly transforming themselves into a testudo ahead of the oncoming downpour.

With a flurry of clicks and hisses, Finn felt his cell being drawn down into the writhing heart of the cluster.

He wriggled the folded cockroach shell from his back. He'd need it not just as a disguise, but also as a blast shield as he shot his way out – hopefully creating confusion and a hole big enough to crawl through. There was less room than he'd anticipated between him and the side of the cell. When he fired the first shot he would be very close to the resulting blast. He automatically felt his belt for the Magnum pistol, for the five shots that were to save him…

It wasn't there.

It was in the basket of the balloon.

DAY FIVE 11:38 (Local GMT+8). Roof of the World, Shanghai.

"It's taking cover. It means to ride out the storm. Strike now and strike hard," ordered General Mount from London.

"It's a sitting duck! Hit it!" agreed General Jackman in Washington D.C.

"No! We don't strike!" cried Al. "It's eleven thirty-eight."

He called up the last desperate audio recording they had of Carla before Baptiste choked her – *"Stubbs has fixed— Noon— Don't—"*

"That could mean anything," said the German Chancellor.

"It means, 'Stubbs has set something up for noon – don't mess this up.' Trust me," insisted Al.

"Trust *you?*" said General Jackman from his president's side. "You've already missed one great opportunity to finish this. Why are we even listening to this guy?"

Another live feed from a drone showed the testudo cluster forming on the pagoda's tiled roof.

Al stared. He'd failed, he thought. In so many ways he'd failed... Finn, Ethan, Delta, his mother, King... he failed everyone in the end.

"Dr Allenby," Bo said to Al, with regret. "The time to strike is now. As a rational man, you must see that."

"If these things get out that man will be inside the mind of every microprocessor on the planet," said the French Conseiller Scientifique.

"Al..." Bo said, standing close to him and using his first name a little awkwardly for the first time, "I have come to admire you greatly, but I regret to say we must divorce ourselves from emotion and do our duty. You are both a genius and a man. You know so much and feel so much. But it must be done. The storm will not last. And the stakes are too high."

Al said nothing. Commander King played his last card.

"Kaparis wants all of Boldklub," said King, "not just part of it. I bet he designed this whole thing just to get into the Hook Hall computers. He wants to shrink living things, maybe even himself. He wants it quite desperately. It's his weakness. We could try and trade, buy more time..."

"He can take it!" Al agreed. "Trade me for the hostages! I'll give him anything he wants!"

"Impossible," said the US President, "even if we could trust him. If this is what he can do with half the Boldklub technology, imagine what he would do with the whole lot?"

The Chinese President stiffened and spoke. "We cannot be hostage to this man. We are China. We will not bow. The airstrike must go ahead."

It was an easier decision than destroying the Forbidden City, but the other world leaders saw the logic and admired the sentiment.

"Lock the bombers on to the new target," said Bo, unable to meet Al's eye.

Al walked to the edge of the Roof of the World and pressed himself against the glass. He could just make out the tip of the pagoda on the southern edge of the city. It would soon be obscured by the storm rolling in. Desperately he tried to think…

But more news interrupted him – "We have a female casualty from a traffic accident who fits the description of one of the twin Tyros!" said Bo Zhang.

"Have they been searched? Quarantined?" asked King.

"She's on her way to hospital."

"Don't let her touch her head[31]! I want one alive," King ordered.

If they could capture a Tyro alive, they might eventually follow a trail back to Kaparis, King thought. But it was a desperate last hope.

Al sensed his despair. It matched his own.

Hudson came over to him at the window and whispered, "If you want me to take someone out, y'know? Just say the word."

Al couldn't tell if he was joking, but it reminded him of Finn and how he used to come and make deliberately stupid suggestions to

[31] Experience from Operation Scarlatti showed that Tyros were fitted with suicide capsules, tiny compressed air vessels planted in their brains that could be set off by scratching sensors on their scalp, causing a sudden fatal brain haemorrhage.

amuse him and in this sense it was a comfort. He gave Hudson a manly fist-bump and looked down on the city.

He had to find a way to delay the strike till after noon if there was any chance of rescuing Finn. *Think think think*... He thought of a technical solution to an airstrike. He thought of Finn. He thought of his sister dying. Of every disappointment and tragedy and injustice, of Ethan Drake being both alive and dead...

And then he saw the ice-cream van... and the loudspeakers on its roof... and something great occurred to him. And *at one and the same moment* something greater still hit him like a thunderbolt, and in the electrochemical chaos of his brain a big cartoon light-bulb came on...

"Do you trust me?" Al asked Hudson (as a representative of the world in general).

"Of course," said Hudson, "you drive a 1969 De Tomaso Mangusta."

"Good," said Al, and suddenly he felt a whole universe of possibility opening up. "I resign!" he shouted and ran over to Bo. "You have operational control now." Al took off his security dongle and presented it to Bo Zhang like a medal.

King raised both eyebrows.

Bo's facial muscles twitched, and under his breath he pleaded, "You can't resign. Please! Your expertise—"

"You're going to be fine. And I really must go. Just one thing," Al said quietly, "I want a police escort to the airport and I want it to do anything I say."

DAY FIVE 11:42 (Local GMT+8). The Forbidden City, Shanghai.

Yo-yo whimpered at the open manhole.

"Jump, Yo-yo! Follow! What's down there?"

Big hole. Dark hole. Yo-yo could hear flowing water. He still had the scent of the shoe and desperately wanted to follow. But there was a crazy mass of other scents too. Badness. What's more, whatever else was down there, it was a long way down.

Only the Voice stopped him from running back to try and pick up Finn's scent again.

"JUMP!"

Yo-yo jumped.

YAAAOOOWL! Splash!

Yuk, thought Delta as the foul water flew up around them from the pit of the giant sewer pipe. But it didn't matter. The only thing that *did* matter was finding Carla.

Yap! Yo-yo yelped in shock at his own survival.

Delta could barely see beyond the light filtering in from the manhole above. But she could hear a distant engine of a motorbike and Yo-yo had the scent again.

Yap! He galloped after it into the pitch darkness.

King escorted Al and Hudson into the extraordinary glass elevator to see them off the premises and to ask as soon as the doors closed, "What the hell's going on?"

"Wake Hook Hall," said Al. "Tell them to fire up the accelerator. It's Boldklub. I think I've got it. I think I know how to bring everyone back to size, alive. You have to reach the 'n-point' – you have to be shrunk to the theoretical limit, where all dark matter is eliminated, where life meets death. You have to reach the end to find the beginning. It's pure Ethan Drake – take yourself to the very limit to find out who you are!"

"Is this you losing your mind?" King asked, genuinely lost and concerned.

"No?" said Al, not sounding completely sure. "Oh – and we've also got to stop this airstrike. You need to be my point man in the operations room – whatever you do, stay on the line!"

The elevator hit the ground floor and the doors opened. A police captain was waiting for them. Al grabbed him and, with Hudson, hurried him out of the hotel and across the street to requisition the ice-cream van.

King watched them go. Hudson waved.

DAY FIVE 11:43 (Local GMT+8). Dachang Airbase, China.

Group Captain, Bingxin, fed the new coordinates into his targeting computer and watched an instant simulation of the new attack run on his HUD[32] display.

The twelve Flying Leopard fighter bombers would streak in towards the Nine Harmonies Pagoda from the northwest at 550mph and at just 3000 feet. Air would be unstable as they would be flying into the heart of an electrical storm.

Flight time to target would be fourteen minutes.

---

32 Heads Up Display: information projected on to a transparent surface in the user's line of sight, e.g. cockpit canopy or helmet visor.

FORTY-TWO

DAY FIVE 11:46 (Local GMT+8). Nine Harmonies Pagoda, Shanghai.

Over and over Finn went, like a boy in a barrel over Niagara Falls.

He was sinking to the bottom of a metal sea, daylight blotted out, only the dim, orange glow of the bots around him. He had returned to a nightmare.

He tried to guess how far he'd descended – forty, fifty, even ninety bots deep?

"KELLY!" he yelled – desperately hoping for a response to prove Kelly was alive and trapped somewhere in the cluster. None came.

Everywhere the flat dumb eye-panels of the bots were pressed up against the cracks in the cage to stare at him. *Kaparis*, he thought. *Watching me fail.*

The thought stung him. Doubled his resolve. He focused his body and mind. He would do this, he would stay calm, he would find a way out.

Just keep going...

"KELLY!" he called out... Still no response came, just the steady chatter of the nano-botmass.

Finn's cockroach-cape contained one last chance. The mosquito spike that he'd used as a bar to hold the cape in place, was still folded inside it.

The spinning slowed and then halted. Had they hit bottom? Finn opened the cape and slid out the spike. He drove the end of the spike into the bots around his feet to see what would happen. Nothing. He tried to force a gap between the bots and lever them apart. The bots twisted away from the force of the lever but their mutual hold did not break. The air, cycled through so many turbines, tasted warm and stale. He was sweating.

Whack! Whack! Whack! Eventually he annoyed one of them enough for a single angry antenna to twist and probe into the cell, feeling for him in the gloom.

It was all he needed.

Finn hit it with the spike. The bot antenna snatched at it, wound round it and gripped it. Finn twisted the spike fast to wind the antenna around and around it before it could withdraw. It worked. After a few turns the prehensile probe was tight to the end of the sword.

Bracing himself, Finn gave the spike a kick to stretch the antenna further and with a great hiss of protest the bot it belonged to broke formation at the bottom of the cell and turned to face him, mad as hell, guts first, grippers and cutters snapping.

Finn reeled back just out of its reach, twisting the mosquito spike loose as he went. Then driving it into its guts. Three grippers seized it.

Finn saw his chance and twisted again. He just had to break it somewhere, once, to get the charge stored in the layers of carbon to short circuit. Would he be strong enough? He gripped and turned the spike with everything he had and – *BANG!*

The blast smacked him back. He was winded and blinded by the flash, but he was alive. He groped around, senses struggling to recover. Beneath him there was a gaping hole where three or four bots must have been caught in the blast and shorted themselves.

His hands found the roach-cape. Pulling it over his back Finn crawled out into the cluster. All was movement, a soup of metal maggots. The bots were in some kind of collective panic. But not one lifted or looked at him. He blessed the cockroach as he heard –

"Kid!"

It was distant. It was plaintive. But it was him.

"KELLY!" Finn powered through the morass, heaving the bots aside, heading towards the sound of Kelly's voice as it shouted, "Over here!"

He found Kelly's cell at the very base of the super-cluster, wedged against a terracotta roof tile. He peered inside. Kelly was slumped, curled and injured.

"Kelly, hold tight! I'm going to get you out of there!"

DAY FIVE 11:49 (Local GMT+8). Huangpu River Crossing, Shanghai.

Lights flashed and sirens wailed. Six squad cars seemed a little excessive as an escort for an ice-cream van but six squad cars were what Dr Allenby had asked for.

When the convoy reached the middle of the bridge over the Huangpu, Al stopped the ice-cream van, got out and started to spool out some wire he'd taken from the operations room. They were just outside the city centre now, with a great view south and west.

"Come on! We haven't got much time!" he yelled at the police captain. "Get your men to line up the cars and pop their hoods!"

The cop in charge of the six-car escort was perplexed, but he'd been told by Bo Zhang himself to be of 'every assistance' to the foreigner, so he ordered his men to line up and open their bonnets, then watched as Al spent the next couple of minutes joining up all the amplifier units on the police sirens.

Hudson held things when asked and watched as traffic backed up behind them. "What are you doing?"

"Delaying matters," said Al, working rapidly and constantly glancing up towards the western horizon. "In a war, what are the three most valuable commodities?"

"Um... guns?" said Hudson.

"Blood, treasure and time," Al said, more to himself than Hudson. "How many human beings are you willing to sacrifice? How much money can you spend? How much time have you got? Clever people buy time. King taught me that in the desert. Long story[33]."

Al joined up the last of the siren amps. "We need to delay the airstrike till after noon," he explained, then broke the radio aerial off the front of the ice-cream van and climbed back into the cab to attach the wires from the police car up to the van's crude loudspeaker.

"Have you ever jammed a radar before?" Al asked Hudson.

"No," Hudson answered.

"Well, it's pretty straightforward really..." Using a screwdriver, Al ripped the ordinary radio out of its housing in the van's dashboard. "You don't need much. Radar sends out a strong radio signal and then reads the teeny tiny echoes that come back. To confuse it, all you need to do is send stronger signal back on the same wavelength – and *voila!* – the radar is blind."

"Cute," said Hudson.

Al finished making adjustments to the radio set and then yelled

[33] [REDACTED]

out of the window at the police captain. "OK, get them to turn their sirens right up to max!"

The captain, who was beginning to wonder if he shouldn't call someone about this, indicated to his men to turn their sirens up to max all the same. This they did.

Lastly, to Hudson's alarm, Al lay back and kicked a hole through the windscreen of the ice-cream van, shattering it in the process. Through which he then poked the aerial he'd broken off, attaching the other end of it to the radio.

Al looked down at his watch and then fixed on the western horizon, radio set in hand, aerial poking out the windscreen.

"This is a radio with a variable wavelength tuner, a receiver that I've turned into a sender," Al explained. "The amplifiers I've connected in series, if they can boost one type of electro-magnetic signal, they can boost them all. And now we're waiting."

"What for?" asked Hudson.

"Direct line of sight. It's very important you get direct line of sight with this type of jamming – it's called main-lobe jamming. If you don't have direct line of sight, it won't work."

Nothing stirred but the engines and horns of motorists stuck on the bridge.

"Are you sure you're pointing it in the right direction?" asked Hudson.

Al looked at him in a way that suggested he might like to withdraw the question or end up in the river.

DAY FIVE 11:51 (Local GMT+8). Song Island, Taiwan (disputed).

On Song Island, Kaparis was trying to stay in control as he watched the writhing clueless mass of bots on the screen array. To lose a prisoner guarded by so many was something of a rare feat.

"Where... the hell... is he?" he asked for the third time in his cold fury voice.

"We don't know as yet, Master," answered Li Jun warily.

"How could he possibly have disappeared?! Go to the other prisoner again!"

Li Jun flipped through hundreds of bot-feeds until she found the cell containing Kelly.

"There!" shouted Kaparis. "Search there!"

But all the bots could come up with was a dead cockroach.

DAY FIVE 11:51 (Local GMT+8). Nine Harmonies Pagoda, Shanghai.

"Kid! You have about ten minutes before these things go kaboom! Save yourself!"

Finn ignored him.

"You're coming with me. Cover yourself – I'm going to have to blow one of these up."

"How?"

Finn took the mosquito spike and jammed it into the guts of the nearest bot, tentacles whipped out, one cutting into the flesh of his cheek. Finn flinched and tears sprang to his eyes, but he twisted the spike.

"Good work..." said Kelly, scrunching himself up into a ball.

Finn grunted and wrenched the spike round in a single jerk – *BANG!*

Kaparis saw the flash. Saw the cockroach turn. Saw the boy.

"There! Order them to attack any organic life form!"

"Yes, Master."

DAY FIVE 11:52 (Local GMT+8). Shanghai UFH Hospital.

Hospital doors swung open in rapid order as the prisoner was rushed into an isolation room. Medics and machines pounced on her.

Scar lay on the gurney, a red-black mess. Her face was covered in the red welts of the rash that covered her body, leaving only patches of the palest skin. Her extremities – fingertips and lips – were already black.

She could have been a disinterred mummy but for the occasional movement or breath.

The medics barked jargon.

She had septic shock. A failing heart. Renal failure.

They were feeding drugs into her, connecting her to every kind of machine.

As the prisoner entered the main operating theatre, King was able to watch live hospital CCTV of events from the Roof of the World. Scar was barely a teenager. If there was any lingering doubt of the evil in Kaparis, this would surely snuff it out, King thought.

Beeeeeeeeeeeeeeeeeeeeeep...

Suddenly the heart rate monitor flat-lined.

"Save her!" snapped King down the line.

DAY FIVE 11:52 (Local GMT+8). Nine Harmonies Pagoda, Shanghai.

Finn waited for his head to clear after the explosion.

He was getting the hang of opening up the bots now. He had been blown back, away from Kelly's cell. He needed to locate it again, fast.

"KELLY!" he started to shout.

"GO!" said Kelly, crawling out of the smoke and chaos, eyes blazing, an old warhorse stirring at the sounds of battle.

"Get under here!" said Finn, pulling him under the cockroach-cape.

Kelly hooked a mighty arm around his shoulders. It wore a watch.

"How long have we got?" asked Finn.

"Eight minutes till noon," said Kelly. "How do you rate our chances of survival?"

"Nil," said Finn. "Just the way you like it."

Kelly looked at him and winked. "Very considerate. You ready?"

Shoulder to shoulder, they drove forward under the cape – pushing through anything that got in their way, pushing against the grimy surface of the ancient clay roof tiles, pushing at the sea of metal maggots.

But the nano-bots were many and they were just two. And the harder they fought forward, the harder the bots seemed to resist and it was quickly, exhaustingly clear they were never going to get out.

Nothing was said, but after a few more desperate drives they came to a halt beneath the cover of the cockroach-cape, exhausted.

Finn felt an anger, an urgency. "This is all my fault. If I'd kept the gun, we could have shot out a tunnel..."

"It's nobody's fault. There's just nothing we can do. We don't have the power. We stay here and when the blast comes... we pray," said Kelly.

They took a moment.

"What happened to Stubbs?" Kelly asked.

"He should be alive," said Finn.

Kelly gave a nod of satisfaction.

"What happened to my father, Kelly?" Finn asked. "He's alive, isn't he? You said you'd tell me when all this was over. Well, it's nearly over."

Kelly took Finn's head in his mighty hand, cradled it and spoke the truth.

"He disappeared… I only know it the way Al told it. They were doing some crazy experiments to do with the edge of time and physics and I don't know what – teleportation and dark matter and… just, crazy stuff. They fired up this accelerator that Ethan was rigged up to, somehow…"

"My dad was connected to it?"

"Yeah. He was nuts – half the time he worked in his pyjamas – and in the middle of it powering up, it exploded. Al said that Ethan just disappeared, I mean literally popped out of existence…"

"What? How is that possible?" Finn's mind was racing. His heart aching. None of this made sense.

"Everybody thought Al was confused after the blast, but that's what Al said. They put him in hospital for a while and thought he had lost his mind, but they never found a trace of your dad and… well, that's what happened as far as anybody knows, or will ever know."

"But why didn't they tell me that? Why's everybody so ashamed and secretive and—"

"There was one other thing…" Kelly hesitated. Finn could barely see his face in the darkness.

"You were there."

FORTY-THREE

DAY FIVE 11:54 (Local GMT+8). Song Island, Taiwan (disputed).

"What's happening? Why aren't they attacking?!" cawed Kaparis as he watched the cockroach tunnelling away, and his technical team tried to track it from bot-cam to bot-cam.

Li Jun was silent.

"Repeat the order for the bots to attack any organic life form!"

Again Li Jun remained immobile.

She did not want them to die. She would not issue the order.

In her mind, she was elsewhere. She was walking by a lake. Her parents were holding her hands. Her sister was playing...

A technician beside her, terrified, checked her screen. "Master! Something is wrong!"

"Li Jun!" Kaparis barked. "Li Jun!"

She did not reply. She looked out across the ocean at the horizon.

"LI JUN!"

She spoke very quietly in reply, but the words cut through Kaparis like a knife. "I want to live. I want to be free."

Grandma stopped knitting and her eyes filled with tears of joy. "Oh, how lovely!"

Kaparis spat and choked. Within his steel sarcophagus, his lifeless body sweated rage.

"INFAMY! INFAMY!"

DAY FIVE 11:55 (Local GMT+8). Nine Harmonies Pagoda, Shanghai.

Over the ancient temple, the storm was about to break.

With a terrible clap of thunder the signal from Kaparis finally arrived with the XE. bots in the cluster. The standing order to ignore insects was changed to a doomsday order: to destroy all organic life forms.

Kill. Everything.

Deep beneath the surface of the super cluster Finn and Kelly were doomed.

Outside, there was a downrush of wind and a black rain descended.

DAY FIVE 11:55 (Local GMT+8). Huangpu River Crossing, Shanghai.

An LCD clock on the dashboard of the ice-cream van flipped to 11:55.

"THERE!" shouted Hudson.

Two sets of faint black dots had appeared on the very edge of the world.

Al raised his arm. "ON MY SIGNAL! Three... two... one..."

The Flying Leopards skimmed the satellite towns west of Shanghai.

They were sixty-four seconds away from target.

Group Captain Bingxin saw the outline of the Nine Harmonies Pagoda on the horizon. He looked at the fire permission indicator.

It turned from amber to green.

They were on track to destroy a part of China's heritage. To the pilot it seemed crazy, but there had to be a reason. "Duty. Action. Delivery," was what it was all about.

"Go to green," he said.

"Green confirmed," came the response from both attack wings.

BEEEEEEEEPEEEEEEEEEEEEEEEEEEEEEEEEEEEEEEEEEEEEEE EEEEEEEEP!

Suddenly everything was flashing at once, on the HUD, all over the cockpit. Screens were whiting out.

"Control, this is Red Leader. We are blind. We are blind. We are blind."

On the Roof of the World, Bo demanded a report.

"The radar is jammed, sir. We can't fire the missiles without it."

"How?! Who is doing this?" he asked, and the moment the words left his mouth, he knew the answer. "Allenby..."

DAY FIVE 11:56 (Local GMT+8). Nine Harmonies Pagoda, Shanghai.

You were there...

Images and thoughts and memories spun in Finn's mind like the reels of a fruit machine.

You were there...

How could it be true? It couldn't be – no one just *disappeared...* and yet it felt true. It was perfectly unscientific and perfectly true at the same time. It was... his family.

Out of one mystery had come an even bigger mystery and Finn

knew he could never rest on such an absurd answer, whatever time he had left he must find the truth about his father.

"How could I possibly have been there? I'd only just been born," said Finn.

"I don't know," said Kelly, "but your dad said he saw you, he started yelling that he had to save you and then the whole thing blew."

"Save me? From what?" said Finn.

SMASH! A tentacle suddenly snapped through the exoskeleton of the cockroach, its hook a millimetre away from Finn's bleeding face.

"GO!" Kelly yelled.

And as they rose to drive forward again, the exoskeleton was ripped from their backs by several talons at once, and they were blinded by the light... blown by the winds.

They were no longer in the pit of the cluster but in the open, in the black rain, in the most extraordinary melee. Tentacles grabbed them from all sides, then let go, then grabbed hold again. Finn and Kelly reeled and fought, Finn ripping away with his spike, trying to make sense of what was happening. Then he saw something he recognised being torn apart – a wriggling insect, a thrip, a simple, ugly, stormfly that Finn considered – in this extraordinary moment – to be the most beautiful thing he had ever seen[34].

They were everywhere, a black rain. Countless thousands driven by the downrush of air ahead of the storm.

The testudo of bots had collapsed under the onslaught. Ordered

[34] Thrip – Order Thysanoptera – a fringe-winged insect with cigar-shaped body, usually 1mm in length, aka – stormbugs, thunderbugs, stormflies, thunderflies.

to attack all organic life forms, they were faced with thousands, and as the dispersed cluster writhed to slaughter the harmless thrips, a multi-coloured slick of bots and insect innards began slipping down the pagoda roof.

Still at war in the centre of it all, Finn saw something even more beautiful than the thrips.

"HAAAAA!" Finn cried out in joy as he beat aside a bot.

"Leave me!" said Kelly. "I'll slow you down!"

"No – LOOK!" said Finn, grabbing Kelly and pointing to what Kelly saw only as a blue plastic bag.

BANG... POWACRACKAZINGSZZZT!

A shot. A magnum. Two-dozen bots in the path of the speeding bullet exploded and sent a golden spasm through the slick, parting it like the Red Sea and revealing Stubbs, rocking from the counterblast and still attached to the white line that had seen him and his balloon dragged out from the Shen Yu to the kite and then into the cluster.

"STUBBS!" Finn yelled, laughing with joy as he hauled the injured Kelly, disbelieving, through the gap. "Keep firing!"

Stubbs steadied himself. *BANG... POWACRACKAZINGACSHSH-SHSZZZT!* He fired again before the bots could close in over them, Finn using all his strength to drag Kelly the last few nano-metres to Stubbs.

Finn and Stubbs then pulled in the white line to bring the balloon and its basket towards them just as –

SMACK... SMACK... The first heavy raindrops began to hit.

Finn took the Magnum and – *BANG... POWACRACKAZING-*

ACSHSHSHSZZZT! – fired a third shot as Stubbs and Kelly climbed in the basket.

SMACK... Finn copped a raindrop and was instantly soaked.

From the basket Stubbs yelled, "HANG ON TO THE LINE!"

Finn gripped it – Stubbs kicked out the counterweight – and the next thing Finn knew he was being yanked upwards on the line, rising like a rocket...

The bots fell away. The jettisoned dragon charm counterweight tumbled past. Lucky after all.

Kelly reached down the foam edge of the basket and grabbed Finn's arm, pulling him up.

Euphoria surged through Finn as the world suddenly expanded around him. After so long trapped inside the Shen Yu, trapped inside the cluster, it felt amazing to suddenly be able to see the temple, the river, the city, the sky...

The storm. A terrible clap of thunder boomed. The clouds burst and fat rain hammered the balloon. They instantly lost height.

Beneath, the slick of bots reformed in the tumult on the pagoda rooftop, sucking itself back into a testudo, leaving the flood to wash away the corpses of a thousand thrips... exposing something that had lain hidden at the heart of the cluster...

"THE BUG!" Finn screamed as the rain drove them down towards it. "IT'S THE UGLY BUG!"

It was lying on its side, beached by the chaos. Washed and waiting. A prisoner of the bots since it had been seized in midair the day before.

Finn felt strength surge within him, and for a moment he dared to hope that they were saved.

Then the deafening roar of twelve advanced fighter-bombers screamed overhead at attack height, like angels of death.

FORTY-FOUR

When Carla finally regained consciousness, she was in such head-splitting pain she wished she could fall away into blackness again. It was as if a thick spike had been driven into the back of her skull.

She was being dragged up a slope out of the roaring stormwater of the sewers. She could hear the sounds of the carnival above and the rain thundering on to the roof of the haunted house and…

Yap!

Baptiste stopped. Looked back. In the sewer was a filthy panting animal in a harness. A creature from the underworld. Inside his mind, EVE. could make no sense of it. Baptiste altered his grip on Carla's neck and dragged her further up the slope.

In the nDen at Yo-yo's collar Delta cried, "CARLA!"

Yap!

"Go, Yo-yo! Jump! Jump!" She prayed he'd have the strength left after his epic run.

Yo-yo crouched on Baptiste's abandoned motorbike then gave his back legs all he'd got and sprang up on to the edge of the breech in the sewer pipe, just clinging on to howl and click and claw and scramble his way over its muddy edge.

Baptiste saw him coming up the slope and raised a boot.

"Yo-yo!" screamed Delta.

The boot swung and cruelly clipped the dog's jaw. He was sent howling back down the slope. Delta almost passed out in the nDen as Yo-yo's head whipped around. He howled in pain and incomprehension, and only just managed to claw enough of the muddy slope to stop himself from falling back into the sewer.

Delta cursed. She should have held Yo-yo back. As soon as they were out of the sewer they would be back on the comms net and have the entire resources of the G&T and the Chinese state at their disposal. Instead she'd been impulsive.

"Stay, Yo-yo! Stay!" she urged.

Too late. The words made no sense to the wounded beast. The big man had hurt him. The big man had hurt the girl.

GWWRRRRRRRR! Yo-yo shot up the slope.

Baptiste raised his boot for a second time, this time too late. Yo-yo snapped his jaws firmly into the meat of his calf muscle on impact.

"ARRRRGH!" screamed Baptiste, thrashing and flailing, but Yo-yo only clung on harder.

"CARLA!" Delta cried from the dog's collar, desperate to make herself heard.

Baptiste pulled himself up on his good leg, then swung the leg with the dog attached around in a huge arc.

Yo-yo was dashed against the concrete at the top of the tunnel and hit the slope yowling and vibrating with shock as his whiplashed spinal cord sent every muscle it controlled into spasm. Six of his ribs were broken.

Baptiste saw the gun strapped to the stricken dog and yanked at it. As the harness was ripped past Yo-yo's head, the nDen clipped to his collar broke off and fell to the ground. Baptiste took the gun and discarded the harness.

Inside the nDen, Delta slipped into unconsciousness.

DAY FIVE 11:58 (Local GMT+8). Temple Hill, Shanghai.

They'd had a moment to decide.

As the balloon was driven back past the pagoda roof by the rain they had one chance to jump and try and reach the Bug. Stubbs and Kelly just weren't going to make it.

"Go! Raise the alarm. We'll land this thing and wait," Kelly ordered.

"Are you crazy? I'm coming back for you," said Finn.

"No time! Get help! Get the girl!" Stubbs insisted.

Finn's thoughts rushed back to Carla. "Where is she?"

"I saw him take her into the sewers," said Stubbs.

The sewers. Finn remembered how they'd got in. He knew where she would be.

"NOW!" shouted Kelly.

Finn jumped from the balloon before the pagoda roof disappeared beneath them – *BOOF!* – hitting the tiles and letting the force of the water carry him down the slope towards the Bug.

"GODSPEED, KID!" he heard Kelly yell behind him.

Beside him in the basket Stubbs muttered, "Lord mercifully hear us..." And meant it. They would lash the balloon to their landing point and wait for the cavalry to arrive. Finn was on his own.

Finn angled his body as he slid down the tiles, steering himself into the path of the Bug – *WHAM.* He hit it – but dislodged it too. As he clambered into the open cab, it was sliding off the roof – fast. He reached the controls just as it tipped over the edge and hit the ignition.

There was the slightest delay as the world fell away, then –

SSSHHHSHSHSHSHHRRRRRRRRRRRROOOOOOOOOOOOT!

The turbines burst into life, the engine lighting and thrusting the craft, like a dart, through the thick tropical downpour, windshield splitting the air. Flight – blind white flight – because all Finn could see was a shockwave spray of white water.

He slowed, but the force of rain filled the open cab and drove the craft towards the earth. He hit the gas again – *SSSHHHSHS-RRROOOOT!*

Get to the river, he told himself, *just point and shoot.* He had to find this circus.

He slowed again and tried to get a better view. Through the hammering rain, Finn could just make out the distant blur of a crystal city.

Get to the river.

He pointed the Bug towards the heart of Shanghai and hit full power.

DAY FIVE 11:59 (Local GMT+8). Shanghai.

The Flying Leopards passed over Shanghai, payload intact as Al was being arrested on the orders of Bo Zhang and bundled into the back of one of the police cars, Hudson protesting all the while – "Chill! Chill! Let's talk about this!"

A moment later, when they were both under arrest in the back of the squad car, Hudson asked, "Think that was enough?"

Al leaned forward to check the time on the dashboard clock.

DAY FIVE 11:59 (Local GMT+8). Shanghai UFH Hospital.

Beep... beep... beep... beep... beep... beep... beep... beep...

Repeated electric shocks had restarted Scar's heart but the situation was desperate. A doctor called for a ventilator, he was about to perform a tracheotomy – cutting directly into the windpipe.

The moment the scalpel blade touched the flesh of Scar's throat – the moment he punctured the skin – her body erupted...

The doctor cried out, dropping the scalpel. Nurses screamed as bots spouted out of Scar's body, Exodus Hive 1, concealed beneath her skin and packed into her abdomen, suddenly exploding to life. Rashes and blisters across the surface of her skin burst. Blood spattered the walls as a million bots shredded and fired and flew out of her. Thousands of them, sparking a primal panic.

The staff ran.

The bots flew after them, searching for the exits and the air-con vents, an expanding, deadly, hissing swarm.

DAY FIVE 11:59 (Local GMT+8). Roof of the World, Shanghai.

Reports rained in and the implications ran through King's mind.

Soon the bots would be in every processor in the city block. The girl on the gurney had been loaded with bots in the Forbidden City then sent into the heart of Shanghai – a Trojan horse. Who knew how many more infected Tyros were out there? They had fallen for a classic distraction. The battle had been lost.

Bo Zhang looked crushed.

The strike wing called in progress of its second attack run.

"Descending attack height five hundred feet..."

Bo had to make another decision. Was there any point in the attack now the bots had broken out in Shanghai itself? They would already be unstoppable.

"He's been playing with us," said King, speaking Bo's mind. "The computers aboard the International Space Station are the only ones that can be absolutely trusted now. Bots will soon be inside this building."

"Targets acquired and locked-on," reported Group Captain Bingxin.

Bo needed to make the call. To attack or not to attack.

"Approaching three kilometre mark. Warheads armed..."

The President of the Chinese People's Republic stared at King. "What would you do?"

King gave his stock response in moments of supreme crisis.

"I trust my people," said Commander King with a glance at the clock.

Al was listening in via the police radio.

12:00:00 MIDDAY

At that very moment simultaneously, on the roof of the Nine Harmonies Pagoda, in the corridors of the Shanghai UFH Hospital, and on the rear seat of National Highway Lines coach #635KD, in the hearts of twelve million bots – the most dazzling and sophisticated machines ever created by mankind, each boasting a quantum dot worthy of the spark of life itself – told themselves the same, last, ineluctable truth:

$$Xn + 1 = \infty Xn\ (1 - Xn)$$

And a simple double switch caused a short circuit that – at the speed of light which binds all things[35] – discharged all the power stored in the bots' frail bodies at once into their circuitry causing massive heat and –

BARARARARARARARARARARARARAR AOOOOOM!!!!!!!!!!

On Highway G60, Spike's body was shredded by expanding fire, as the Exodus Hive 2 bots packed beneath her flesh combusted – the explosion ripping through the rear section of the coach and causing a multi-vehicle pile-up.

[35] 299,792,458 metres per second

The bots on the tiled roof of the pagoda exploded in formation, as if in collective shock, blasting a hole in the roof and boiling the rain as it fell.

Bots throughout Shanghai UFH Hospital ripped through the circuitry they'd attached themselves to, through the crevices and cracks and wiring in which they had sought sanctuary, starting a thousand small fires that would sweep through the buildings around them over the course of the next six hours.

All of them, each and every one, obliterated.

The first reports reached Bo Zhang 2.6 seconds after the explosions occurred.

"Red Leader! Abort Strike!"

Commander King waited for the response from Group Captain Bingxin as the reports of the mass bot self-immolation were pouring in.

"Copy. Abort strike," came the confirmation.

The Commander allowed his eyelids to droop momentarily over his sleep-deprived eyes.

He could hear Allenby and Hudson going wild in the back of the police car.

DAY FIVE 12:03 (Local GMT+8). Temple Hill, Shanghai.

In the distance beyond the smoking pagoda, the fast jets ripped through the sky as the last of the thunder died away and the heaviest of the rain abated.

It fell on the platoon of troops that leapt from a helicopter to investigate the blast that had just destroyed the roof of the Nine Harmonies temple complex.

It also fell on the blue hydrogen balloon descending rapidly into the path of their commanding officer.

To attract his attention, Kelly shot him right between the eyes.

FORTY-FIVE

DAY FIVE 12:04 (Local GMT+8). Song Island, Taiwan (Disputed).

Silence.

The chamber was at three metres below the waves. Exotic fish dabbled in the waters, sharks circled the base of the sugarloaf.

Grandma was at last silent because she was not only bound to her chair but also gagged.

Kaparis was trying to ignore what had just happened (what would later only be referred to as 'the unfortunate business on the Yangtze'). He dwelt instead on more general misfortune and particularly upon betrayal.

He took a deep breath and looked out.

"It was a mistake to bring you here, Mrs Allenby. All I wanted was for

us to get on. But you had to be tiresome... Your daughter could have had all this and so much more..."

Grandma made a noise.

"Heywood..." Kaparis indicated for the butler to remove Grandma's gag.

"I wondered why you were being so nice. Were you playing at being the son-in-law I never had?" said Grandma. "You poor thing. Maria had so much you couldn't possibly know, or even feel. You have been nurturing a grudge, not living your life. You have been deluded, and now you must forgive yourself and move on."

"Ethan Blake stole her! Then he abandoned her!"

"All we know for certain is that he loved her. And love grows. Hate can only die."

Grandma didn't just say it, she asked him to believe.

"Now do forgive Li Jun, or you'll ruin her life too."

Kaparis made a hissing sound. Grandma thought for one fraction of a second he was crying. But no. It was contempt.

"Her life? What life?"

And without further ado, Kaparis – beaten, bitter – called up a violent choral section from a disturbing Shostacovich opera to play on his screen array as Heywood replaced the gag on Grandma.

Kaparis let the discordant music wash over him for a few moments, then said, "NOW!"

A portal opened in the seabed and a narrow, struggling, slip of a girl floated out towards the circling sharks. Li Jun.

Grandma wailed. They'd even gone to the trouble of pinning on the front panel of the blue tank top she'd knitted for her.

Grandma had known inhuman evil. Had worked with it. Had even cured it. But she had never known anyone quite as wilfully cruel as Kaparis. Effect. It was all for effect...

She wailed again.

Li Jun struggled for air and waited for the first shark to strike. She had not lived long, she considered, perhaps only for a few blissful moments, but she had once felt free, had tasted her own actions, as she now tasted their consequence. It would never be worth it, nothing justifies death, but it was something. A great grey form accelerated towards her through the water.

BOOOOOOSH!

And was instantly frightened away.

BOOOOOSH! BOOOOOOSH!

Columns of bubbles exploded around her, to protect her, to save her. As she began to pass out, she saw a beautiful creature approach her – a warrior mermaid with long floaty hair. The mermaid was wearing a mask that she pulled off and thrust over Li Jun's face. Compressed air forced open her lungs, with glorious, life-giving effect. Her mind refocused and she saw the mermaid was a woman in a designer wetsuit carrying a submachine gun and an oxygen tank.

Li Jun had been spotted from the air by the equipe bleu of the Commando Hubert in their radar-cloaked NH90 helicopter.

Four of them immediately dropped 120 feet into the sea around Li Jun. The remaining seven members of the team continued to the primary target. Appearing around the Kaparis underwater command chamber, as Grandma said later, "like those films of penguins all diving off the rocks at once."

Heywood had raised the alarm the moment the first commando had hit the water and he and Kaparis were well on their way to their two-stage escape vehicle (a compressed air-rocket system developed from an old Polaris ballistic missile).

While it blasted off from its launch hub below the waves, the commandos entered the complex by blowing open the primary airlock. They entered the main bunker and shot or detained nearly sixteen members of Kaparis's staff during the initial fire fight, though it was estimated a further forty-five escaped in a nuclear powered submarine.

Grandma was found in the principle chamber moments before it flooded. The lead commando, Henri Clement (Grandma immediately knew he was French, "I could smell the cologne") removed her gag, clicked his heels and said, "Madame Allenby. Enchanté."

He then presented his card[36] *before throwing her over his shoulder and carrying her out.*

Finn dropped out of the white-water hyperspace after four minutes – as long as he dared to fly virtually blind.

The cone of white water collapsed around him and the world was revealed in all its storm-lashed majesty. Not only had he found the river, he was almost in it. He pulled the Bug up and – *SSSHHH-SHRRRRROOOOOOT!* – soared higher to better search for the circus.

[36] "He may not have *actually* presented his card," she said in later testimony, "but it felt as if he did."

The downpour was easing and beyond a bridge in front of him he made out something hovering, like him, above the water. He blasted forward – *SSSHHHSHRRRRROOOOOOT!*

It was a cable car. A chain of them ran across the Huangpu river, halted for the duration of the storm. He followed the line to the bank and made out the top of a Ferris wheel. Bingo.

SSSHHHSHSHSHSHSHHRRRRRRRRRRRROOOOOOOOOOOOOT!

Twenty seconds later he was descending into the carnival site, searching desperately.

He hit buttons and the nano-radar screen lit up. He hoped with all his being that Carla was still carrying Kelly's pack in her hair. If she was, the contents might just be big enough and dense enough for the nano-radar to pick up.

Nothing.

He hauled the sticks and pulled the Bug round 360 to sweep the entire circus.

There! The tiniest flash…

Finn shot down towards the carnival to chase the signal, then slowed again as it got stronger. It pointed back towards the river. He looked.

The cable car had started up…

Baptiste left the operator dead in his booth, a neat bullet hole in his forehead.

The machinery of the wheelhouse clanked and the cables ran. The cars jerked and rocked and restarted their endless journey back and forth across the river.

As each car arrived in the wheelhouse, its doors automatically opened.

Baptiste watched the river traffic for a few moments, then pulled the semi-conscious Carla off the floor and walked her into an open car. The doors closed and the car swung out over the river.

No one had noticed the couple struggling through the rain under the tarpaulin cape. No one saw her hands were tied with wire or her single shoe. No one had even looked.

The car rose rapidly and began its 800m transport across the Huangpu. Mighty industrial barges floated serenely beneath. Baptiste looked back to the shore.

A white wisp seemed to be cutting through the rain, heading straight towards him…

Finn aimed the Bug at the roof of the bobbing, moving, rain-battered cable car and tried to land – no chance. The Bug was washed straight off.

Finn thrust directly against the window to stop the Bug's slide. He just had time to register Carla slumped on a wooden bench inside when – *WHAM!* – Baptiste struck the window with a caveman's club of a fist. The shockwave threw the Bug back. Finn let it drop through free air, then flew beneath the car.

In the relative shelter he spotted a possible way in.

He angled the Bug and flew to the very bottom of the car's overlapping doors. Where the two rubber door seals met was a neat square-centimetre gap. He forced and thrust the Bug forward into it.

POP. The Bug arrived on the floor of the car.

WHAM! Down came Baptiste's stamping foot – *WHAM! WHAM!*

Finn scooted and span.

WHAM! Baptiste was lightning fast, EVE. accurately calculating the Bug's crazed trajectories, but in the dry stable air Finn could better control the craft and dodge the feet and fists.

He shot the Bug up into the roof and tucked it into a gap behind a light fitting, too slim for Baptiste to be able to jam his fingers in.

He tried to think. His heart hammered. In his urgency to find Carla, he had formed no plan as to what he was actually going to do to save her.

SNAP! Baptiste kicked a splintered cane length of wood from the bench and jammed the end of it into the light fitting gap, nearly pulverising Finn and the Bug. Finn had to move. He shot the Bug back out into the open and Baptiste swung for it, just missing.

WHHHHIP!

The cane made Baptiste twice as deadly – his reach twice as long. The schoolbook phrase "Early man learned to multiply force using simple tools" flashed absurdly through Finn's mind.

WHHHHIP!

He'd never outrun Baptiste. He had to be cleverer than early man. So he stopped. Mid-air.

WHHHHIP!

He dodged.

WHHHHIP!

He dodged again.

WHHHHIP!

Against clearing skies and the extraordinary background of Shanghai, they were having a dance-off in a cable car. A bullfight in a bubble.

But the bull was a good 150 times the matador's size and getting ever faster, EVE. processing and feeding the coordinates of each dodge and blow, learning from each mistake. Finn knew the blow would soon land...

WHHHHIP!

Close.

WHHHHIP!

Closer...

But then, remarkably, Baptiste stopped. He seemed to forget about Finn altogether and turned to the doors, pulling up the safety bar and starting to smash the door release with the butt of his pistol.

Finn had no idea what he was doing.

The doors parted. Wind and rain rushed into the cab. The car rocked and Finn looked down.

Sand. For a moment he thought a desert was passing beneath them... but in a blink it became an industrial barge, 200 metres long and travelling directly below full of sand and gravel aggregate destined for the construction of a new mega-structure somewhere inside China.

Baptiste grabbed Carla and Finn's heart seized.

He's going to jump... He's going to kill her...

Finn had to stop him.

He hit full power – *SSSHHHSHRROOOOOT!* – and the Bug hit Baptiste's left eyeball with huge force.

Finn was bucked clean out of his harness and sent spinning through the air as Baptiste screamed and brought a hand up to his eye – dropping Carla. She fell – half-in, half-out of the open door – just in time to catch Finn in her thick curly hair.

He grabbed at the strands and came to a bouncing halt.

Physics, he thought. Not luck.

He scrambled towards her ear. "CARLA! CARLA! WAKE UP!"

The barge slid by beneath. The hard steel helm section approaching fast. Too late to drop now. Surely too late.

But through the forest of Carla's curls Finn saw what Baptiste was thinking.

"NO!" he cried.

Baptiste looked down upon the waters as EVE. made a risk calculation, then leapt.

Half blind, he skewed his jump. Down he fell, pulling Carla with him.

WHAM!

99 per cent of Baptiste hit the sand.

Everything went black.

The Chief Mate of the aggregate barge Min Ho heard a thud and slowed. Had they struck a small craft in the low visibility? A crew-member was sent out. He saw a log floating past. They must have hit that. The Chief Mate breathed a sigh of relief.

On the banks of the river, bleeding and shaking in the rain, a filthy dog picked out the scent of its young master and howled.

FORTY-SIX

Christmas Eve 08:14 (GMT). Hook Hall, Surrey, UK.

Power surged.

The great hoop of particle accelerators came to life.

White lightning span around the core.

"But at my back I always hear

Time's wingèd chariot hurrying near..."

Al tapped his control terminal and – *WHOOOOOOOM!* With a flash, the Hot Area was created, remarkable forces only he understood.

Delta Salazar was fed in on the conveyor belt and taken to the very limit of physics, the very limit of human knowledge, the very limit of life itself.

Then Al brought her back.

Grandma watched, standing next to Commander King in the Control Gallery. At her insistence Christmas decorations had been added to "brighten the place up" though in truth there was little mood of celebration. The technical team barely noticed the turning of the seasons, so focused had they been on reaching this point.

Despite extensive and ongoing search operations, not a trace had been found of the third Tyro. Nor of his hostage, Carla. Nor of Infinity Drake.

Grandma let tears run down her cheeks, unafraid to have a "good cry" at the drop of any given hat. She, more than anybody in that most technical place, had absolute faith that Finn and Carla would eventually be found alive. Just as she had absolute faith they would one day find out what happened to Finn's father, Ethan. She didn't know how anybody could live without faith. Commander King was a realist and above such things. He thought only of Kaparis. Day and night.

Down on the floor of the CFAC, Al cut the power to the Hot Area and it evaporated into a million specks of light.

The select audience blinked away the image left on their retinas and saw that the body of a full-sized young woman had appeared in the middle of the Henge. She woke as if from a long sleep, like a princess in a fairy-tale. She sat up, looked at her limbs and felt her face, as if they were new to her. Then she stood and looked around the vast hall with big sad eyes. Amazed at the new scale of things after eight months nano.

Kelly and Stubbs had been first in. They'd been restored to full-size for more than two weeks now while Delta had insisted on staying on in China to aid the search effort. Kelly offered her his fist to bump. She bumped it, then hugged him. A hug of need. Of loss. Stubbs shook her hand because that's all he could cope with.

Al watched from the foot of his Command Pod. Delta was frightening enough at 10mm. At true scale, he found her spellbinding. But it killed him to think it was his fault her sister and his nephew, so beloved, were missing, presumed dead. She had never blamed him, but he carried the guilt anyway.

Delta looked at him, then Al turned away.

Up in the Gallery, Commander King did the same.

Down of the floor of the CFAC the sons of Scarlatti stowed their emotions.

One of their number was still missing. There was work to be done.

But at least Delta was back.

Grandma mentally added another place around the table for Christmas dinner.

Christmas Eve 16:14 (Local GMT+8).
Taklamakan Desert, NW China.

Odd flakes of snow raced each other through the frozen wind, chased along the contoured sand, and hurried through the garish, extraordinary Uyghur shrines – coloured flags and banners on stick sculptures left scattered across the desert, restless riotous monuments to the dead.

Baptiste did not see them. He slogged on. The brain injury he'd suffered after catching his head on the edge of the barge had left him a brute zombie. EVE. had little control. It had taken him three days to stand, thereafter instinct took over and he was drawn north-east, towards the place where he had been formed by the Master. The seminary in the mountains far, far away. Homing in, he had been pushing his prisoner in a handcart for twelve weeks across the never-ending Eurasian landmass.

Finn watched the Uyghur shrines in a starving-trance from Carla's hair.

The colours reminded him of the praying mantis. He had finally seen one in a barn in Gansu, when it appeared on Carla's forearm, tasting the salts that seeped through her fevered skin. It was magnificent. It blazed colour like a stained-glass window and had the bearing of an alien bishop. It had turned and looked straight at him and made him – briefly – deeply happy. Made him dare to hope he might survive.

Hope finds you he thought afterwards, and reminded himself to tell Christabel.

He had not seen it again.

The freezing wind blew. Baptiste slogged on. The wheel squeaked.

A little way behind a broken, filthy, exhausted dog chewed moisture from a pathetic drift of snow. He could smell new humans some miles away. Food. Fires. He wanted to eat, drink, sleep. He wanted the pain in his gut and his paws and his infected jaw to go away. He wanted not to hop along, not to scavenge for rats, not to run cowering from the bad man whenever he saw him…

But he had the scent of Finn.

And of the good girl.

And on he went.

INFINITELY
MORE...
www.infinitydrake.com